MATCHMAKING BY BLACKMAIL

"You cannot marry without love, Clay." Emily touched his sleeve. "Please, don't throw your life away on this castle and Cathaven's money. It isn't worth it."

Clayton had turned his back on love after Serena had left him. Emily vowed never to go through that again. "I lost everything in the tobacco shipment, Em. I have nothing left."

The hope in Emily's eyes faded. "I cannot in good faith give you a list of women for your choosing. There are some who would marry you just for the money, and there are some who would marry you as a means to escape their family. Either way, it would be a terrible loss for you, don't you see?"

"I don't want your pity, Em. I want your help."

His sister scowled. "Yes, and Briana is not for you."

Though he had believed Miss Garland a perfect candidate, a nice list of possible brides from Emily would help considerably. "For your information, I don't think Miss Garland's mother would turn me away. Do you know she mentioned marriage last time we met?"

Emily crossed her arms over her chest, reminding Clayton of a general he once knew. "If you dare hurt Bree, I'll never speak to you again."

"Give me some credit, Em. I will handle this in the most delicate manner."

"Very well. Your blackmail worked. I will have your list of suitable ladies by tomorrow."

The Convenient Bride

Teresa McCarthy

A SIGNET BOOK

SIGNET
Published by New American Library, a division of
Penguin Group (USA) Inc., 375 Hudson Street,
New York, New York 10014, USA
Penguin Group (Canada), 90 Eglinton Avenue East, Suite 700, Toronto,
Ontario M4P 2Y3, Canada (a division of Pearson Penguin Canada Inc.)
Penguin Books Ltd., 80 Strand, London WC2R 0RL, England
Penguin Ireland, 25 St. Stephen's Green, Dublin 2,
Ireland (a division of Penguin Books Ltd.)
Penguin Group (Australia), 250 Camberwell Road, Camberwell, Victoria 3124,
Australia (a division of Pearson Australia Group Pty. Ltd.)
Penguin Books India Pvt. Ltd., 11 Community Centre, Panchsheel Park,
New Delhi—110 017, India
Penguin Group (NZ), cnr Airborne and Rosedale Roads, Albany,
Auckland 1310, New Zealand (a division of Pearson New Zealand Ltd.)
Penguin Books (South Africa) (Pty.) Ltd., 24 Sturdee Avenue,
Rosebank, Johannesburg 2196, South Africa

Penguin Books Ltd., Registered Offices:
80 Strand, London WC2R 0RL, England

First published by Signet, an imprint of New American Library,
a division of Penguin Group (USA) Inc.

First Printing, September 2005
10 9 8 7 6 5 4 3 2 1

PUBLISHER'S NOTE
This is a work of fiction. Names, characters, places, and incidents either are the product
of the author's imagination or are used fictiously, and any resemblance to actual persons,
living or dead, business establishments, events, or locales is entirely coincidental.

    The publisher does not have any control over and does not assume any responsibility
for author or third-party Web sites or their content.

To Bob and Patricia

*Thank you for your support
and for being the best in-laws a daughter could have.*

Love always . . .

Chapter One

*S*he was in love.

His favorite food was roasted duck with plum sauce. He enjoyed bayberry soap with his bath. And he liked raspberry tarts for breakfast. There wasn't much sixteen-year-old Briana Garland didn't know about Lord Clayton Clearbrook.

Standing in the shade of a cluster of oak trees blocking the afternoon sun, Briana glanced through the window of the massive ballroom of Elbourne Hall and let out an audible sigh. Metal clashed against metal as the fencers slid over the newly shined dance floor of the Duke of Elbourne's country estate.

He looked positively magnificent.

Coffee-colored hair flew about his handsome face, giving him the appearance of a pirate on the high seas. Long, powerful legs lunged against his enemy with such perfect form it made her shudder. Lord Clayton was four years her senior and her ideal man.

"Oh, don't be taken in, Bree. They are not that dashing," Lady Emily pronounced, leaning her elbows on the outside ledge of the open window, gazing into the ballroom.

Briana felt a blush climb up her throat. Caught up in the world of dueling swordsmen, she had almost forgotten about her friend.

The duke's only daughter rolled her eyes. "They are my brothers, not at all the type of gentleman one would want to dream about. The ninnies don't even know we're watching them."

Briana shifted her gaze back to the swordplay as the weapons hissed through the air. Clayton was pitted against his brother Marcus, who was a year older than he. Stephen, the youngest of Emily's brothers, born a few years before his sister, stood on the side, jeering his siblings on. Curses flew from one end of the room to the other and Briana's color deepened.

She was staying at Elbourne Hall this summer, as she had for the past few years. Her mother, a longtime friend of the duchess, had made the arrangement in hopes that Briana would attach herself to one of the Clearbrook brothers. Not that Briana should set her eyes on Roderick, who was in line to be duke, her mother had said, but one of the other boys would be agreeable enough.

"I did not say they were dashing," Briana said, trying to justify her attentions.

Emily's eyes twinkled. "You didn't have to. Many of my friends think my brothers dashing and all that rubbish. But that is where you are different, Bree. You will not throw yourself at them like most females."

Still resting her elbows on the sill, Emily leaned her chin against her palm. "Depend upon it, they are able to turn grown women into pudding in the wink of an eye. I daresay it is the most disgusting thing you ever want to see."

Briana tried not to blink. *Oh, she had seen it.* Her gaze strayed to Lord Clayton, and she literally had to hold back another sigh when she caught a glimpse of those mesmerizing violet blue eyes. Even his jaw held a certain stubbornness that captivated her.

She smiled inwardly. His tall, lean form encased in buckskin breeches, along with his commanding air of self-confidence, only added to his appeal. And although all the Clearbrook males had many special qualities, memories of Lord Clayton's kindness were never far from her mind.

It was less than two years ago when she had fallen off her horse and he had rushed to her side, wiping the tears and dirt from her face. "Miss Garland, if you are trying to deprive all the young men in this county of your beautiful eyes, you are doing a deuced good job of it. They are fairy eyes." His violet blue gaze danced with mischief and she laughed between her tears.

Since then, her affection for him had grown, and today she finally realized it was love.

There were many times he had caught her reading in the

duke's library and never once had he scoffed at her. In fact, he had done just the opposite. They had actually carried on intelligent conversations about whatever book she was studying at the time.

To her, Lord Clayton Clearbrook was wonderful, a man any girl would want to marry.

"If you must know, Em, I have never seen anyone fence before. I have read about it, to be sure. But seeing the real thing is quite exciting."

"They are using blunted ends, so there is no chance they will die," Emily said calmly. "I declare it is not at all exciting." She flung her arm toward the dance floor. "Look at them. They act as if they were swashbucklers on the high seas."

"They look like swashbucklers," Briana said quietly.

"Oh, they box, too. And take lessons at Gentleman Jackson's. Papa says they should not practice on themselves, but they do anyway. It is all an act for the ladies. But they have soft hearts, even Roderick, who will be duke one day. And I do love them and they me."

Eyes sparkling with mischief, Emily jumped away from the window. "So, you see. Our plan will work. I can get them to do almost anything I want."

Briana worried her bottom lip. She had no doubt who would win in the battle of wills. Since Roderick was away, with their father, the other brothers were mere puppets in Emily's hands.

Baring a devilish grin, Emily pressed her hand against the jasmine flowers climbing the wall beside them. "Remember that day I had them take me back to the village for a special ribbon I had seen in the shopkeeper's window?"

Briana nodded, her lips curling upward. Emily's grin was infectious. "It was last year and your father was furious. A storm was ravaging the countryside. We were soaked to the bone."

Emily chuckled. "Yes, and we had to stay at Lord Kingsdale's home to dry. Mama was livid. She never liked him, even though he is friends with Clayton."

"Oh, I thought Lord Kingsdale quite nice. In fact, he likes Egyptian architecture, you know. We talked about it for hours." *But he was no Clayton,* she wanted to say.

"Yes, he was quite agreeable that day," Emily said with a shrug, turning her head back to the ballroom.

Briana picked a white petal off the flowering vine and glanced at her friend. Emily's raven black hair and violet blue eyes, the same shade as Clayton's, were stunning.

"My sister is like you, Em. Pretty and quite the thing. In a few years, I imagine she will sway many a gentleman her way."

Emily angled her head toward Briana. "You are quite pretty, Bree. No one I know has eyes as green as yours. I think Clayton calls them fairy eyes."

Had he mentioned her eyes to Emily? Hope sprang within Briana as she peered back into the ballroom. Male voices echoed about the room, mingling with the clash of steel.

"I don't know about this plan," she said to Emily. Her petal fell to the ground, and she began to wring her hands on her muslin skirt. What would Lord Clayton say when he discovered their ploy? "It makes me nervous. Perhaps we should wait—"

Emily grabbed Briana's hand in a friendly squeeze. "Wait? Why wait? This is the perfect time."

"But Mama will not allow me to learn that dance."

"What does that matter? My mama won't allow it either. What are we to do during our first London Season without knowledge of the latest dances?"

"I don't—"

"Oh," Emily interrupted, as the male voices rose in intensity. "Listen, Bree. They are having a great row now. Fists will soon be flying. It's the best time to approach them."

Briana looked on, the blood rushing to her head. Maybe Emily's brothers would never discover their scheme. Besides, this might be the one time Briana could be close to Lord Clayton, and who knew what would happen when she went to London and had her Season. She would know the dance by then, and he might even ask her for a waltz at Almack's if the patroness gave permission. "I see. When they are thinking of something else, then we attack?"

"Precisely," Emily said, smiling. "When a female has four brawny brothers, she has to fight with her brain because brute strength certainly won't work. Remember that, Bree. It will help you in the Season, especially with the male gender."

No sooner had Briana tucked the idea away when a shout

penetrated her thoughts. She stared in amazement at the fiery exchange taking place. The stakes seemed to be rising.

"Clay, watch out! You'd best be careful with your footing! To the left, you peabrain! Thrust, Marcus! Parry, parry, thrust!"

A growl erupted from Clayton as Marcus gave another jab of his sword.

"Bad form, Clay," Stephen spouted, his voice laced with amusement. "I say, very bad indeed. What the devil were you doing? I told you to go left."

Clayton did not think his brother's words funny in the least. He stepped to the side, his sword slicing Stephen's way. "Button your blasted lips or I shall do it for you!"

Stephen crossed his arms over his chest and laughed. "Oh ho! I would like to see you try! I believe Marcus scored that point, not you!"

Marcus's black hair flew over his temple as he let his sword fall to his side. "Do you two have to go at it again?"

Stephen shrugged and made his way across the room, fingering the pianoforte. "If Clayton says please, I just might stop."

Briana's brows lifted in mute horror as she watched Clayton march toward his brother. "I am going to skewer you with the point of this blade, little brother."

"That's the problem with you, Clay," Stephen said, laughing. "You don't even know the point is flat."

"Emily, they are going to hurt each other," Briana said anxiously.

"No, no, they won't. Now just play along with me, and we will have them eating out of our hands."

"But—"

It was too late to protest. Emily gave an earsplitting whine of distress that made Briana scream herself.

Clayton's gaze snapped toward the window, and all three brothers froze. Out of the corner of her eye, Emily glanced up at Briana. Briana blinked in shock, too paralyzed to think.

"Follow my lead," Emily whispered. "We will be learning the waltz in no time. Here they come."

The click of heels echoed in Briana's ears like the pounding of a huge drum. "What?" she gasped.

"They cannot stand tears," Emily said through stiff lips. "Just do what I do. But for goodness' sake, don't stare at them with those fairy eyes of yours. Your face will give everything away."

"Em?" Clayton said, poking his head out the window. Stephen and Marcus stood anxiously beside him.

Emily cried harder into her handkerchief. Briana dropped her gaze to the ground, her mouth glued shut in terror.

"What the blazes is wrong?" Clayton asked.

Briana forgot the plan and raised her head. Her tongue stuck to the roof of her mouth as she gazed into Clayton's beautiful eyes. They were more blue than violet now. Their color seemed to change with his emotions. She well remembered when they had deepened to a dark sapphire the day Emily had placed a buttered scone on his seat, ruining his new jacket.

No, these were a soft dusky blue, full of concern and worry. Sweat beaded on his brow and across the open neck of his shirt. Briana tore her gaze away.

"What the devil is wrong with you two?" It was Lord Marcus and he sounded quite perturbed.

Briana swallowed past the large lump blocking her throat. Fudge! She was in the thick of it now. Her face burned with embarrassment. She opened her mouth and closed it, feeling like a fool.

"Jupiter and Zeus," Stephen said from behind. "Do you know you interrupted a very desperate battle?"

Briana thought she heard a snicker from beneath Emily's handkerchief. Goodness, the girl had her brothers twisted around her finger like the vine of the jasmine flowers beside them.

The brothers seemed so tall and powerful, it amazed Briana how one wail from a little female could change their steely demeanor to one of intense concern. Briana didn't know much about feminine wiles, but she was learning fast.

"Em," Clayton said, his voice kindness itself, "what's wrong?"

Emily peeked over her handkerchief and dabbed at her eyes. Shiny black hair winked in the sunlight, making Briana all too aware of her own dull auburn locks. Feeling extraordinarily self-conscious, she stepped back into the shadows.

"Oh, Clayton, it's terrible," Emily sniffed. "I am to go to London soon and I have no idea how to waltz. My dancing master, Monsieur Buckette, is ill."

Three male groans hit Briana's ears. Although she truly loved Emily, she thought pulling this act on all three brothers was scarier than meeting the king at court. She wanted to shrink behind the climbing vines and disappear. She was good at fading into the crowd. Sometimes no one noticed her at all.

To her surprise, the three brothers turned their backs and started to converse in low voices. Were they truly going to bow to their baby sister's request and teach the girls to waltz? Or had they already discovered their ploy?

"Well, dash it all, I don't like it above half, but she has to learn," Clayton said in a hushed tone.

"You have a point," Stephen put in. "Every lady should know how to waltz."

"Don't like it," Marcus added. "Don't like her waltzing with any gentleman. Devil a bit. It ain't a seemly dance for either of those imps."

The whispers were no longer audible and Briana started to panic when the brothers shot them curt glances over their broad shoulders.

"Emily," she said, scooting toward her friend, "don't you think—"

Beneath her handkerchief, a smile sprang to Emily's lips. "Wait thirty seconds," she whispered.

"Why does Mother not hire another dancing master?" Stephen's voice rose suspiciously as he turned toward Briana and Emily.

"Because, Monsieur Buckette is at least three score, if not more," Clayton said, narrowing his brow and regarding the two girls. "He's . . . well . . . he's safe."

"There is Sir William," Stephen announced calmly. "I hear he has filled in as a dancing master for Lady Penelope—"

"Sir William?" Clayton said, exasperated. "You have to be jesting. There is no idiot on earth that would have that rogue dance with any female of his acquaintance, let alone a sister."

He peered at Briana and frowned. "Or a sister's friend."

Stephen smiled. "Are you calling Lady Penelope's father an idiot?"

Clayton ground his teeth.

Marcus frowned. "Don't like it above half, but it will have to be us. Don't trust any of those young dancing masters."

"Marcus is right," Clayton put in. "Come on inside, Em. Bring Miss Garland with you. You will learn how to waltz. Give us some time to clean up."

Briana's eyes grew wide. She was astounded that her friend's plan was falling into place so easily. "Emily, I—"

"Shhh." Emily squeezed Briana's arm as the three men sauntered back into the ballroom and up the stairs to change.

"But, Emily, Monsieur Buckette is in fine health. We saw him only yesterday."

"My brothers don't know that." Emily shrugged. "Besides, I think the man had the sniffles yesterday."

"But . . ."

Emily giggled. "Oh, won't it be divine when we take London by storm?"

Briana was becoming more uncomfortable by the minute. Emily always liked excitement, and that was one reason Briana usually enjoyed her company—except for a few times like this, when her taste for excitement forced Briana to, well, lie.

"I would rather be reading about Egyptian artifacts," she mumbled.

Emily laughed. "My brothers won't bite. They are quite tame when they dance. And besides, they like Egyptian artifacts." She pulled Briana along. "Don't worry, silly. I'll make certain you are paired with Clayton. He's not as stuffy as Marcus. But just don't look at him with those fairy eyes."

"I don't have fairy eyes."

"Yes, you do. I've always wished mine were your color. But Clayton has a sixth sense about these things." She giggled. "Except when I stretch the truth. So remember, if your eyes give us away, it's good-bye, waltz, hello, boredom."

Courage welled up inside Briana. *Good heavens, she was going to dance with Clayton!* "I can keep this a secret."

"Of course you can. I never said you couldn't."

A chuckle escaped Briana's lips. "I can be just as stubborn as you about withholding information."

Emily turned to her and frowned. "If you think me stubborn,

don't even test Clayton. If he discovers our trick, well, I vow he will make it hard for me to ever waltz again."

Briana's brows fell into a concerned V. "He will?"

Emily laughed. "I am only jesting, Bree. But he is stubborn. Come on."

Briana managed a half smile as they turned the corner and entered Elbourne Hall. She always had a sixth sense about these things, too. Something was bound to go wrong.

Thirty minutes later, Briana found herself in the arms of Lord Clayton, while Emily was partnered with Marcus and Stephen played the pianoforte.

"One, two, three, one, two, three," Clayton said aloud, swinging Briana about the room. "That's it. Just let your partner take the lead. Everyone will think you two girls have been dancing since you were four."

Briana was acutely conscious of the man's nearness. His hand was firm and strong about her waist, while the scent of bayberry drifted her way, sending a tingling to the pit of her stomach.

A hot ache grew in her throat when she thought about her mother's plan for her to marry a Clearbrook. With a sinking heart, she realized nothing would ever come of it. She had heard Lord Clayton was in love with Lady Serena Brently from London. A diamond of the first water. A lady with lustrous yellow hair and large chestnut eyes. A lady, not a mere girl of sixteen.

And to make matters worse, just last week she had overheard him talking about buying a commission in the army. All the Clearbrook brothers would be going to war soon. Napoleon was causing too much havoc for them to watch sedately from the English countryside.

Her stomach clenched at the thought of Clayton hurt on the battlefield—or worse, even dead. Too embarrassed to look anywhere else, she dropped her gaze to the floor.

"Miss Garland, if you look down at your feet, you will decidedly trip over them. Look up at me."

Briana stumbled and felt Clayton's large hand tighten about her waist. She slowly lifted her gaze. Dark brown hair hung over his right temple, framing eyes that sparkled with a mixture of amusement and compassion. This was the Clayton she liked best.

"That's it, Miss Garland. Now just follow me. Relax."

Briana felt herself floating on air. She circled the room like a princess in the arms of her prince.

"How long are you staying at Elbourne, Miss Garland?"

Briana blinked and accidentally stepped on his foot.

He smiled, sending her heart somersaulting.

"Um, the entire summer, I believe."

He nodded, his lips parting in a heavenly display of even white teeth. "Now, it is your turn to ask me a question."

Her blood froze. "I—"

Emily's twittering laughter broke into Briana's thoughts. Her friend had stepped on Marcus's toe, and he was groaning.

Clayton turned Briana toward the window, while Stephen's fingers ran up and down the pianoforte in a sweet melody of notes.

"Perhaps something about the weather," Clayton suggested.

Briana cleared her throat. "The weather?"

"Yes, the weather." He chuckled. "Or perhaps how fine I look today."

Briana colored and was saved when Marcus laughed. "Spare us the self-adoration, Clay. You're embarrassing the poor girl."

Briana noticed the arms about her stiffen. "He was only trying to help me," she said, surprising herself.

Clayton's lips spread into a wide grin. "There, you see, the lady defends me. Now, tell me about the weather, Miss Garland."

Briana blinked. "I don't . . . um, the weather?"

"Yes. Is it raining out? Or is it pleasant?"

Emily chuckled. "Clayton, you are supposed to teach us to waltz, not talk about the weather."

"Did you hear about Miss Winters?" Stephen asked. The music softened to a whisper as the two couples kept dancing.

Emily gave Briana a wink. Briana tried not to stumble.

"What about the lady?" Marcus asked his younger brother.

"Ran off with Mr. Summers, the dancing master."

Briana laughed.

Clayton looked down at her and grinned. "You know, Miss Garland, when you smile, you are the prettiest girl in the county. Your eyes sparkle like a sea of emeralds."

Briana faltered a step. His brows lifted in mirth as he swung her toward Emily and the dance ended. They practiced a few more times until the girls were decent enough at the dance, and then the brothers left for a ride into the village. Standing in the ballroom, Briana stared in shocked amazement at her friend.

"Well, what did I tell you?" Emily asked, smiling as she leaned against a towering pillar on the edge of the dance floor.

Briana clapped both hands to her cheeks. "It was the most thrilling day of my life. I will never forget it, ever!" *You know, Miss Garland, when you smile, you are the prettiest girl in the county. Your eyes sparkle like a sea of emeralds.*

Emily's face glowed. "My brothers are pudding in my hands. Mama will never know. We handled it perfectly, did we not?"

"I heard that."

Briana's head snapped up to see Clayton's hovering form blocking the entrance to the ballroom. He was no longer pudding in his sister's hands here. His arms were crossed over his chest and dark sapphire eyes stared back at them. Briana gulped.

Emily snatched Briana's hand and carefully hastened past her brother. "Well, what's a girl to do after all, Clay? I mean, if not you or Monsieur Buckette, then who? Sir William?"

"If I had known Mother would not allow this—"

"Well, you didn't know!"

Clayton's eyes were almost black.

Emily took a hesitant step back and Briana began to worry. She decided it was time to take over. Emily was always manipulating a plan; now it was Briana's turn. She felt her lips quivering in mirth when the absurd thought came to her.

"Yes, truly, my lord," Briana blurted out. "You don't want us dancing with Mr. Summers, do you?"

Emily turned to her friend and burst out laughing. "Oh, Bree. That's hilarious!"

Shocked, Clayton dropped his hands to his sides. He stared at Briana as if she had never spoken before. Not giving him a chance to make the next move, the girls took off down the hall.

"Emily, you are going to pay for this!" his voice boomed.

Emily laughed, waving her hand in the air, as if he were nothing but a stranger on the road.

Briana giggled. It was the most perfect day of her life. She was definitely in love.

Chapter Two

Six Years Later

"'And to my godson, Lord Clayton Peter Cathaven Clearbrook, I leave my castle and all its holdings, including any monetary sums remaining after all debts are paid. There is one stipulation and that being—'"

Lord Clayton Clearbrook glanced up at his uncle's solicitor and let out a boisterous laugh. "Oh ho, tell me this is a jest. By Jove, the castle is more of a dungeon than a home."

Clayton's brother Roderick, Duke of Elbourne since their father had died a few years earlier, looked up from his chair in the library of the Elbourne townhouse, trying to suppress a grin. "Now, now, hear him out, Clay. Who knows, there may be something for the rest of us."

Both Marcus and Stephen let out snorts of amusement. A small chuckle even passed Emily's lips.

"This is just what you need," Stephen said. "Taking refuge in that castle up north may save you from all the matchmaking mamas. Don't you see?"

Marcus sat back against his chair, his eyes dancing. "A hideout for all the bachelors like you and me. Why, you don't have to marry at all. It's just what you wanted."

Mr. Banes, the solicitor, cleared his throat. "Forgive me for interrupting, but there is a bit more to the will."

Clayton raised his hand in apology. "Banes, I think this calls for a drink. Anybody else?"

Clayton's siblings were barely able to control their mirth as they declined his offer. Banes, however, sat as stiff and proper as a starched neckcloth.

Clayton shook his head as he strode toward the rosewood sideboard. He had invested almost everything he had in a to-bacco shipment that had been lost last month, and the blasted castle was the last thing he needed.

"I say, I will take a bit of brandy, my lord."

Clayton glanced over his shoulder at Banes's request. The solicitor pushed his slipping spectacles back up his rounded nose and swept his bald head with a handkerchief.

Clayton regarded the man as he handed over the glass of amber liquid. Why, he actually looked quite nervous. But Clayton was resolved—he was not going to take that castle.

He grimaced as he took his seat. It was a deuced good thing his mother had an appointment and wasn't here. The lady had a soft spot for old Cathaven, and she would insist that Clayton take the dilapidated old hellhole and everything that went with it.

Dash it all! It didn't matter. She would eventually learn the details of the will and then he would be sunk.

"I fail to see why none of you inherited the castle," Clayton snapped, glowering at his family.

"You are his godson," Marcus put in, smiling. "Ah, a poor failing on our parents' part, to be sure, but there you have it. Roderick here was left the dukedom, and you, dear Clayton, have been left Uncle Cathaven's delightful castle."

Emily coughed into her hand, but it was definitely a laugh.

Clayton peered over the rim of his glass. "You all realize there's probably a mountain of back taxes to be paid. I could be inheriting a debtor's prison. I won't take it. Besides, the man was a hermit. Heard he took a bath once a year and never paid a penny for anything but the bare essentials. Even Emily hated visiting there with Mother."

Roderick shook his head. "Em has no taste. Love her dearly, but look at the man she chose for a husband."

Clayton let the brandy slide down his throat. His sister had married the Earl of Stonebridge, a man every bit as stubborn as Roderick and the love of her life. They were the perfect couple.

They had what Clayton had once wanted for himself. A loving spouse, a family, a home. But after Lady Serena had run off with a colonel, Clayton vowed never to fall in love again. Freedom and security were his goals now. And devil take it, he would not be saddled with a dirty old castle.

"Em?" he asked. "Have you nothing to say?"

"You are correct," she said, raising her delicate black brows. "Indeed, the man took a bath once a year."

Another round of laughter filled the room. Clayton's hand tightened on his glass as he swung his gaze back toward the solicitor. "I am not taking that castle. Is that clear?"

The small man gazed over the top of his spectacles and pulled at his pointed neckcloth. "I would like you to hear me out, my lord. If you wish, I can simplify this process and merely state the facts."

"Fine," Clayton said in a clipped tone. "Just the facts."

Stephen gave an exaggerated clearing of his throat. "I believe Uncle had a damsel in distress imprisoned in the turret and now Clayton will inherit her, too."

"Let the man finish," Roderick announced, winking at Emily.

"I won't take the damsel either," Clayton said calmly, glancing toward the mantel clock. *I have another damsel waiting for me in London. A very pretty one, in fact.*

"Go on," Marcus said to Banes. "Just do it quickly. We don't need all those fancy words."

The solicitor snapped the papers in his hands. "Very well. As I said, I will try to simplify the process. Lord Clayton will inherit the castle and all its belongings."

Stephen snickered. "All its belongings? Well, well, Cathaven certainly wasn't the penny-pincher I thought he was."

Clayton shot him a cool stare.

"To His Grace," the solicitor went on, trying to ignore the interruption, "my client leaves a small cottage outside Brighton. To Lord Marcus, a townhouse in Bath."

Banes swallowed and peered up at Stephen. "I believe, for you, my lord, I should read the words as they are stated."

Clayton leaned back in his chair and smiled. Cathaven had never liked Stephen. "By all means. Mayhap my baby brother has inherited the moat with all its delightful artifacts."

Emily's lips twitched.

Stephen wasn't affected in the least. "Cathaven was a miser of words as well. This has to be more entertaining than Nigel fighting with Mother's cats."

Clayton couldn't help but laugh at the solicitor's confused expression. "Nigel is Lord Stonebridge's dog, my good man."

"I see. Well, may I continue?"

Roderick waved the man on.

Banes dropped his gaze to the papers. "'To Lord Stephen, the youngest, I leave nothing, for at the present moment I believe he has behaved with the utmost disrespect, declaring me a penny-pinching miser. Therefore, let it be so.'"

Clayton wiped at his eyes, his sour demeanor lifting. "Oh, this is too much."

Stephen's lips thinned. "I have all I need with my Elizabeth. I don't need an old moat from a dead uncle, thank you kindly."

Clayton glanced at Emily, who seemed to be trying to contain her laughter. It wasn't working.

The solicitor reddened. "May I proceed?"

Roderick crossed his arms over his chest. "Forgive us, Banes. Cathaven was . . . uh . . . eccentric, to say the least."

Banes pinched his lips. "Yes, well, except for Lord Stephen, instead of reading the details, I will circumvent the obvious."

Clayton massaged the back of his neck. "Go on, Banes. We are on pins and needles."

Stephen snorted. "This should be interesting."

"Very well," the solicitor said, adjusting his spectacles. "'To Lady Emily, I leave my portrait. The one that hangs above the hearth in the big hall.'"

"His portrait?" Emily blurted out.

Chuckling, Clayton accidentally tipped what was left of his drink onto the plush rug beneath him. Stephen's eyes twinkled. Roderick stood and walked to the other side of the room, his shoulders shaking, while tears came to Marcus's eyes.

"Em," Clayton said, rubbing a hand across his mouth, "we all know you had a soft spot for the old boy."

Emily groaned. "But his portrait?"

"At least you weren't left a dingy castle," Clayton said as he rose and glanced at the solicitor. "You can let the ruins go to the nearest vicarage for all I care. I don't want it."

"But I have not finished," Banes interrupted, shuffling the papers and quickly rising. "There is a bit more, my lord, and it has something to do with your inheritance. The stipulation I mentioned. Thought I would leave it for the end, you know."

"I knew it," Stephen put in. "A lady imprisoned."

Clayton knew the castle would push his finances beyond repair. Shaking his head, he crossed the room and grabbed the handle of the door. "I have an appointment in Town. Roderick can inform me of the details later. Better yet, send it off to my man-of-affairs, and he can inform you of my refusal."

"Wait," Emily said, rising from her chair. "If I have to take old Cathaven's portrait and stick it in my attic, you can at least hear the man out."

The mantel clock ticked in Clayton's ear. "I have an appointment."

"Is it that pretty blonde you are accidentally meeting in Hyde Park again?" Marcus asked, all laughter gone from his expression.

Emily's eyes widened. "Oh! You are meeting Miss Hookston?"

Clayton stiffened. Miss Hookston might be a bit soft in the head, but she was the prettiest thing in England. "Have a bit of decency, Em." He peered at Banes, who was turning crimson, whether from embarrassment or anger he knew not. "It's not as if I am going to marry the lady. Carry on, Banes. I have a minute or two."

Banes drew a deep breath of relief. "Very well, my lord. You are to inherit all your uncle's money."

Clayton gave a dry chuckle. "The man had next to nothing. Even an idiot could guess that when you rode past the place. It would take a king's ransom to fix the ruins."

Banes peered over his spectacles. "But my lord, it seems your godfather stored all his coin in the dungeon."

Clayton leaned against the door, crossing one Hessian boot over the other. "Oh, this is getting quite good. Sounds like one of the fairy tales I read to Emily's stepdaughter, Gabrielle. She would adore this."

Stephen stood, his brown gaze flashing with humor. "Banes,

now let me get this straight. Are you saying my brother is to seek out that dungeon and clear out all the skeletons?"

The men tried to hide their snickers, but it was almost impossible. Even Emily could not help laughing. Banes was turning a deeper crimson, if that were possible.

"You must forgive us, Banes," Clayton said, feeling sorry for the older gentleman. "It's not every day a man inherits a castle with a dungeon full of money from his hermit of an uncle. Had my brother informed me of this little meeting ahead of time, I could have planned my day better."

He looked at the clock again and set his jaw. "I do have an engagement and must not be late. But rest assured, I'm not going to take that blasted castle. Good day."

Clayton opened the door and barely took another step before Banes hurried toward him. "My lord! Please! Hear me out!"

Clayton released a tired sigh. "Don't think this is disrespect for our uncle. Quite the contrary. He was an angry old man, set in his ways, but we did cater to his whims every now and then, and we, or at least I, had a liking for the old fellow. The man was in good mental health until his wife died." He threw up his hands and turned to leave. "It was a devilish shame, but the poor man lost touch with the world, especially when he wrote that blasted will."

"My lord!" Banes clamped his hand upon Clayton's arm, stopping him. "There's more than skeletons in that dungeon."

Clayton lifted a sarcastic brow. "Indeed? Well, my good man, I will not be the one who will be cleaning it out."

"B-but I must inform you of the stipulation if you wish to inherit the castle."

Clayton shot a sharp glance toward his siblings, who were doing nothing to help him. "Thank you for the information, Banes. But as I have said, I will have my man call upon you to make certain that does *not* happen." He started down the hall, his heels clicking upon the marble floor.

"My lord! Have you no wish to know the quantity of funds?"

Clayton kept walking. "How much, Banes?" he drawled.

His siblings filed out of the library to listen just as Banes quoted a sinful amount of money.

Clayton spun on his heels. "What did you say?"

Stephen's head snapped up. "Why, that sneaky little devil."

Clayton hastened back down the hall and grabbed the solicitor's shoulder. "Forget my earlier words. I *will* take that castle and *all* its belongings."

"Clay, oh favorite brother, can you put me in your will?" Stephen said mockingly.

Clayton waved him off. "Now, what about this stipulation? Do I have to live there for a year or something insane like that?"

"Not precisely. You must wed within three weeks of the reading of the will. If you do not have a bride by that time, the entire sum and the castle will go to your cousin Sir Gerald."

"Sir Gerald?" Emily announced in horror.

"Bride?" Clayton shouted.

"Three weeks?" Roderick uttered.

"If not for the money," Stephen said bitterly, "I would let Sir Gerald have the old ruin."

"Gerald is an insufferable oaf," Emily said tersely. "A man like him should never have that amount of money."

"Can't let him have the castle," the duke said with a cold edge to his voice. "I've heard things about that man that would rattle your bones. Everybody back inside. Let's discuss this calmly."

Clayton, too startled to protest, followed the others back to the library, with Banes leading the way.

"Three weeks," Clayton said, trying to assimilate the information as he strode restlessly about the room. "How the devil am I to find a bride in three blasted weeks?"

Banes pulled out a handkerchief and wiped his brow. "I have no idea, my lord."

"What about a special license?" Stephen asked offhandedly.

Clayton regarded his brother's smiling eyes. "And whom do I marry, oh wise one? Do not forget about that miscellaneous detail." His gaze swung toward his sister. "What do you think of Miss Hookston now?"

Emily gasped. "You wouldn't dare? This is foolish. Special licenses are for, well, special things, like me and Jared. We were in love. You cannot think of going through with this."

But Emily was wrong. He was already listing the possibilities in his head. No, he wouldn't have a marriage based on love. Lady Serena had burned any notion of that. While he had been serving his country under Wellington she had decided to marry someone else. But a convenient bride was another matter.

He pursed his lips, intrigued at the notion. There had to be some lady who would fit in with his family, some lady he could set up nicely in the country, some lady who would bow to his commands and be a biddable wife. Yes, by Jove, he could do it. He *would* do it. But it would definitely not be Miss Hookston.

"Hell's bells, Clay," Stephen said, his mouth dipping into a frown. "Tell me you are not really thinking of doing this."

Clayton whipped his head around. "Put a cork in it, baby brother, or I'll do it for you."

Stephen's eyes narrowed. "Will you now?"

The duke raised his hand. "We can work this out. There is my wife's ball this week. What say you to finding a lady there?"

"I say it is the most idiotic thing I have ever heard of," Emily cried. "It's outrageous!"

"I don't think so," Clayton replied calmly. "Besides, I do believe it is my choice."

Clayton avoided Emily's sour expression as he strode toward the window. Inheriting that sizeable amount of money freed him from the family coffers. Not that he didn't receive a quarterly sum handed out by Roderick, but it was a pittance to what he had lost in his investments. He would be a fool to let this go. Yes, he would marry for convenience' sake. He could do it. He could.

"It may be idiotic and outrageous," Banes said, "but quite lucrative. Ethical is another question altogether. Of course, this is none of my affair, but I will say, Lord Clayton, that after I spoke with your uncle when making this will, he mentioned something about his contented life as a married man. Perhaps he may have wanted the same thing for his godchild, duty and all that, you know."

Banes shrugged and stuffed his papers into a leather case. "I will leave you with a copy of the will and send one to your man of affairs. You have three weeks. If you do not have a bride by the stated time, the holdings and all monies will be settled upon your cousin. No need to see me out." With a quick good-bye the man departed, closing the door with a resounding thud.

"Well, he couldn't get out of here fast enough," Emily said. "I daresay it's such a sordid thing, I don't blame him at all."

Clayton dug his heels into the rug as he paced. "Three blasted weeks. It seems impossible. What lady in her right mind would marry me in such a short amount of time?"

"None!" Emily exclaimed. "Oh, depend upon it, you could have some simpering female like Miss Hookston, but don't let her pretty looks deceive you. She knows exactly what she's doing."

"And I know what I am doing," Clayton said, exasperated. "Miss Hookston may be a beauty, but believe it or not, she is not the kind of lady I wish for my wife. What I need is a detailed list of possible candidates."

Silence. All heads turned when the mantel clock chimed the hour. Clayton's narrowed gaze traveled over his siblings.

"Confound it! Would you rather Gerald inherit the money?"

Emily's shoulders drooped.

Clayton's mouth twisted with frustration. "When I entered this room today, marriage was the last thing on my mind. Dash it all! The very last thing!"

Stephen threw a booted foot upon the hearth and tilted a smile Clayton's way. "It happens to the best of us. Who knows, old boy, you may end up just as blessed as Roderick and me."

Clayton let out a dry laugh. *He should be so lucky.*

Emily's hands formed two stiff fists by her sides. "I fail to see the amusement in finding a wife." She regarded Stephen. "And I doubt Elizabeth would find this funny." She darted a gaze toward the duke. "Or Jane, *Your Grace.*"

A flush swept across both gentlemen's cheeks.

"Em," Clayton said, hoping his sister would relent, "what about one of your friends?"

"Oh!" Emily marched toward the door. "You are impossible!"

Turning toward the window, Clayton caught sight of Banes stepping from the walk and into his carriage. *Three weeks! Who the deuce would fit into his plans and marry him in such a short amount of time?* Clayton stared back at Emily.

Her eyes burned into his. "I would never give you leave to marry one of my friends!"

Hmmmm, one of her friends . . .

A pair of intelligent emerald eyes suddenly came to mind. Of course! Miss Garland! The girl wasn't bad to look at, with her dazzling auburn hair and those fairylike eyes. And it didn't matter to him that her nose was always in the books.

At least he could have a decent conversation with the lady. Of course, he wasn't fond of her matchmaking mama, who had been hounding him for years. Still, he recalled the girl's kindness and biddable nature. There was that one time when he had been teaching her to waltz, but that did not signify. No, not at all.

His lips curved into a satisfied smile. "Em, I believe Miss Garland is staying with you for a spell, is she not?"

Emily wagged a stern finger at him. "Don't you dare!" With a huff, she turned and left the room, slamming the door behind her.

Roderick raised a mocking right brow. "If I don't miss my guess, I think that means you are to stay far away from the lady."

Stephen fixed his eyes on the door and frowned. Clayton looked at him in disgust. "Do not tell me you are leaving, too?"

"I daresay Emily has a point." Stephen plowed a hand through his brown hair. "I love my wife and don't plan to have her separated from me because of an old man's will. If you were to marry for convenience and I helped you, Elizabeth would be livid."

Stephen had almost been pushed into a marriage of convenience with Elizabeth over a stupid wager. Though the couple had worked out their differences and eventually fell in love, Clayton knew the same thing wouldn't happen to him. Love would not be involved at all. He pointed Stephen toward the door. "I am not one to meddle in my brother's marriage. Off with you, then."

Stephen gave a sigh of relief and started across the room.

Clayton turned. "Roderick, are you with me on this?"

His eldest brother stiffened. "I am a duke. I can do whatever I want. No woman dictates my life."

Jane might have something to say about that, thought Clayton, but he had desperate need of Roderick's assistance and he kept that thought to himself. "Then you will help me?"

Roderick played with an ivory letter opener on his desk. "This is the end of the Season. The parties are winding down. As I said, we are hosting a ball in a few days, but I fear that will not leave you enough time to make a choice. You need a more intimate setting to make your move."

Stephen turned with his hand on the door. "By George, never say it came from me, but I believe Lord Grimstoke is having a house party at the end of the week. I think you might find a reasonable female in the mix."

Reasonable female? Clayton dragged a hand over his face. What choice did he have? Emily was going to deny him the one biddable girl who would fit perfectly into his plans.

He heaved a resigned sigh and peered up at his brothers. "Never thought I would be saying this, but devil take it, which ladies would you suggest?"

Stephen yanked open the door. "This is where I take my leave. Ah, good afternoon, Jane."

The duke let the letter opener slip from his hands when he heard the duchess's name. The man's eyes softened as his wife's baby blue eyes peeked into the room.

"Roderick, dear. Forgive me, but I was wondering when you will be finished. I have need of the carriage for some shopping and the groom told me you wished to come along."

The duke gave her his sweetest smile. "Indeed, I do."

Roderick hurried to his wife's side, taking hold of her hand and kissing it. "I have a little side trip planned just for the two of us," the duke whispered.

Jane's face colored, and Clayton gave Marcus a hard look. Down to one sibling. It was quite apparent Roderick was out of the game. Blast it to pieces! The duke had been married almost a year, and by Jove, staring at the couple, one would think it had been only a week of wedded bliss!

Roderick lifted a wary gaze. "Gentlemen, I will leave you to the details. My duty awaits."

Clayton sank into a nearby wing chair and groaned as the door snapped shut once again. "Duty! You would think all my brothers would help me out in a time like this."

Marcus crossed the room and grabbed the decanter of brandy, a wicked sparkle in his eyes. "Yes, well, married life can do that to you. You'd best be sure of what you want."

"Hell's teeth. I never planned to be married, not after—"

"Lady Serena?" Marcus said, not glancing his way.

Clayton's face went grim. "History. But the worst of it is I lost everything in that shipment from the West Indies."

His brother peered at the glass in his hand. "Everything?"

"Everything. And if I don't take that blasted castle, I will be dependent on dear old Roderick and the family coffers."

Marcus pulled the bell cord. "I had no idea things were that bad. Then this mission calls for a bottle of a finer substance."

"Make it two bottles. If we have to make a list of ladies, I want to make it as painless as possible."

Chapter Three

"*Y*our mother entrusted me to find you a husband. And I intend to do just that, even if I have to move the search beyond the Season."

Briana Garland looked up from her seat in the moving carriage and frowned at her godmother's remark. Oh, she loved the lady dearly, but sometimes Agatha was as stubborn as she was.

Miss Agatha Appleby had been childhood friends with Briana's mother, Lady Garland, and there was nothing Agatha wouldn't do for the lady or her godchild, including finding Briana a husband. And since Lady Garland had withdrawn to the country to recuperate from her persistent headaches, Agatha had become Briana's sole chaperone for the London Season.

"I have obligations other than marriage, Agatha."

The elderly lady's black parasol hit the floorboard with a loud clap. "Fustian! Obligations providing for a women's home? As a Christian I believe in your cause, but as a single woman you will be shunned by the world."

Pressing her lips together, Briana stared out the window of the vehicle as it rolled down the London streets toward the Duke of Elbourne's townhouse. Whether Agatha liked it or not, Briana intended to follow through with her plan.

She was going to visit her friend Jane, the Duchess of Elbourne, hoping the lady could help her find a home for her proposed women's shelter, a project that Agatha obviously believed would result in social suicide.

Briana leaned her head against the cool pane of glass, her

throat tightening. What did she care about Society anyway? It's not as if she ever intended to marry.

"Briana, did you hear me?"

Briana turned. Her gaze collided with a pair of steely gray eyes. "I heard you. But *you* do things and you are not shunned."

Most people would take one look at Agatha, with her salt-and-pepper hair and plump body, and think her a sedate older lady consumed with thoughts of tea parties and peaceful drives in the country. But this harmless-looking lady had been secretly involved in the war against Napoleon for years. No one would ever think she worked for Whitehall.

Briana certainly hadn't thought such a thing, not until a few months ago when Agatha had come to her for help in the area of Egyptian architecture, which had led to the deciphering of certain mathematical formulas.

For whatever reason, Agatha had needed answers fast. Briana had provided the answers, but her suspicions about her godmother had grown to astronomical proportions.

Briana badgered Agatha for her own answers.

It all came to a head when Agatha needed more help in her so-called research. Though it proved a shaky period in their relationship, with great thought Agatha had finally confessed her involvement with the government and asked for Briana's silence. Briana begged to be part of the lady's secret world. The answer had been an emphatic *no*.

But Agatha saw qualities in Briana similar to those in herself, which Briana, knowing the soft heart beneath that hard exterior, took full advantage of, and at a weak moment the stubborn older lady, gave in to Briana's persistent requests to be part of Agatha's secret life. What was the difference anyway? Briana was providing Agatha with answers. This way she was part of the team.

Of course, Briana's work for Whitehall was done at home, a desk job of sorts, but Briana was thrilled. She didn't have access to exactly what was going on. But it didn't matter if Briana knew only a small piece of the operation. That momentous time in her life had brought her out of mourning for her father and sister and into a new world of excitement and intrigue.

The lady's black parasol thudded against the carriage floorboard. "For heaven's sake, child! I am an elderly spinster! I am allowed to do what I want! Taking care of single females in their delicate time, well, it's simply not done by another unmarried woman, especially a young female as pretty as you. The scandal, child."

Briana touched her hair. Did the lady ever think that their work with Whitehall was scandalous? Of course that was secret, but still . . .

"For one thing, I am not pretty. Auburn tresses are not at all the thing." Briana raised a hand to her nose. "And freckles are considered a sin. Nothing I do helps."

"La, my dear, you are prettier than ever, and you possess a brain most gentlemen would give their right arm to have."

"I have no wish to capture a gentleman's attention," Briana said, wishing the driver would pick up his pace and hurry to the Elbourne townhouse. The very idea of finding a husband was beginning to grate on her nerves. Agatha was becoming more obsessive about the subject every day they were together.

For the past few weeks they had been staying in London with Agatha's nephew, Lord Stonebridge, and Lady Emily. Briana enjoyed her stay at the earl's home, and she especially loved the children and catching up with Emily, but even Emily had been hinting about a husband for Briana. And Emily could be quite mischievous if she wanted.

"My dear girl," Agatha said, "fading into the walls is all well and good if you are trying to escape a scandal, but as a lady on the search for a husband, it won't do at all."

The carriage had begun to slow down and Briana was counting the seconds. This was definitely a subject she did not want to touch. It opened too many wounds. How could she tell her godmother that allowing herself to love a man would only cause her pain? The man would eventually leave her, either physically or emotionally, and that was never going to happen to her again.

"I like not being seen, Agatha." *It saves me from heartache.*

"I have noticed that lately, especially this Season. You used to be such a happy child. Maybe not as outgoing as Emily, but you enjoyed being with people. I heard Lord Rockham asked you to ride with him in Hyde Park the other day and you declined."

Agatha took Briana's hand in a warm clasp. "What happened to the girl I used to know?"

Briana swallowed, not trusting her emotions. *That Briana is dead,* she wanted to say. *That Briana was an innocent soul, full of dreams and foolish wishes.*

Emily was wed to the man she loved, and for her, marriage was wonderful. Jane was like a daughter to Agatha. She had married Emily's brother, Roderick, the Duke of Elbourne, and the loving couple were seen everywhere together.

Briana closed her eyes. Somehow her friends had found men they could trust. Briana never would. She just didn't see it happening for her. Trusting a man could be hazardous to her heart and her freedom. Hadn't her sister paid the ultimate price? The past was indeed a lesson for the future.

"What happened?" Agatha repeated, her voice full of concern.

"Oh." Briana looked up, squeezing her godmother's hand. "After I declined the offer, Lord Rockham asked Miss Celia for a ride instead. I didn't mind at all."

Agatha's gaze narrowed on Briana's forced smile. "I am not asking about Rockham. I am asking about you. And do not lie to me. Those eyes of yours tell me you were buried in the past."

Briana dropped her lashes. "My sister died alone and afraid. I can never forget that or how my father sent her away."

Agatha clenched her hand on her parasol until her knuckles turned white. "Your father was an idiot."

Briana blinked back the pain. "What father would send his daughter away? Clarice was with child, Agatha. A child with child!" Briana wiped a hand across her eyes. "He wanted nothing to do with her. Oh, he admitted his fault later, but it was too late. Too late for everything."

Her father's actions had horrified her. He had died a few weeks after Clarice did. The doctor had mentioned a heart ailment, but Briana knew it had been caused by a mixture of grief and guilt over his daughter's death.

Agatha bent toward the window and dabbed at her eyes.

"Drowning in the Thames, such a terrible accident. It's your father whom I'll never forgive."

Briana swallowed past the large lump in her throat. Many people were convinced Clarice had taken her own life. Briana didn't want to believe it, but the situation had been desperate and Clarice was such an impulsive child.

Her sister's terrible misfortune had been enough to destroy Briana's trust in men. And why should it not? Sir Garland had thrown his daughter out of the house in a fit of rage. The man who had gotten her sister with child had left Clarice to carry the burden alone. And then Briana's own love had abandoned her, only to get himself killed. It wasn't safe to depend on a man at all.

A horse neighed and a gust of warm air filled the carriage as the footman opened the door and let down the stairs. They had arrived at the Elbourne townhouse. Grateful for the interruption, Briana grabbed her reticule to leave.

But to her dismay, Agatha waved her parasol at the footman. "Close the door, James. We will be with you in a minute." The footman nodded and slowly clicked the door back into place, replacing the stairs.

Briana sank back in her seat. Though Agatha had business in Town and would return in a few hours, the lady was not about to leave Briana until the conversation had some closure.

Briana rubbed her hand across the leather seat. "I think my father's pride was hurt when he discovered Clarice's predicament. I forgave him a long time ago, but I will never forget."

"Well, your papa's dead now, child, and you need a husband. Since your mama is recovering from those devilish headaches, I must take the initiative—"

Briana lifted her chin. Her mother's headaches had gotten worse after Clarice's death. The lady had never forgiven her husband for what he had done. "I am not going to marry."

"But you are out of mourning now. Plenty of gentlemen have been asking about you this Season."

Plenty? There was only Lord Rockham, who was twice her age and widowed with five children. "The mourning period for my sister and father has given me time to think."

"Indeed, it has. I believe wearing black made you realize

you could easily disappear into a crowd more than ever before."

Briana felt her color rise. It was true. After returning to her customary clothing for the Season, she found the talent of fading into the background quite useful when one did not want to find a husband. Dull shades worked very well.

"I see no reason for you to be so stubborn about this, Briana. A women's shelter can be supported by other groups."

Briana shook her head. "No. I aim to see that Clarice's death was not in vain. There are too many ladies in trouble, and if I can help one of them, I will."

"My dear girl, you are as stubborn as ever."

"My sister fell into some man's trap, and our father let her down. I have to do something."

Agatha sighed. "But you cannot save the world."

"I can do everything I can to save another woman from such a terrible fate. The shelter will house women who are with child and have no one to care for them. After their babes are born, I intend to find positions for them where they can take their children with them, or if they want, they can give the baby up for adoption. That is the least I can do."

"But a husband can give you the respectability to do such a thing. Don't you see?"

"I don't need a husband. A man left Clarice in her delicate state. My own father let Clarice down. A husband would be a yoke around my neck. He would own everything I had." *Including my heart if I let him.*

"Not if he loved you—"

"Love? I used to believe in it. Once, when—"

Agatha raised a discriminating brow. "You fell in love with that lieutenant, did you not? It was when I was staying at Hemmingly and you were caring for your mother. I always had a feeling about him."

"I don't want to talk about it."

Briana had missed Agatha during the few years she had been without the older woman's support. She had seen her godmother during the year of mourning, but for three years previous she had been taking care of her mother in Bath, hoping the waters would cure the lady's headaches. That was when she met Lieutenant Alistair Perry.

"He was supposed to sell out his commission in the spring of 1815, was he not?" The compassion in Agatha's voice touched her.

"Yes." *He promised me he would leave his regiment. And I believed him. He said he loved me, but he loved the army more.*

"But Napoleon escaped from Elba," Agatha continued, to Briana's dismay, "and your lovely lieutenant was killed."

Briana bit her lip. She didn't want to recall Alistair's death at Waterloo. The pain had eased in time, but her distrust of men was still there and she didn't see it changing in the near future. Alistair was a good man, but he had left her.

Oh, it didn't mean that all men were bad, it just meant that Briana would not make the mistake of putting her heart and soul under a man's power ever again. "I think we have more important things to discuss than the past, Agatha."

"My dear, you cannot let a death stop you from living. Now, what do you think of Lord Clayton? I believe he is a trustworthy gentleman."

Briana's head snapped up, taken completely by surprise.

Good heavens! She certainly didn't want to bring back memories of a schoolgirl crush when she had thought herself in love with the handsome lord and his fine violet blue eyes. As the years had passed, she realized the man's charm and good looks had swayed her innocent mind. Still, his kindness had touched her, and she had never forgotten how he had taught her to waltz.

"I believe my mother has been speaking to you. Ever since we have been out of mourning, she has been hounding Lord Clayton every chance she gets. Do you know, a few months ago she had him cornered at the Elbourne soirée?"

Briana's cheeks burned as she recalled her mother's hunt for a husband. "I was only two feet away when I heard her ask him about marriage! Two feet, Agatha! I was never more embarrassed in my life." The man had made a swift retreat to the library and was never seen again the entire evening. It was obvious he had been horrified at the thought of marriage to a boring bluestocking like herself. Briana had not spoken to his lordship since.

Agatha meant well, but at times she wasn't very practical.

The very notion of Briana and Lord Clayton as a couple was ludicrous. The man would never look at her twice. And she was no sixteen-year-old now. Indeed, she had put him out of her mind!

Agatha scoffed. "Had a feeling your mama had been meddling. But this idea of a women's shelter, good though it may be, will only hinder your search for a husband."

Upset, Briana reached for the door of the carriage. "Jane is ready to help me find a facility for my shelter."

Agatha frowned as Briana pulled on the handle. "It's not as if I won't help you, dear. Perhaps we can find a husband for you at Lord Grimstoke's party. You know his daughter, Violet—maybe she can help."

Knowing it was better to say nothing on the subject of Grimstoke's party, Briana kissed Agatha on the cheek, stepped down from the carriage and blinked into the late-afternoon sun.

Agatha waved her parasol in the air. "I might be a bit late, dear. I'm certain Jane won't mind if you stay a little longer."

Briana nodded as she walked up the steps of the duke's townhouse to see the duchess. She understood Agatha's concerns about her finding a husband, but she wasn't about to tell the lady the true reason she was attending Grimstoke's house party.

As Briana stepped into the Elbourne townhouse, her brows puckered with guilt. Before the butler closed the door, she glanced over her shoulder, watching Agatha's carriage clatter down the street in the direction of Whitehall.

Briana's position with Whitehall, and with Agatha in particular, had mostly involved paperwork. But as of yesterday that had totally changed. Briana was going on assignment.

The opportunity for her to attend a house party where there could be an exchange of information regarding an assassination plot against the Regent was something Whitehall could not ignore. Ever since Prinny had been booed by crowds in January when he traveled through the city to open Parliament, every threat against the Regent was taken seriously. Not only that, but

Whitehall had informed Briana that Agatha was in charge of the mission.

Briana drew in a ragged breath. In a few minutes the lady would be told that her goddaughter was going undercover as well, and when that happened, heaven help anyone in Agatha's path . . . and that of the lady's trusty parasol.

Clayton sat on the stone bench in the gardens of Elbourne Hall, tugging at his neckcloth with one hand and holding his list of possible brides in the other. He raised his blurry gaze toward the sunset as his brother's shadow swayed over him. "Miss Hookston ain't on the list. Shouldn't be, anyway."

"The devil with her," Marcus said with the slow drawl of a man who had consumed his share of Roderick's wine cellar. "You have three ladies to choose from, Clay. That should be quite enough."

During the past few hours, the brothers had downed the last two bottles of the duke's favorite French wine, among other things. Clayton had quickly come to the decision that if Roderick could not stay and help choose his future bride, then the duke could dashed well give up his favorite drink.

Clayton flicked a finger over the names. "Miss Cherrie Black, Lady Georgette, and Miss Diana Price." Grinning, he picked up the empty bottle on the ground. "Roderick's brandy is nothing compared to this."

Marcus chuckled. "Depend upon it, the turn of the century was a very good year. But if you would like to have your head attached to your body when you depart the premises, I would suggest you take it upon yourself to dispose of the evidence."

Clayton let the bottle slip to the ground as he returned his gaze to the list of eligible maidens. "She will have to live in the country."

Marcus plopped down beside him. "Because you wish to travel and live in Town during the Season. We have already covered that. All these ladies adore the country."

Clayton's finger stopped on Lady Georgette. "She must like children. Seem to recall this lady ain't fond of them."

The light in Marcus's eyes dimmed. "Then by all means

strike the witch off. We don't need someone like her in the family. Wouldn't do well at all."

"But I don't have the pen. You left it in the library."

"I didn't leave it—you did."

The fog in Clayton's brain was beginning to clear. "It don't matter. I forgot to take a copy of the blasted will anyway. Banes mentioned he left one for me."

Marcus put an arm on his brother's shoulder. "You know, Clay, I've been thinking Grimstoke's house party is not such a bad idea after all."

Clayton rose to his feet, combing a hand through his disheveled hair. He grabbed his jacket lying on the bench. "Been thinking the same thing. The man is a bit stuffy, but he would never dismiss a Clearbrook. Won't be hard to obtain an invitation."

"Stuffy?" Marcus replied in disapproval. "That is an understatement. Grimstoke ruined some lady two summers ago."

Clayton's brows went up. "Ruined her?"

"No, not like that. She was caught on a boat with Lord Hughs. Some innocent outing that went awry because of the weather. Grimstoke claimed the girl was compromised and demanded they marry. Both refused. The girl was shunned from the *ton* and now lives in America. Blasted shame."

Clayton shrugged into his jacket. "I won't be caught on a boat with a lady unless I intend her to be my wife."

"I don't think that's funny, Clay. I think what you're doing is dangerous."

Marcus rose and picked up the empty bottle that Clayton had dropped on the ground. "Even more dangerous is Roderick when he is in one of those moods. He won't be too happy, you know. We had best refill this with something more agreeable than water."

Clayton let out a chuckle as he walked down the garden path, his boots crunching on the gravel. "If that were the least of my problems, I would join you in the refilling process. But duty calls. You can take care of the weighty matter while I pick up my copy of that cursed will. Won't be but a minute."

Stepping into the duke's library, Clayton closed the door behind him and made his way to the desk at the other side of the room. His head was aching like the devil.

And dash it, he didn't like the idea of making a list of potential wives at all. But if he wanted that deuced money, he would have to give in to Uncle Cathaven's demands. A bride of convenience would suit his needs perfectly.

Raising his gaze to the steady ticking of the mantel clock, he scowled when he thought of the lost rendezvous with Miss Hookston. He fixed his eyes on the desk, snatched the will, and stuffed it into his jacket pocket.

"Hell and thunderation," he mumbled. He could be—

At the sound of a light snore, he snapped his head around. Who the devil was that? His eyes widened at the sight of auburn curls peeking out from the side of a wing chair near the bookshelves.

A smile worked its way to his lips as he treaded softly toward the hidden intruder. Why, it was Miss Garland, sleeping like a baby with her slippers tucked beneath her bottom and a book in her lap. He tilted his head to scan the title and his eyes widened with respect. *Archimedes, the Great Mathematician.*

She was called a bluestocking in many circles, but he'd had no idea of the depths to this woman's knowledge until now. Oh, years ago he had conversed with her many times in this very room. They had talked of such things as crop rotation and how many stars were in the sky. But Archimedes? He laughed to himself. He seemed to recall she enjoyed studying Egyptian history, too. On her visits to Elbourne, she had adored his mother's cat, Egypt, had she not?

He shook his head as another thought came to him. He pursed his lips, pulled out his list, looked at it, then switched his attention back to the sleeping lady. No one on his list possessed any great intellect. At least nothing like Miss Garland's.

And what about his future children? He didn't want them to be a bunch of nitwits, did he?

As quietly as he could, he pulled up a chair and studied the woman. Two delicate white hands slipped from her lap to the side of her face as she cuddled against the arm of the chair. He smiled. That was definitely a snore. She was probably waiting for Jane to return from her shopping excursion with Roderick. But if Clayton knew the duke, he had made a romantic side trip with his wife. Miss Garland might have a longer wait than she planned.

Another delicate snore. Clayton suppressed the urge to laugh. The lady would be mortified if she knew he was staring at her. Flickering light from a nearby candelabrum fingered upon her head, setting off her locks in fiery red streaks.

She let out a little whimper and Clayton felt an instant tug on his heart. There had always been an innocence about this girl that had attracted him. He vividly recalled the day he had taught her to waltz. She had been a shy little thing, but in the end she had surprised him when she snapped back with a comment that had both infuriated him and charmed him.

But she was Emily's friend—off-limits to him and anyone like him. He was definitely someone this lady did not need, even though her harassing mother seemed to think otherwise.

Not realizing he was smiling, he observed the spray of freckles about her nose. Society regarded the dots on any female as a sign of ugliness, but to Clayton, Miss Garland's freckles gave her character. She was different from most ladies, in her looks and her manner. She wasn't beautiful, but she was pretty in a fragile sort of way.

He leaned forward and dropped his gaze to her berry lips. The sweet scent of vanilla pulled him closer, and in an unguarded moment he almost kissed the sleeping beauty. Muttering an oath, he quickly rose and pulled at his neckcloth. *That deuced wine must have been stronger than I thought.*

He kept staring at her lips and rubbed his hands along his face in frustration. He blamed his actions on the castle and the blasted will. Yes, yes, it was Uncle Cathaven and that stupid bridal clause turning his brain upside down. The entire situation had upset his balance.

Narrowing his eyes, he leaned down once again, only to have a peek. He was doing it for his own good, to prove she meant nothing to him. But before he could stop it from happening, two unfocused emerald eyes blinked back at him in horror. The next moment *Archimedes, the Great Mathematician* took to the air and the lady shot up with a scream.

Clayton quickly threw a hand over her mouth and jerked her

body against his. "Devil take it, woman. Do you want the entire household to come running to your rescue?"

She seemed slender and fragile beneath his grip, but to his amazement, she tilted her face to meet his and her fine green gaze skewered him like a piece of meat on a spit. *Why, the little termagant.* "I'm letting you go. Just don't start screaming again." He slowly lifted his hands, but the touch of her lips against his palm sent a tingle of awareness through him.

"What were you doing standing over me like that?" she snapped, a rush of pink tinting her cheeks.

She may be slender, but fragile? He felt the list in his pocket and looked at the lady, his lips twisting into a wry smile. Why should Emily determine if this lady was appropriate for his bride or not? "Why indeed?" he muttered.

Briana stared at Lord Clayton, as if she had never seen the man before. He looked, well, he looked like Lord Rockham when the man wanted to take her for a ride in the park.

This towering lord was certainly not the twenty-year-old she remembered from her summers at Elbourne Hall. He was leaner, tougher, more rugged, if one could say such a thing about such a beautiful man. The war had done that to him, she thought. There was a certain hardness about him now.

"I beg your pardon," she said, a little harsher than she had intended.

He stood there, too devilishly handsome for any man, making her feel like some bird-witted female. Still, she couldn't forget the way he had pulled her into his strong embrace, trying to keep her quiet. He didn't have to place his hand over her mouth to do that.

"I beg your pardon, Miss Garland. I came in for some papers off my brother's desk and heard a snore."

She glared at him. "I do not snore."

The man had the audacity to laugh, but was stopped short when the clatter of feet sounded down the hall.

"They heard the scream," he said, glancing at the door.

"What the devil is going on in there?" It was the duke's voice, and the man didn't sound amused.

Trying to calm her erratic pulse, Briana picked her book off the floor just as the duke and his wife came rushing into the room. "What on earth—"

The duchess stopped and turned, a look of astonishment crossing her face as she stared at Clayton, then Briana.

His Grace lifted his right brow. "Clayton?" There were more questions in that one word than in an entire speech.

Before Lord Clayton could answer, Briana crossed the rug and took the duchess's hands in hers. "Oh, Jane, while I was waiting for you, I fell asleep in the chair. And you will never guess what happened. It was so silly. When I awoke, I found—"

"A mouse," Clayton put in as he stepped forward.

Jane looked horrified. "A mouse? Here? In my house?"

Briana swallowed in admiration at Lord Clayton's quick comeback. "Yes, it was a gray little thing with big whiskers."

Clayton's smiling eyes froze on her face.

"There are no mice in this house," the duke said firmly.

"Are you calling Miss Garland a liar?" Clayton asked.

The duke's lips thinned. "I didn't say that."

Jane glanced at the two men, then tucked Briana's arm in hers. "Come into the drawing room, Bree. I am so sorry we were late. Roderick had an impulse to make another stop along the way."

Roderick cleared his throat.

Jane blushed. "Well, you did. But if you care anything about me sleeping here tonight, you'd best clear it of any mice."

Roderick glared at his brother. "I will clean all the beasts from this room, never fear."

"The entire house, Roderick," the duchess said. "I mean it."

"Of course, dear, the entire house."

As Briana turned from the room, she heard the duke mention something about his favorite wine. Clayton seemed to find the duke's comment terribly funny.

"I believe it was a mouse by the name of Marcus, and then there was his brother, too, Your Grace. Thirsty little devils."

The library door slammed behind the ladies and Briana jumped.

The duchess laughed. "Don't worry. Roderick and his brothers always act like that."

"Yes, I saw them go at it many times when I stayed at Elbourne."

"They adore each other."

Briana smiled. "If that's adoration, I wonder what love is."

The duchess's blue eyes sparkled. "Love is wonderful, Bree. Simply wonderful. Now, let's go over what kind of home you need for that women's shelter. I have a few ideas that may help you. If you would only let me run things, it would simplify matters."

Briana shook her head, knowing that Jane was trying to shield her from the *ton*'s gossip. "I need to do this. Not for me, but for Clarice."

Jane's blue eyes softened. "It will be a difficult venture for an unmarried female, but I will do all I can to support you."

Briana heard the shouting in the library and wondered what the duke would say about that.

Chapter Four

*B*riana sat in the Earl of Stonebridge's drawing room, watching with increasing trepidation as the frown on her godmother's face deepened.

The previous evening Agatha had been so upset during the carriage ride home from the duke's, she had almost broken her parasol by gripping it so tightly. She had stared into Briana's eyes, looked away, and compressed her lips into a harsh line of disapproval. A minute later she spoke in a brusque tone, announcing she would speak with Briana the following morning.

At the time Briana had been grateful for the silence because her encounter with Lord Clayton had confused her. But now, she wondered if giving her godmother time to think about the situation had been the wrong thing to do.

As to Lord Clayton, the harder she tried to forget about yesterday's incident, the more it raced about in her brain. The handsome lord had rekindled feelings she had thought long gone. He was a dangerous sort, always playing with her heart.

Even though Alistair had returned to the army, he had been safe. Their relationship certainly wasn't as intense as what Jane and Emily had with their spouses, even before they had married.

She wondered if it had ever been love between her and Alistair. She just wasn't sure about anything anymore.

"It's not as if I am going off to fight Napoleon, Agatha."

The older lady was walking about the room, her trusty parasol tapping the floor with each agitated step. "Napoleon is resting comfortably at St. Helena, so fighting him is not possible."

"But it's only a house party."

Agatha turned, her gray eyes narrowing considerably. "A house party? It is an assignment from Whitehall to find a spy in the trenches, child. There is every reason to worry. They should have never asked you. I don't care if there is a chance in a million that the enemy will be there. I don't want you involved."

Briana glanced at the door to make certain it was closed. Living in the earl's London townhouse had been wonderful, but sometimes privacy was at a minimum, especially with three-year-old Gabrielle and a new baby in the house.

"If it were anything high risk, Whitehall would have sent in the army," Briana said calmly. "I am only helping you."

Agatha's lips puckered. "I don't need help, and I don't see why Whitehall decided to go over my head on this!"

Briana wasn't going to touch that comment. It was better to play upon her assets. "The invitations were sent out weeks ago. Everything about this mission fits in perfectly."

"Yes, and it seems the Director of Operations thought so, too. I am not happy about Headquarters going behind my back like this. I was to be the only one involved."

Agatha pointed the parasol at Briana and lifted a gray brow. "I don't like it. Your mother wouldn't approve."

Briana smiled, not the least bit afraid of Agatha's trusty parasol. Some men avoided the alleged weapon at all costs, but to Briana it was a loving reminder of her godmother's eccentricities. "My mother knows nothing about this, and you are not going to tell her."

"Your mother entrusted me to find you a husband. And I intend to do just that."

Briana picked up her tea and sipped the warm liquid, peering over the rim of her cup. Finding a husband was the last thing on her mind. "I am two and twenty. I believe I can make that decision by myself."

"I know what you have decided, but as your godmother, I have a solemn duty to see you married."

Briana laughed. "Good grief, I am no child. I can take care of myself."

"I should never have included you in my dealings with Whitehall, even if it was just paperwork."

"Though secret it may have been, I was only adding up columns of numbers and going over some research for you. It's not as if I was in the front lines at Waterloo."

"You have a high intelligence, my girl, but don't think to use it on me. I needed someone like you to help me, but this—this is outrageous! Since you had clearance on my behalf, you now hold a position I never intended you to have."

A bark erupted from the corner of the room.

Agatha's steely eyes glinted with triumph. "Nigel, you are of the same opinion, I believe."

The earl's massive dog barked again. The parasol swung wide. "Ha! See, he doesn't like it one bit either. Paperwork is one thing, child, facing the enemy quite another."

Briana settled her cup on the rosewood table to her left. There was no stopping Agatha when she started her little speeches, so all Briana could do was try to calm her godmother down.

"I understand your concern. However, we both know this is probably a wild-goose chase. Nothing will come of it. Afterward, I will see to a few things in London, then visit my mother. This is, in truth, the only excitement I have had in years."

"Excitement? Bah. You should be married to some nice gentleman instead of searching out spies and whatnot. I am not too old to do my duty, young lady. Do not forget who I am."

"But—"

The parasol thwacked against the fireplace. "I will do everything in my power to see you don't go. It's not as if I haven't done anything like this before."

Briana bit down on her anger. "This is too important to keep me behind and you know it. Your people need someone like me who can fade into the crowd. I am perfect. As you said yourself, there may have been a leak already. In fact, you might be the one in danger. I don't think it a good idea for you to go along at all."

"I don't want you hurt." The lady's words flowed together while her bottom lip trembled.

Briana's heart clenched as she picked up Agatha's tea and handed it to her. "I won't be hurt."

Agatha took the cup and sank into a wing chair beside the hearth. "There has been talk of Grimstoke being involved. This could be more than just a hunch. We are talking about a possible link in a plot against the Regent's life."

"I am aware of that. But could this be a decoy to throw Whitehall off course? Grimstoke is Prinny's good friend. It all seems a little far-fetched if you ask me."

Agatha's eyes closed and she shook her head, as if remembering something she would rather forget. "There have been greater men who have given away their best friend, my dear. Never let your heart get in the way of your work."

Briana brushed her hand against Nigel's soft fur as the dog moved beside her. Her heart was never going to get in the way of anything ever again. "I can fade away easily enough. If Lord Grimstoke is passing on information that can hurt the Regent, he must be apprehended along with the enemy."

Lines of worry creased Agatha's brow. "Whitehall should never have asked you. They have other people who do these types of things. Trained specialists, for heaven's sake."

Briana took the elder lady's hand in hers. "It will probably come to nothing. Lord Grimstoke said something to the prince in anger and now Whitehall thinks the man is an enemy of the Crown. It's all so absurd. Look at it this way: Maybe I will be able to clear Violet's father of any wrongdoing."

"It is more complicated than that, I am afraid. There are particulars you need to know."

Briana's curiosity rose. "Particulars?" What had Whitehall not told her?

Her godmother rested her parasol against her gown and sighed. "The source is thought to be a servant or a family member of Grimstoke. Possibly even a guest at his party."

Briana leaned forward, her senses humming. "And this unidentified informant has led Whitehall to believe some exchange will be taking place?"

Agatha nodded. "Whoever the source is, they gave us quite specific information. How they passed on the communication, I don't know. It is not being shared with me."

Briana glanced at the door, then shifted her wary gaze back to Agatha. "Servants have been known to make the best spies."

A wry smile flashed across the older lady's face. "Anyone can be a spy, my dear. Don't let one's outward appearance fool you. But in this case the source has led us to believe there may be a missive exchanged in Grimstoke's library somewhere in the vicinity of his desk."

A bubble of laughter escaped Briana's lips. "In the vicinity of his desk? That is the most ridiculous thing I have ever heard. You must be jesting!"

Gray eyes sparkled back at her. "I admit, it does sound rather absurd and could mean nothing, so why don't you stay here with Emily and the children while I go on that wild-goose chase?"

Briana's green eyes tapered into suspicious slits. "You are not getting rid of me that fast."

Agatha blinked, looking close to tears. "I lost my true love more than ten years ago, child. You are as close to me as Emily and her family. I don't want you hurt."

Briana put her hand in Agatha's. "I won't be hurt. I promise."

"Promises cannot be kept as we wish them. I know that from my own experience."

Briana felt for her godmother, but she wasn't ready to step aside. "For all we know, it's just as you said, and this entire mission will lead to nothing at all."

The door swung open and both ladies turned their heads. Lord Clayton stepped into the room and Briana's heart gave a sudden kick. Was it only yesterday that he had held her?

Even though he was the third son of a duke he had a certain air about him that demanded instant attention. And it didn't hurt that he looked magnificent in his navy blue coat and tan breeches.

A slow smile spread across his lips. It was a smile that had given hope to many women in the *ton* that this man would choose them for his bride. "Ah, forgive me, ladies. I had no idea you were here. I was to meet with my sister."

Violet blue eyes twinkled at Briana. Though it wasn't unusual for Emily's brothers to walk into the room unannounced in the middle of the day, she found it unsettling that this man, who had caught her sleeping in the duke's library, was standing before her now.

The memory of the way he had held her flashed in her mind. The scent of bayberry. The gentle force of his hand against her mouth. The softness of his eyes. The quickness of his mind. And he remembered it all. The insufferable man!

"Good afternoon, my lord," Briana said, growing hot with embarrassment. Uncomfortable under his scrutiny, she pulled her hand from Agatha's, accidentally knocking the creamer onto the rug. Nigel jumped and barked, tipping over the teapot. Agatha tried to calm the dog, but to no avail. The dog kept yapping.

Agatha looked up. The parasol swept through the air as the lady tried to keep Nigel away from the steaming tea and cream. "You took us by surprise, my lord. Nigel! Stop that!"

The scene seemed to amuse Lord Clayton. "It looks as if poor Nigel was taken by surprise as well."

Briana leaned over to dab at the rug with her handkerchief. Nigel barked louder, thinking it was a game. A shrill whistle pierced the air. All heads snapped in the direction of Lord Clayton, including Nigel's. Briana stared at the towering man in stunned amazement.

"Forgive me," he said smoothly. "It was my unannounced visit that caused this mess. Let me call for help."

In three long strides he was across the room and pulling the bell cord. "From previous encounters I have found that Nigel can turn the calmest settings into a production fit for the stage." His wry grin shot straight through Briana's heart.

"Well," Agatha sighed, walking toward the door, parasol in hand, "you are quite right about that, my lord."

Briana stood and peered anxiously at her godmother. Why was she leaving her with this man? "Agatha?"

Agatha glanced Briana's way, a definite twinkle in her intelligent gray eyes. Without a word to her godchild, she switched her gaze back to Lord Clayton. "If you are to meet Emily, I am certain she will be here in a few minutes. Probably checking on the babe. So, if you would be so kind as to keep my goddaughter company while I see to a few things. I don't think a chaperone is necessary with the door open, now, is it, my lord?"

Lord Clayton's eyes flickered with mischief. "Certainly not, madam. You can trust me."

Agatha looked him up and down. "Indeed."

Lord Clayton made a quick bow and held the door open for Agatha to depart.

Briana was so mad she could spit. *Agatha! Don't you dare leave me!* But before she could open her mouth, the point of that trusty parasol sailed past the door and disappeared.

Dropping back into her seat, Briana gaped at the mess on the floor. What could she say to this man? What should she say to this man after yesterday? She stared at Nigel's big brown eyes. The dog seemed to understand her situation better than anyone else did.

Lord Clayton took a seat across from her and picked up the empty teapot, setting it back on its tray. "So, Miss Garland, we meet again."

Briana slowly raised her eyes to gaze at him. She wasn't afraid of the man. It was just that he was so . . . so charming and infuriating at the same time! "So we do," she said sweetly.

Her eyes slanted slightly, daring him to mention yesterday's fiasco. He was nothing at all like Alistair. Where Alistair held a quiet, soft gentleness, this man held a strong, authoritative air that suggested he could obtain anything he wanted.

He cleared his throat and leaned back in his chair, his grin twisting her heart until she could barely think anymore. He was remembering yesterday. She could see it in that gaze. Drat him and his alluring smirk. Alistair had never made her feel like this.

"Your mother is well?" he asked politely, the smile slowly fading as if he suddenly remembered *her mother.*

It was all Mama's fault, she told herself. Lady Garland should never have mentioned marriage to this man. The poor lord had to act like the perfect gentleman and sit with her until Emily appeared.

But if Briana knew anything about Agatha, the lady would make certain Emily was late. Not only that, her godmother would make certain to detain the maid who was to clean up the mess as well.

"My mother is ill with the headaches, my lord. She is resting in the country. I am staying with my godmother and the earl until the end of the Season."

He nodded, glancing up at the mantel clock. It seemed he was contemplating the weight of the world. Yesterday didn't mean anything to him. What a goose she had been even thinking it had.

Little did she know that in the back of Clayton's mind she was a slim but potential candidate for his bride, even though Emily had commanded otherwise.

Oh, Clayton knew he would never love Miss Garland. But he could respect her. She had spirit, gentleness, and intellect, all wrapped tightly into one neat little package. If Emily didn't come through with a list, he was definitely putting Miss Garland on his.

"The, uh, weather has been rather fair for June," he said, wondering what was going on inside that little red head.

"Yes, it has been rather fair."

He tapped a finger against his knee. "Your mother is faring better, I presume?"

He distinctly remembered the summers this female had spent at Elbourne Hall. Briana Garland had been a sweet, biddable girl without a spiteful bone in her body. Her meekness had amused him more than once during those carefree years. But now, well, she seemed different. A bit more unyielding than he remembered, and definitely able to stand on her own two feet. She had pluck.

Two lovely green eyes stared back at him, and a strange sensation swept through him. "Better? I believe I mentioned that my mother is recuperating in the country, my lord," she said stiffly. "And she is not better."

"Ah, I see."

"Headaches!"

"Yes, headaches will do that." He sat up straighter. Now, this was quite odd. The lady seemed rather annoyed with him.

After a few more minutes of dull conversation, the maid finally came in to clean up the mess, bringing another round of tea. Miss Garland put her hand to the pot. "May I pour?"

Clayton looked up into those stubborn green eyes and felt a rush of pleasure. When had the female become so alluring?

Before he could answer, Nigel gave an obnoxious bark and decided to jump between them. With a horrified yelp from Miss Garland, the teapot flew from her hand toward Clayton's lap.

"Yeooooow!" Clayton shot out of his chair as hot tea splashed onto his breeches. He slapped at his thighs, feeling the burning liquid seep into his skin like flaming coals from hell.

Nigel howled while Miss Garland jumped up and down, dabbing a handkerchief to his legs.

"I am fine, madam," he hissed between his teeth. "Quite fine!"

She pulled back, her cheeks turning pink. "Forgive me. I didn't mean to throw it at you."

Clayton backed up, his hands in the air. "Just stay where you are." He was trying desperately not to curse.

Two green eyes went wide. "It's not as if I meant to do it!"

Clayton eyed her suspiciously, his legs still smoldering. "Of course not," he said through a stiff jaw.

Her lips began to tremble. By Jove, he hated tears. "There is no reason to cry."

Her delicate brows narrowed. "I am not crying!"

"Well, where the devil is Emily?"

"You do not have to shout!"

"I am not shouting!" he yelled back.

Nigel barked.

"You are shouting, my lord!"

Clayton bit back another curse as he watched the lady's delicate white hands deposit the teapot back onto the silver tray. The burning on his legs seemed to be subsiding. But her bold retort had surprised him. Again.

His gaze clung to the base of her swanlike neck as she brushed Nigel aside. Then it traveled to the freckles that seemed to dance in the sunlight. Her berry lips were broad and full.

They were indeed kissable, he thought. It wasn't the wine yesterday that had made him think that. His eyes suddenly narrowed. What the devil? Wait a deuced minute. Were her lips moving? Indeed, they were. She seemed to be mumbling to herself. And by Jove, he thought he heard the word "idiot"!

"What did you say?" he asked, rather perturbed.

"Nothing."

She looked up, her spine stiffening. Her lips had turned into a thin line of disobedience. Biddable she was not! What the devil had he been thinking?

His hands clenched at his sides as the scent of vanilla assaulted him. "I believe the word I heard came from either you or Nigel, and since dogs cannot talk, I assume it came from you."

Her tiny chin lifted higher, daring him to say it.

He jerked his jacket tighter to cover the wetness on his breeches, knowing he should leave the matter be, but a little demon of anger rose up inside him, and he refused to back down.

"Miss Garland, I distinctly heard you say 'idiot.'"

Chapter Five

"Clayton, I am so sorry to be late. I—"

Emily stopped at the threshold of the drawing room, her gaze flicking from the spot on Clayton's breeches to Miss Garland's pale face. A frown settled across her brow.

Clayton understood the meaning of that fixed stare, and dashed if he would be taking the fault for this situation. Perhaps he had been a bit detached, but it certainly did not call for tea in his lap!

"I had an accident with the tea," Miss Garland said apologetically, turning to his sister. "Nigel startled me and, well, I jumped. Next thing I knew, the tea was flying into your brother's lap."

A mischievous smile quivered at the corner of Emily's mouth.

Clayton's lips thinned. "I fail to see the amusement in this." He turned toward Miss Garland. It was obvious the lady was having a rough time holding on to her laughter as well.

Her green eyes twinkled under dark lashes. "Forgive me, my lord. I am such an *idiot*."

Emily could barely control her laughter as she took another glance at his breeches. "No, you are not an idiot. Is she, Clayton?" his sister added, pretending she had something in the corner of her eye.

Clayton ignored the question. "I will be in search of your husband's valet, *dear sister*. After I find another pair of breeches, I will meet you in your husband's study."

He gave Miss Garland a curt bow. "Your servant, Miss Garland."

"Oh, Uncle Clay!" came the little voice from behind the door. "You came for my tea party!"

Clayton groaned. It was Gabrielle, Jared's three-year-old daughter, and the blond-headed imp noticed everything. Being quite intelligent, she also had a mouth that knew more words than most girls her age. And yes, he had promised her a tea party the next time he came calling. Hell and thunderation!

"Oh, no!" Big blue eyes locked onto his breeches. "Did you have an ackident?"

"Accident," Emily corrected, pressing her lips tightly together to hide her grin.

Clayton glared at Miss Garland, whose shoulders were beginning to shake. Oh, the lady was quite a fine actress. He should have caught on years ago. It would have been funny if it were not so humiliating.

Gabrielle came across the room and slipped her tiny hand into his. He felt about a foot tall.

The little girl tried to whisper, but her voice penetrated the entire room. "Mama said I have to tell her when that happens." She pointed to his wet spot.

Nigel gave a whine of distress.

Clayton bit down on his tongue. He could only be glad the earl was not home. Jared would have ripped him to ribbons if he had caught him in this embarrassing predicament.

Gabrielle tugged Clayton toward Emily. "Is he in trouble now, Mama? Will he miss my tea party?"

A few feet away, Miss Garland burst forth with laughter and left the room.

"What exactly happened in there?" Emily stood in her husband's study, perusing a book from the earl's shelves.

Clayton planted his hands to his hips, wanting his sister's full attention. But the devil of it was, Jared's breeches were too blasted uncomfortable. It was deuced hard to act manly when he knew two women had been laughing at him.

As he yanked at the waist, he noticed his sister was thumbing through a book on Egyptian architecture. No doubt the volume was pulled for the red-haired tea-spiller, he thought, watching Emily's lips starting to tremble.

"If you can contain your amusement, I may be able to explain."

Emily glanced over her shoulder, her violet eyes dancing. "I—I am not laughing."

"Dash it, Em. It was all Nigel's fault."

His sister closed the book with a snap. "That dog would never cause any trouble."

Clayton's brows went up. "Really? I have heard differently. As a matter of fact, I have it from a higher authority that good old Nigel trapped you beneath Jared's bed."

Emily's face reddened. "That was a long time ago."

"Before you were married?"

"Nothing happened," she said, her chin set into a stubborn line.

"Point taken. That is exactly what I am trying to say."

Emily placed the book on a nearby end table and crossed her arms over her chest. "You tried nothing with Briana? You weren't so foolish as to ask her to be your bride? Your convenient bride, I might add."

Could his sister read minds now? "What do you take me for?"

"You are known to be an excellent horseman, a superb swordsman, a decent rifleman"—she paused—"and an excellent flirt."

Clayton reddened. "I don't know who you have been talking to, but it isn't true."

Emily shrugged.

"Nothing happened! It was an accident!"

"I believe you."

"Then why are you so short with me?"

Emily's arms fell to her sides. "I'm worried about Briana. Since her sister and father passed away, she has not been the same."

A cold ball of guilt began to grow in his stomach as he thought about his conversation with the lady. All he had been thinking about was that deuced will. He clearly had not been listening to her—he had been so wrapped up in his thoughts. Perhaps Miss Garland was correct after all. He was an idiot.

Clayton walked across the room and paged through the book Emily had pulled. "I had forgotten about the drowning incident and what effect it would have on her. But what the devil is wrong with talking about the weather and her mama's headaches?"

Emily's eyes burned into him. "How could you have forgotten about Clarice's death?"

"I didn't forget. I remember reading it in the papers. I hadn't forgotten they had been in mourning the previous year either. A man doesn't forget a thing like that."

"You were thinking about the will and not paying attention to Briana, weren't you? As a gentleman, it was not well done of you. You used to do the same thing when we were children."

He clapped the book closed. "It's not as if I said something terrible!"

Clayton knew he would have to find the lady and apologize. Emily was correct. It was not well done of him.

"Did her sister commit suicide?" he asked bluntly.

The fight seemed to go out of Emily. "Oh, Clay, I don't know. They say she drowned in the Thames, just like you said."

Clayton shook his head. "All females should learn to swim."

"She knew how to swim, Clay. Don't you remember that time at Elbourne? Briana and her sister came out that summer. You were swimming with your friends from school in the nearby lake. I think Lord Kingsdale was with you. Clarice dove under the water and bit your ankle. In the meantime, Briana and I dumped your clothes in the bushes beyond the road."

The mention of Kingsdale brought a frown to Clayton's face. He had parted ways with the man a few years ago when Kingsdale had vehemently begun to oppose many government policies. He had become part of an eccentric group that wanted complete change.

Oh, Clayton knew there were some things that needed to be changed in England, but Kingsdale had been over the top. He was a liar bent on always having things his way, not only in government but with the women he encountered. Like a spider, he lured females into his web, and once they were in his clutches he struck with a vengeance.

A muscle ticked in Clayton's jaw as he recalled watching the man spin his plans at Vauxhall Gardens so many years ago. It was evening, down a secluded path, and Kingsdale thought he was alone with the lady. But he had not been alone. Clayton had intervened, rescuing an innocent maiden from Kingsdale's hands, making the man furious. Afterward the two men had severed their friendship. Their childhood memories were no longer a reason to forgive and forget.

"Yes, I remember," he said to his sister, inverting his frown. Emily knew Kingsdale enjoyed the study of Egyptian artifacts, but Clayton suspected she didn't know the man's heart was as hard as that of the pharaoh from the story of Moses. In truth, Clayton was glad to no longer have contact with the man.

"We had good enough sense to keep our breeches on, but when I caught up to you, you were sitting innocently next to Father, telling him what a wonderful day you'd had."

"Yes, and Briana was embroidering near the fire. We could hardly contain our laughter."

"I imagine it was your idea," Clayton said, raising a speculative brow.

"No, it just happened. We saw a lady walking along the road with her maid and thought it would be hilarious to leave you and Lord Kingsdale without proper attire. Briana wanted nothing to do with it. But after Clarice bit you, the game was on."

"I admit, it was amusing. But only years later, mind you. Kingsdale was furious."

Clayton did not want to think what the man would have done if he had been alone with the girls. It had taken Clayton years to uncover Kingsdale's unpleasant side.

"It was silly of us girls, but poor Briana didn't swim. We were going to wade in the lake when we found you boys. You never had a chance. And since you had ruined our plans . . . "

Clayton frowned. "Clarice was what?"

"She was twelve then. We were about fifteen. You know, I think she was only seventeen when she died."

"She was a silly little chit, but pretty as a princess."

"But she's dead. And poor Briana still feels the pain. I suppose it was like that for me when Papa died."

Clayton strolled about the room, his hand rubbing the back of his neck. "Yes, well, I suppose it was." He paused. "You know I care about you, Em, and I do care about the feelings of others, even Miss Garland's. However, sometimes one must be practical. You must know why I made this appointment to see you."

Emily's brows dipped. "Don't say it."

Clayton glanced over his shoulder. "What?"

"Don't ask me to help you find a bride."

"Em, I'm in dire straits here. You're my devoted sister. If not you, then who?"

Emily tilted her head. "You know, I always wondered what happened between you and Lady Serena."

"She married a colonel," he stated in a cool tone.

"Yes, well, I know that. Everybody knows that."

"His rank was higher than mine," he bit out. "Anything else?"

"She was a fool."

"Love is for fools."

Emily stiffened.

He shook his head. This deuced will was making him insane. "I'm sorry. I didn't mean that. You and Jared have a wonderful marriage. It just isn't for me."

"I know what you mean. You want a biddable wife? A woman who will stay in the country while you enjoy the entertainment in Town. You don't want to involve your heart in any way, matter, or form. Tell me I'm wrong."

"Oh, for the love of the king, I'm not asking for much. It would be a marriage of convenience, but I certainly don't want my bride to throw me into debtor's prison after a year of marriage. A husband is responsible for his wife's actions, you know."

She put a hand on her hip. "So you want someone with some brains, but not too many."

"Do you want Gerald to have the money?"

"No."

"Then help me." Clayton stood with feet apart, hands behind

his back, waiting patiently for her answer. Surely his sister knew some maidens who would fulfill his requirements.

Her violet eyes darkened. "My mind is blank on the subject."

Clayton's fists clenched. "With or without your help I will find a bride."

"You cannot marry without love, Clay."

"Love is not a requirement. Our parents married without love, and we turned out quite fine indeed."

"Did we?" she said in a pained whisper. "Did we truly, Clay? It wasn't easy knowing that Mama desperately loved Papa and he didn't return that love."

"Hell's bells, Em! What do you want of me? My soul?"

She touched his sleeve. "I want you to marry a lady who loves you. I want you to have what I have now, what Mother has now. What Roderick and Stephen have. It is possible, Clay. Please, don't throw your life away on this castle and Cathaven's money. It isn't worth it."

Clayton shrugged away, picking up one of the earl's alabaster bookends. His parents had loved him. He knew that. But their life together hadn't been easy. After the duke had died, the duchess had fallen in love with a gentleman who adored her. Clayton had never seen his mother happier than she was now.

Emily, Roderick and Stephen had all found their true love. But Clayton had turned his back on love after Serena had left him. Had he loved her? He wasn't sure anymore. But he'd vowed never to go through that again. No one would have part of his heart, love or otherwise. He had been a soldier and he quickly learned that a vulnerability, mental or physical, could get you killed, and it dashed well wasn't going to happen to him.

He set the bookend down. "I lost everything in the tobacco shipment. I have nothing left."

There was a slight pause before Emily spoke. "I can understand how you feel, but you have us. Roderick or Jared could give you some money, even lend—"

"No! I will not beg!"

"It won't be begging. We're family. You are entitled to your monthly sum."

"Many gentlemen live like that, but I cannot. Yes, that amount may keep me in London. I could gamble, go to New-market, even travel a bit. But I want control over what I do. Since I lost my fortune, I would become dependent on the family. Roderick would always have a say."

"No, he would never interfere in your life."

There was a loving gentleness in his sister's tone that tore at his heart. He didn't want her sympathy or her pity.

"Oh, yes, he would. Roderick is the head of the family now."

The hope in Emily's eyes faded. She understood all too well the wish to be independent. She had her own skeletons. "I cannot in good faith give you a list of women for your choosing. There are some who would marry you just for the money, and there are some who would marry you as a means to escape their family. Either way, it would be a terrible loss for you, don't you see?"

"No, I don't see. I can make a decent choice. Don't you trust me?"

"I certainly cannot stop you. Most likely I will know the lady of your choosing. I can only wish you well."

"Then you will not condemn me?"

She held his gaze. "No. I love you, Clay. But I want you to have what I have."

He marched toward the door. "I don't want your pity, Em. I want your help."

"What are you thinking?" Emily asked in alarm.

Clayton peered over his shoulder, his lips curving into a wicked smile. "Marcus gave me a short list, but I think I can do better. You refused to help, so I am left to my own devices. I cannot promise you anything."

Emily's eyes widened. "Oh, no, you don't!" She ran to the door and flung her arms wide, blocking him from leaving.

He glanced at her. "What? You think to stop me?"

"Yes. Briana is not for you."

He returned her determined gaze with one of his own. "I think you are wrong."

"Oh, you are despicable! Just because she adored you as a child does not mean she adores you now."

His chest swelled beneath his waistcoat. "She adored me?"

Emily's lips puckered. "You know very well she followed you around like some duckling waddling after its mother."

Clayton vaguely recalled the girls following him everywhere when he had been home. But Emily had been with Miss Garland every step of the way. He had thought simply, well, it had never occurred to him the little bluestocking with the green eyes *adored* him.

Though he had believed Miss Garland a perfect candidate for his list, after today's tea-spilling incident, he was definitely having second thoughts. And a nice list of possible brides from Emily would help him considerably. He decided to goad her a bit.

"For your information, I don't think Miss Garland's mother would turn me away. She has been after me for years. Do you know she mentioned marriage last time we met?"

Emily glared at him. "Then by all means marry the mother!"

Clayton laughed. "Ah, very amusing."

Emily crossed her arms over her chest, reminding Clayton of a general he once knew. "If you dare hurt Bree, I will never speak to you again."

"Give me some credit, Em. I am not an unfeeling oaf. I will handle this in the most delicate manner."

Her keen gaze swept over his person. "Hmmmm, very well, I will give you a list of ladies that would suit you."

Clayton tried to act shocked. "You will?"

"Yes. Your blackmail worked. I will have your list by tomorrow."

Chapter Six

"**And** what say you to the weather, Princess? Do you think it will rain?"

Briana fit rather snugly in a child-size chair in the Stonebridge nursery as she carefully picked up the miniature teapot pouring air into the nearby cup where Gabrielle was seated.

Gabrielle giggled, bringing the cup to her lips and slurping the tea air. "Papa says it's going to rain, but I want to play outside." She set her elbows on the table and leaned forward, her blue eyes sparkling. "But Fairy Ladies can change the weather."

Briana threw a hand to her chest. During the past few weeks Lord Stonebridge had teased her, calling her the Fairy Lady whenever she had her head in her books. His lordship would say Briana seemed to be in another world.

Maybe she was—just like Gabrielle was today. Of course Briana knew the earl had not come upon the witty name alone; it had come from dear old Emily, the true teaser in the family.

"But I am not a Fairy Lady, Princess. You must be mistaken."

Gabrielle pointed a white finger at her. "But you are the Fairy Lady! Papa told me! You go . . . you go other places!"

Briana's eyebrows rose at the vehemence of the girl's claim. That comment definitely had the earl's imprint.

Briana loved the study of mathematics and could lose herself in the Pythagorean theorem for hours. She also had a fascination for Egyptian architecture. The pyramids never ceased to amaze her. She understood about going other places easily.

enough. She smiled reassuringly. "Well, then, I guess I am the Fairy Lady."

Gabrielle smiled with pride and scooted onto Briana's lap. "I know you are the Fairy Lady." With her tiny finger, she traced the freckles on the bridge of Briana's nose. "You have lots of feckles. Papa said that if I touch a feckle on a Fairy Lady, I can make a wish." A cool finger pressed lightly on Briana's nose, and the little girl squeezed her eyes shut.

Feckles, not freckles? Briana adored this little girl.

"Feckles are magic," Gabrielle whispered, opening her eyes. "Very magic. And I can make a lot of wishes when I touch them."

Two innocent blue eyes stared at Briana. "Do you know what I wished?"

In her mind's eye Briana could see the earl laughing. But the thought of his love for his daughter touched a chord in her heart that had been numb too long. "Oh, no, Princess, you must not tell me the wish or it won't come true."

"Oh!" Gabrielle slid off Briana's lap and immediately began to set the teacups back on their saucers for another round. "I won't tell. I promise, I won't!"

Briana laughed. "Princesses keep the best secrets."

"And do princesses like tea?"

Briana's head turned at the distinct male voice filling the room. Lord Clayton stood just inside the door, his violet blue gaze looking more mischievous than ever. His words seemed to hold a certain challenge, and she boldly met his gaze. Had he asked the earl's valet for another pair of breeches? A smile sprang to her lips, for indeed the clothes were a snug fit.

She looked away, suddenly embarrassed. His easy stance emphasized his well-formed muscles and narrow hips, making her all too aware of his powerful presence. This man, with his dark features and compelling eyes, certainly didn't look like an idiot.

Why had she ever uttered that word? *Because he goaded me,* she thought, feeling her cheeks turn red. And she had to admit, for a few seconds he had acted like an idiot!

Gabrielle ran toward him. "Uncle Clay! I have tea! Do you want some?"

The man's smile filled the room with sunshine as he lifted the little girl into his arms. "Only if it is princess tea."

Gabrielle broke into laughter. She tried to inch higher in his arms. "I have a secret," she said, one eye peeking at Briana.

Lord Clayton's lips quivered. "I keep secrets, too."

Gabrielle's face pinched with thought. "I can tell you," she whispered, "but you can't tell anyone. Ever."

The man's inquisitive gaze shot to Briana and he winked.

Heat flooded Briana's face. Gabrielle was cupping the man's strong jaw with her two petite hands and leaning into his ear. What was the girl telling him?

The man threw back his head and laughed.

Briana bristled, wondering if he meant to be so alluring.

A multitude of conflicting emotions surged through her. Why did he have to like children? Wasn't being handsome enough for him? His kindness along with his imperfections made him more appealing than ever. A handsome bachelor who adored children was a dangerous combination—even though he did act like an idiot from time to time.

She rose from her chair, having no wish to be in such close quarters with the man. Her heart was already leaning in his direction, and she was in no position to give it away for free.

She had gained too much knowledge in the past few years, and as a woman of learning, she had no reason to let her emotions take over now. She couldn't forget Clarice, her father, or Alistair. She wouldn't forget. Ever.

Good grief! What fanciful notions were taking over her brain anyway? The man wanted nothing to do with her. She was only his sister's houseguest, nothing more.

"Miss Garland, you are not leaving?"

Frowning, Lord Clayton let Gabrielle slip to the floor. "Forgive me for my intrusion. I should have announced myself. But my sister asked me to stay for dinner. She is having duck with plum sauce. It is a favorite of mine."

I knew that, Briana wanted to say. *You also like raspberry tarts. And you smell of bayberry soap every time I'm near you.* Instead, she waved a hand over the table and tried to figure out a way to avoid this man. "We were having a party. But—"

Before she could excuse herself, Gabrielle grabbed hold of

her uncle and dragged him into the nursery. "And now we can have a big party! Like Mama has in the drawing room!"

Within seconds the little girl had connected her free hand with Briana's.

Clayton's brows went up as he regarded the situation. "I dearly hope my niece is pouring."

There was a teasing laughter in his expression that gave Briana all the more reason to leave. She didn't mind being laughed at, and she didn't mind a good joke, but this man was playing with her emotions. She didn't like that at all.

"Perhaps the princess would like to be with her uncle . . . alone," she said, slipping from Gabrielle's grip.

The girl shook her head, jumping up and down. "No! No! I want a big party! I want Nigel, too! Don't go away!"

She spun toward the door and scampered from the room. "Nigel! We're having a party!"

Lord Clayton shuddered at the sound of Nigel's name. "Confounded creature," he muttered, making his way toward the hall. He looked over his shoulder as Briana followed him. "You are not leaving our little party, are you?" The challenge was evident in his eyes as he turned around and blocked her way.

She froze. Of course she was leaving! The insufferable man! But she certainly didn't want him to think she was running away from *him*! Even though that's exactly what she was doing!

"Certainly not," she said calmly, turning toward the window.

She thought she heard him chuckle during the icy stillness that fell between them. As the minutes passed, she couldn't find anything to say to the man, and the awkwardness increased.

She was embarrassed that she had lost her temper earlier, but sometimes Lord Clayton infuriated her. He was nothing at all like Alistair. She picked at the lace on her sleeve. And handsome lords did not willingly join tea parties!

"So, you have magic *feckles*, do you?"

The seriousness of the man's voice made her grin. She turned toward his towering figure, watching a smile spread across his entire face. Merciful heavens! She was not exactly afraid of him. It was just that he was so undeniably attractive.

"They are called *freckles*, my lord. Society detests them."

"Ah, I see."

"Yes. Diluted hydrochloric acid does not seem to help. Neither does the lemon juice my mother gives me."

He started to walk toward her. His eyes locked onto her face as if he were inspecting every freckle she had.

She backed up against the small doll cradle. Her heart began to beat double time. What exactly was he trying to do?

"You are not afraid of me, are you, Miss Garland?"

"W—why in the world would I be afraid of you?" He came close enough that she could smell the familiar bayberry soap he had used in his morning bath.

"Because you seem to be avoiding me."

"I—I am not avoiding you." She walked toward the tea table, clanking the dishes about for another round of pretend tea.

He leaned against the wall and stared at her. The intense look on his face was similar to the one he had given her in the drawing room. Well! She was certainly not going to be the one to run away and give credence to his suggestion that she was avoiding him.

Managing a tiny smile, she took a seat at Gabrielle's small table, hoping the girl would arrive soon.

It seemed an eternity before he spoke. "What do you think of marriage, Miss Garland?"

Briana almost fell off her chair. "W-what?"

His forehead seemed to crease with concentration. "Marriage. I was wondering your thoughts on marriage."

Was he mad? It was the last thing she expected from this man. "I don't think this an appropriate conversation, my lord."

"I meant no harm. I was only wondering why you are not married. It seems an innocent question to me."

He might be a lord, but she was not some simpering female he could tease. "And an arrogant one, my lord. For your information, I am not a diamond of the first water, and my dowry is quite small compared to those of most ladies of the *ton*. Does that satisfy your curiosity?"

"For some ladies of quality, a small dowry would be a disadvantage in the marriage mart, but most females would not let that stop them. Even a bluestocking such as you, Miss Garland."

Briana pressed her lips together. The blood pounded to her brain, and she clenched the teaspoon in her hand. The arrogance of the man!

The smile in his eyes incensed her as he pushed off the wall and strode in the direction of the window seat. Without missing a beat, he began sketching on Gabrielle's easel.

Minutes passed before they spoke again.

"And what do you say of marriage, my lord?" she asked prettily, her blood simmering.

Two violet blue eyes peered over the easel. "Marriage?"

"Oh, forgive me for asking, my lord. It seems speaking to a bluestocking is not on your list of things to do."

He laughed then, a deep male laugh that resonated in her heart. Here was the boy Briana had known when she was a child. Arrogant, yet amusing. Witty, but charming. Handsome, yet insufferable!

He raised his brows as she walked toward the door. "You are not leaving? What about the tea party?"

Oh, she certainly was leaving!

A bark sounded in the hall, along with the thwack of little feet. Briana frowned.

"I found him!" Gabrielle shouted. "We can have a big party now! And Cook is sending some cake and 'emonade! Here it comes!"

A maid was behind the little girl, bringing in a tray of sweets, along with a small pitcher.

"Lemonade?" Briana asked, wishing it were only she and Gabrielle at the tea party.

"Uh-huh." The girl bounced into the room and pulled at her uncle to sit on one of the tea party chairs. Clayton's long legs hit the table with a thud.

"Too big!" she cried.

Clayton's lips puckered. "Well, Princess, what if I push my legs out straight?"

The little girl clapped her hands and smiled. "Just right!"

"Oh, no!" She frowned. "Only two chairs!"

She put a finger to her chin and looked across the room at Briana. "I know. You can sit on Uncle Clayton's lap!"

Clayton snorted.

"I think not," Briana said firmly.

"But I am the princess!" Gabrielle sat on her chair and stuck out her bottom lip. It was obviously time for the girl's nap.

"Yes, Miss Garland, she is the princess," Clayton said, a hint of amusement in his voice.

The maid had left, and Gabrielle and Lord Clayton were staring at Briana, waiting for her to make the next move.

Wanting to kick Lord Clayton from his chair, Briana knelt beside the little girl and said calmly, "May I pour, Princess? But after one glass, I will have to leave. The king awaits."

Gabrielle giggled. "Nigel wants some 'emonade, too. He likes it!"

The dog barked and brushed Briana's arm at the same time she was picking up the pitcher of lemonade. Her hand slipped and Clayton jumped back. But it was too late. Nigel had pushed Briana aside, sending her off balance, and the lemonade splashed onto Clayton's lap, pitcher and all.

An oath sprang to Clayton's lips as he slipped off his chair and onto the floor. Briana gasped, trying to regain her balance, but to her horror she fell onto Clayton's chest.

Gabrielle stood up and laughed, pointing her little finger at them. "You look silly!"

A steely arm wrapped around Briana's waist. "My dear girl," Lord Clayton said, "remind me never to ask you to pour again."

"Well, well, what have we here?"

The cool, disapproving tone of the earl's voice penetrated Briana's ears.

Gabrielle squealed in delight as her father stepped into the room. "It's a tea party, Papa! But it's not tea! It's 'emonade!"

"That's wonderful, Princess." Taking the girl into his arms, the earl directed his firm gaze toward the couple. "May I have a word with you, Clayton?"

The arm around Briana's waist tightened just as another voice broke into the room.

"What in the world—"

Blushing, Briana looked up to see her godmother's gray eyes taking in the scene. The older lady stood behind the earl, her face a mask of disapproval.

"I can explain," Briana said apologetically.

Lord Clayton let out a groan, and his arm suddenly loosened. He rolled onto his elbow, and in one fluid movement he rose, taking Briana with him. The breath whooshed out of her lungs as she swayed to the side.

Lord Clayton stood behind her, his hands pressing gently against her shoulders to steady her. "Easy."

The gentle whisper jerked at her heart.

"We were having a tea party," Lord Clayton said. "Nothing else."

Gabrielle clung to her father's neck, having no notion of the tension swirling about the nursery. "It was 'emonade, Papa."

Jared patted his daughter's head. "Yes, lemonade. You already told me that, poppet."

A bark interrupted the conversation, turning Gabrielle's head toward her tea table.

"Oh, no! Nigel is eating everything!" the girl screeched.

The massive brown dog began to slurp at the spilled drink on the floor and sniff the cakes.

Gabrielle kicked her feet, trying to get down. "My 'emonade!" She slipped from her father's arms and chased after the yelping dog, pushing him away from the mess. "Bad doggie!"

"I can explain," Briana said, trying to make her voice heard over the noise. She thought she heard Lord Clayton muttering, calling the dog an infernal beast.

Agatha shook her head and stretched out her hand for Gabrielle. "Come here, dear. We can give Nigel some lemonade in the kitchen."

"But he ruined everything!"

"Now, now, you know it wasn't all Nigel's fault."

Agatha raised a curt brow Clayton's way, then took her leave of the nursery with a crying Gabrielle in tow.

Briana frowned and stared at Clayton, who had made an unusual snorting noise. Was the man actually laughing?

Jared's voice penetrated Briana's thoughts.

"Clayton, if you can tear yourself away from the tea party, I would like to see you in my study as soon as possible."

With those stinging words, the earl turned on his heel and left the room.

Picking up a chair, Clayton watched Miss Garland's face turn as red as her hair. "A rather embarrassing predicament, Miss Garland. But I believe we fared quite well. Again."

Her green eyes flashed, and Clayton almost laughed. It was obvious she was struggling to stay calm.

"You think this all rather amusing, do you?"

"I daresay, it was rather amusing, was it not?" He bent down to pick up the empty pitcher. "However, I fail to see why you are always dumping things on me."

Instead of playing the meek little miss, Miss Garland stiffened. Her hands bunched at her sides, and those berry lips pressed together to form a stubborn line of defense.

Clayton was captivated by the transformation. The lady was a puzzling mix of femininity and brains. How very intriguing.

"You are no gentleman."

Devil take it. She certainly had spirit.

Clayton followed on her heels as she marched toward the door. Surprisingly, he felt a sudden lift to his step.

"I believe it was you who dumped the tea on me earlier, Miss Garland, and if I am not mistaken, it was also you who dumped the *'emonade* on me. Or are you losing your memory as well as your balance?" *Hmmm, that did it!*

She spun around on her delicate slippers and pushed out her chin. "You are poking fun at me, my lord. I saw it in your eyes the minute you stepped into this room. Why, I saw it the minute you stepped into the drawing room downstairs.

"Well," she sputtered, "have your little amusement at my expense. Have your little ladies at Vauxhall Gardens and the opera. Have your rides in Hyde Park with Miss Hookston and Lady Whatever. But do not think I am subject to your rakish entertainment!" With a huff, she tucked a stray ringlet behind her ear and glared at him.

Clayton blinked. So she knew about Miss Hookston, did she? How very interesting. "Your pardon, Miss Garland. I had no intention of bringing you down to my lifestyle."

"Oh!" she cried, turning from him.

Guilt sliced his heart at the sound of her sniff.

"Listen here," he said more calmly, pulling out his handkerchief, "I own it was an embarrassing situation, but it's not as if I whipped you."

He walked around to face her. She jerked her head away, but he had seen the tears on her cheeks. She wanted to appear strong and in control, but beneath that red head was a mind of sensitivity. Even more fascinating.

He raised his handkerchief as a peace offering. "I am wiping the *feckles*, Miss Garland. A Fairy Lady cannot cry or they will all wash away and so will the wishes."

Miss Garland slapped his hand. "Do not make fun of me!"

Clayton gently grasped her wrist. To his surprise, a shock ran through him. "I never make fun of ladies." His voice was husky and full of apology.

Her watery eyes looked up into his, and something in the air simmered. She smelled of the roses from his mother's garden with a hint of vanilla. Sweet, fresh, and vibrantly alive.

Not knowing why, he raised his finger to touch the bridge of her pert little nose. "One feckle, one wish."

A smile edged out of the corner of her mouth, and though the feel of her skin against his own upset his balance, he continued his count. "Two feckles, two wishes. Three feckles . . ."

"You are insufferable, my lord."

He leaned closer and pushed a stray tendril away from her temple. Devil take it, she was a little sea nymph with those green eyes and that fiery hair. The second her mesmerizing gaze locked onto his face, temptation swept through him like a wildfire, and suddenly he wanted to taste those berry lips.

Hell and thunderation! What the deuce was he doing?

Shaken at how close he had come to kissing her, he quickly stepped back, swallowing hard. "I never said I wasn't insufferable, Miss Garland." With a slow bow, he handed her his handkerchief. "A memento of our tea party."

Smiling, she took it in her hands.

"Friends?" he asked with a charming grin.

She shook her head regretfully. "No, I don't think we can ever be friends," she said rather softly.

Her candid remark annoyed him more than he wanted to admit. Yet the flash of sadness he'd seen in her eyes told him she had been harmed in some way. By a man? He wasn't certain, but whatever this young woman had endured seemed to have hardened her.

With a twinge of regret, he realized this wasn't the innocent girl he recalled from his youth at all. "I must work on that line, must I not, Miss Garland?"

Before she could answer, he surprised himself and kissed her hand. "I believe I have an appointment with the earl."

Her eyes widened at his boldness.

"Oh," he said in wry amusement, "don't worry. I have decided to pass on the duck and plum sauce. Another engagement. So, if you will please excuse me. *Au revoir*, my dear lady. *Au revoir.*"

Briana's gaze followed Lord Clayton as he strode from the nursery. Was it her imagination or had he just asked to be friends? One minute he seemed annoyed with her, the next, well, it seemed he was going to kiss her. She shook her head. No, she was the one going insane. She made her way across the room toward the easel. What had he been drawing? Stick figures to pass the time while he teased her about marriage?

She dropped her gaze to the sketches, and her stomach plummeted. The top paper was a sketch of her. A few freckles were sprinkled across her nose and there was a tiara on her head and at the very bottom were the words "Fairy Lady."

Lord Clayton had more talent in his one finger than she had in all the watercolor and art classes she had taken in a lifetime. The man was full of surprises. What else was he hiding?

She flipped through the rest of the drawings. She had been in the nursery on many occasions, but never once had she paged through the sketchings. Amazed at her find, she fell back against the window seat, holding the papers in her hand. One had Gabrielle sitting on Nigel's back. Another had Gabrielle pouring tea. Her heart turned when she stopped on the one with Gabrielle sitting on the earl's lap and both of them laughing while Nigel jumped in the air beside them. Lord Clayton had even sketched the smile lines around the earl's eyes. It was remarkable.

The man would break her heart if she gave him half a chance. Being friends with him would be a slow death indeed. And his question about marriage . . .

She stiffened. What on earth was she thinking?

Yet the memory of his arms around her earlier that day during the lemonade spill reminded her of the time he had taught her to waltz. She finally had to admit that when she was in his arms, he gave her a sense of security that even Alistair had never given her. His arrogance annoyed her, but his tenderness entranced her.

Her brows narrowed as she took one last look at the sketch. The man could charm a flea off a pot of honey if he wanted to.

She had to keep her distance from him—now and always. Because if she weren't careful, she could be one of the many fleas smashed beneath the heel of his shiny new Hessians.

Chapter Seven

*C*layton strolled into the earl's library, not at all moved by the impatient look in Jared's eyes. "You wanted to see me?" he asked with a sarcastic twist to his mouth.

The earl threw his hands behind his back. "I am not her father, only a very distant relative at that, but you were caught in a compromising position."

"I am here because you are my friend, Jared. I don't want anything between us. Nothing was going on except that your beast of a dog tried to interfere in a princess tea party."

Clayton noted the earl's expression tighten as the man walked about the room. By Jove, to hell with Emily's list and his! If he had to be leg shackled it would be to a woman with some wit and tenderness. Miss Garland might be in a bit of a huff over their strange meetings the past few days, but he told himself his future children would benefit prodigiously with a mother such as her.

"If it worries you, I intend to marry the girl."

Lord Stonebridge whipped around so fast Clayton thought he might burn a hole in the rug. "What the devil did you say?"

Clayton knew Jared shared Emily's fondness for Miss Garland, but he wasn't quite ready for the heated flash of protection he saw in the earl's eyes.

"I need a bride, Jared. You know my circumstances."

"Not Miss Garland," the earl warned.

"Why not? A marriage of convenience would suit us both."

"Is that what you had planned all along, then? In front of my daughter? To compromise the lady?"

Clayton clamped his jaw tight, biting back a swift retort. "Any other man would be called out for that."

"She has no man to speak for her," the earl ripped out. "What do you take me for, some bumbling idiot? I will not let my wife's good friend fall into some marriage of convenience with you or any other man."

"The lady may be under your roof, but she is not your ward."

Jared spread his hands on his desk and leaned forward, his eyes darkening. "I won't have it."

Nigel gave a bark as he trotted out from behind the desk.

Clayton shot the beast a hardened glare. "Does that blasted canine have to be everywhere?"

"Did you hear me?" the earl ground out.

Clayton was irked by Jared's arrogant tone, and it took all his willpower not to walk out on the man. "Rest assured, you have made your point. However, I made my way down here because I am your brother-in-law. But be that as it may, I will do as I wish."

The earl slapped his hand against the desk. "You cannot marry her for a confounded castle!"

"It is for more than a castle," Clayton said harshly.

"Ah, but it is not all about you, is it?" The sarcasm in the earl's voice was evident.

"I am not that shallow, Jared. I intend to treat her well. It would be a mutual agreement between two intelligent parties."

"Do you know how hard the past few years have been for her? Someone has to see to her welfare. That mother of hers is always ill with something."

"Yes, and that mother of hers is always seeking me out."

"Marry the mother, for all I care. But stay away from Miss Garland. Do I make myself perfectly clear?"

The fatherly tone in the man's voice sparked Clayton's anger. "I am not a dragon, hauling her into my cave. She will have the choice to say no. But a woman in her circumstance would never decline such an offer."

Jared straightened, crossing his arms over his broad chest. "Oh ho! You think much of yourself."

Clayton reddened. "I didn't want to marry. But I cannot pass on this opportunity." He thought of Lady Serena. She had never loved him. He knew that now. And what was she to him? Simply a prize to be won? What kind of life would they have had, deceiving one another? In his proposed marriage of convenience, there would be no deception at all.

"Miss Garland can keep to the country. As a child she always loved it there. I can give her a comfortable home and her mother can stay with her as well. I hear Sir Garland was in need of funds when he died. This will be a marriage of convenience that will work well for both of us."

"It won't work for both of you. Take it from a man who went through a *marriage of convenience*. You may be fond of the woman, but you will be miserable."

"Miserable? I've been miserable. I don't want to be there again. The castle, the money, they are not something I asked for, but by heaven, I'm going to take this opportunity. See if I don't."

The earl's face softened. "Clay, for your sake, let this go."

"I am not about to let it slip through my fingers. I have three weeks to make my choice. Miss Garland is at the top of my list. Though a bit of a bluestocking"—*and a bit stubborn,* he wanted to add—"she seems quite agreeable. And," he emphasized, "she is not some simpering female who has to be at my side at all times."

Jared's brows dipped considerably. "I don't think your sister would take kindly to that description."

"You know that's not what I meant," Clayton snapped. "I meant that Miss Garland has the capability to live in the country without me. I will visit upon occasion, but my life will be here in Town. Besides traveling to Newmarket and racing some dashed fine horses, I will have my clubs and other entertainment to keep me busy. Not something a country wife needs or wants."

"And what about children?"

A pair of twin girls with auburn curls came to mind, and Clayton smiled. With Miss Garland as their mother, they would be smarter than most men he knew. And in this day and age, having brains was not a bad thing at all. "Of course I plan to have children."

Jared let out a rush of air. "I should shoot you right now. You know that, don't you?"

Clayton could not resent the earl coming to the lady's defense. In fact, he was glad Miss Garland had a respectable gentleman shielding her from the advances of unwanted suitors, but this was the outside of enough. Jared knew him.

"You have what you want," he said to the earl. "A wife, children, a home. I am only asking for a bit of that."

Jared's face hardened again. "You don't know what the hell you want anymore," he said. "All you're thinking about is that castle and the money!"

The dog let out a groaning howl of distress.

With a scowl twisting his handsome features, Jared marched across the room and swung open the door. "Yes, I know, Nigel. It hurts my ears, too."

The dog dashed into the hall with another wail.

Clutching the door, Jared regarded Clayton with a disapproving stare. "I don't like it. You should love your wife. I don't care what the rest of the *ton* does or doesn't do. It isn't right, Clay. It just isn't right."

"I thought I loved once, too, Jared. But I was wrong. The lady ran away, thinking she would have a better life with an older man. So you see? A marriage based on what you have is not for me."

Another lady holding even a part of Clayton's heart would set him in a weak position, and as Wellington had learned in the war against old Boney, any sign of weakness could get a man killed.

"Then you're a fool, Clay. A deuced fool."

Briana had started down the stairs but halted when Nigel came rushing toward her. "Hello, boy." Smiling, she patted his thick brown fur. "Ah, I understand. You are running from someone. Did Gabrielle get ahold of Agatha's parasol again?"

The dog let out a yelp and licked her hand.

"Not Gabrielle, huh?" She laughed and pushed him up the steps toward the nursery. "Go on, then. I suspect your favorite girl will be there soon."

The massive dog dashed up the staircase and disappeared

around the corner as if a nice juicy roast were waiting for him on a silver platter. With a low chuckle, Briana continued down the stairs. *If only life were that easy.*

She paused at the bottom step when two angry voices met her ears. The sounds were coming from the library. Lord Clayton and Lord Stonebridge were shouting at each other.

"I thought I loved once, too, Jared. But I was wrong. The lady ran away, thinking she would have a better life with an older man. So you see? A marriage based on what you have is not for me."

Briana fought the impulse to run back up the stairs along with Nigel. It was Lord Clayton's voice and it shook her to her very core. Whatever tiny hope she had had of marriage with the handsome lord fizzled into nothing. Any childhood dreams she had suppressed instantly dissolved.

She had heard stories about Lady Serena's flight with some high-ranking officer and she thought the lady a fool. But she had never realized how much it hurt him. He held wounds of sorrow and grief that mimicked her own. A seed of empathy began to grow inside her, and she didn't like to admit it, but the imperfections in his character made her like him a little more. And his loving Gabrielle didn't hurt him either.

Her heart squeezed and her eyes stung. So, he didn't believe in a love-filled marriage. What did it matter? Hadn't she known the truth about her and Lord Clayton a long time ago? What kind of imaginary life had she been spinning?

A strange ache began to spread through her limbs. Why should she care anyway? Why should she ever trust a man again? She had already made her decision before she'd heard whatever Lord Clayton had to say or before she had ever felt his pain.

Besides, he wasn't even thinking about her.

He was only confirming her very thoughts, her very plans for the future. A man would only ruin her life. Wasn't it a man who had left Clarice with child? She put a hand to her mouth and choked back a sob as memories flooded her. Sir Garland and Lieutenant Alistair Perry had made a fine impression on her life as well, almost like Lady Serena had made on Clayton.

No, she thought, turning around and climbing the steps to her bedchamber, trusting the opposite sex was not an option.

After speaking with Jared, Clayton realized he was making a rash decision and admitted to himself that perhaps he should at least try to find another bride instead of Miss Garland, but the lady was never far from his mind.

"Here is the amended list," Marcus said, handing over the paper to Clayton.

Clayton sat down in the chair at White's, shaking his head. "Only three more names? You are as much help as Emily. She gave me a list of widows ten years older than me."

Marcus's smile died. "This is not polygamy, Clay. Whittle the six down to two and then make your choice. I may be your brother, but that doesn't mean I like what you're doing."

Clayton pointed to two names. "Never heard of them."

Marcus took a sip of his wine, avoiding Clayton's gaze. "Twins. Just out of the schoolroom. Father's a rich earl up north."

"Wonderful. How old are they, sixteen?"

"Seventeen."

Clayton grimaced. "I am not out to rob the cradle."

Marcus's glass clanked against the table. "No, but you have made it known that you need a wife."

Clayton began to wonder if his entire family was against him in this. "Who the devil is Miss Dunkly?"

"You remember, the female with the silly laugh. Christian name, Roberta. Not bad to look at. Has quite a dowry. I do believe she wouldn't mind the country. Stays there most of the time anyway." Marcus chuckled. "Loves horses."

Clayton winced, recalling the lady's snorting laugh. "You never liked me, did you?"

"You could drop the whole thing." Marcus's expression turned serious. "Perhaps you could invest in a plantation in the Caribbean. I can loan you some money."

"No," Clayton said, curling his fingers around the paper. He had no wish to be in debt to his family. He had this one chance, and by heaven, he was going to take it! "I will do this, Marcus."

"Dash it all, Clay, I can't stop you. You always do what you want anyway."

Clayton heaved a sigh as a pair of bright green eyes came to his mind. "Tell me the truth." He drummed his fingers on the table. "What do you think of Miss Garland?"

Marcus frowned. "Miss Briana Garland? Em's friend?"

"The same. She and Miss Appleby are staying with Em for a bit. Lady Garland is in the country. Headaches, you know."

"Ah, yes, the mama." Marcus stretched out his right leg as he surveyed Clayton with a humorous expression. "The lady who looks like a penguin. Mother's friend, is she not?"

"At least the daughter doesn't look like the mother."

Marcus smiled. "No, Miss Garland has those green eyes that could turn a man inside out if she only knew how to use them. And those freckles are, well, no matter what the *ton* says, I think they are rather sweet. Adorable, in fact."

Clayton made a fist beside his glass. "Don't tell me you have a fondness for her?"

"Oh, she is a rather pleasant girl. Quite scholarly, they say. Not a beauty in the conventional way."

"I think her rather pretty," Clayton said in a clipped tone.

Marcus studied his brother for a few seconds. "Yes, I would say she was rather pretty indeed. Wasn't it her sister who drowned in the Thames? Father died immediately afterwards."

"Yes. The lady and her mother came out of mourning end of last year."

Marcus twirled the handle of his wineglass. "Now, why would you be interested in Miss Garland, I ask myself? I admit it, she does have a brain, always popping into the library, especially when she was at Elbourne. Seen her at the lending library a few times. Blends into the books as if she lives there. Bluestocking if there ever was one. 'Course there is one bookish gentleman who works there, and I believe he definitely has eyes for the lady."

He pursed his lips and regarded Clayton. "If you ask me, I think she's hiding something."

"For your information, I didn't ask you."

Marcus's lips twitched. "Those eyes of hers are quite the

thing. But I have to be honest—lately she wears the most dowdy of gowns. Not that I am a fashion expert."

"No, that you are not," Clayton said sharply. What did his brother know about anything anyway? She'd just got out of mourning.

"But I do believe if the lady was stuffed into the right clothes she might present—"

"What the hell did you have to drink?" Clayton snapped. "I don't need an entire dissertation on the lady."

Marcus looked annoyed. "You asked me. I told you."

"Forget I asked."

"You do know Em would call you out with swords if you dare take one step in that direction."

Clayton scowled. "What the devil are you blabbering about?"

"Miss Garland, you idiot!"

"You know, I am sick and tired of being called an idiot."

"You are, if you think you'll be happy marrying some chit for that castle. I've tried to help you because you're my brother and you asked me. But you could have any woman you wanted, Clay. Don't make a mistake just because you feel time's running out."

"I'm not making a mistake. I'm not interested in a marriage based on love. How many couples in the *ton* live like that?"

Marcus's lips narrowed into a thin line.

"Convenience is the only thing I ask for. A bride who will let me set her up in the country is what I need. She will have everything to her heart's desire. If she wants to journey to London, she need only send word to me and it will be done."

Marcus leaned across the table. "How old are you, seventeen?"

Clayton's chair scraped against the floor. "Thanks for all the help. I wish I could be there when you search for a bride."

Marcus frowned. "That day is coming, I fear. Being the second son of the duke gives me no choice in the matter."

Clayton stood. "You seem resigned to that fact."

Marcus looked up. "Devil take it, Clay. You have the choice of marrying for love. I am the second son of the duke. I will look for love if I can find it, but the title must be secured. It is my duty. All my life I have been told I must marry for the sake of the Elbourne name. You have time on your side."

Clayton had never heard this confession from his brother. "You don't want to marry?"

"That's not it. But I want to travel. Be an ambassador of sorts. Give something back to the world. What lady would ever want to leave her country for ports unknown? It's inconceivable."

"You never gave the slightest hint you wanted to leave England."

Marcus shrugged. "Back to you. Whom do you find the most appealing? You must have other ladies in the running."

"There is that opera singer, and then the actress at Drury Lane, but I daresay they would not make good wives."

Marcus's eyes sparkled. "No, I don't think they would. Neither would Miss Hookston. However, Miss Cherrie Black will be at Grimstoke's party, along with a few others. If you have to make a choice, you will have two weeks with them."

He leaned back in his chair. "Em won't like it a bit if you go after Miss Garland. I, for one, would stay clear of the lady."

Clayton folded the paper and shoved it into his pocket. *Stay clear of the lady? Maybe, maybe not.* "Should be enough time."

"And the special license? Have you thought about that little insignificant detail?"

"Of course. The archbishop is staying in the nearby village. Visiting relatives, I believe."

Marcus raised a sardonic brow. "How very fortunate. Once you find the girl and she agrees, you rush to the archbishop's side and obtain the special license. And the man can even marry you if you wish. What lady could ask for more?"

His expression sobered. "You know, Clay, did you ever once think that perhaps a female might refuse your offer?"

Clayton thought of Miss Briana Garland. No. She would never refuse his offer. She might have a slight temper when provoked, but he could keep her under control. A little charm and she was his.

He was getting deuced tired of all this bickering about lists and brides. Why even attend the party at all? Miss Garland would be the perfect wife. Why go back and forth about the issue? The answer was right before him. She would have her mother for company, and the two females could travel to their hearts' content. His family would warm to the idea soon enough, even Em and Jared.

He grinned. Tomorrow he would seek Miss Garland out at the Elbourne ball. This list would be used only as a backup plan.

"What the devil are you grinning about now?" Marcus asked.

Clayton gave a soft pat to the list in his jacket pocket. "I appreciate your help, but I might not need it after all."

He grabbed his glass of wine off the table and lifted it to his lips, watching Marcus's eyes narrow in confusion.

Jupiter and Zeus, this was much easier than he'd thought. Truly, it was inconceivable that Miss Garland would turn him down now. There were the two tea incidents, but those accidents were insignificant. Hadn't Emily mentioned the girl adored him?

This was going to be as easy as teaching the lady to waltz.

Chapter Eight

*I*f Briana thought she would be able to lose herself in the crowd at the Elbourne ball, she was sorely mistaken. With Agatha buying her an emerald-colored gown from Madame Michelle's, and Emily lending her a pair of diamond earrings and matching necklace, she felt rather conspicuous, to say the least.

She had desperately wanted to wear her gown of pale pink trimmed with white lace, but since it was the duke's birthday and Jane wished everything to be just right, Briana had given in to the duchess's demands, with Emily's and Agatha's help.

A few minutes after her arrival at the ball, Briana was surprised to find herself in the arms of Lord Clayton. He had literally snatched her hand from Lord Rockham's for a waltz.

"I seem to remember I was the one who taught you this dance, Miss Garland."

Briana felt a blush creep up her neck, recalling those innocent years spent at Elbourne. Why had this man sought her out? Had she not told him they could never be friends? After the lemonade incident she had thought he would try to evade her every chance he had. And after overhearing his words with the earl, she could not see any reason he wanted to be with her. She thought he would be seeking out some female with, well, similar values.

She purposely looked over his shoulder, not wanting to fall for his inexhaustible charm. And she was definitely not afraid of him or her heart, even though he did smell of bayberry!

"Miss Garland, I seem to remember informing you that at this time in the dance you are to say something back to me."

More embarrassed than ever, Briana raised her head and replied, "I remember a dancing master named Mr. Summers, my lord."

He let out a rich laugh. "You are not as shy as you appear, are you?"

Briana noticed Agatha waving her gloved hand from across the room and winced. The woman was in sheer ecstasy over Briana's dancing with Emily's brother. What did her godmother think the man was going to do, ask her to marry him?

Briana quickly shifted her gaze back to Lord Clayton. "As you can see, I am not sixteen, my lord."

His gaze was riveted on her face, and his hand tightened about her waist. "Indeed, you are not, Miss Garland, much to my delight."

His words slid down her body like a silky caress. The charmer! The rogue! Why had he chosen her for the waltz? Perhaps he wanted to get back at her for the tea and lemonade accident the other day. Or perhaps Agatha had begged him to dance with her. The thought was humiliating.

It certainly didn't help matters that his nearness had kindled feelings she had hoped wiped from her heart. And she could not deny there was a strength about him that captivated her, making her feel totally safe in his arms.

Yet there wasn't an unmarried young woman in the room who didn't want to dance with him. The feelings she had were probably the same as they experienced when they were in his arms. Her pounding heart meant nothing at all.

He swung her around the dance floor until she felt dizzy. "You do know I am an idiot," he whispered in her ear.

She accidentally stepped on his toes. "I, uh, beg your pardon, my lord."

"I am trying to apologize for my ungentlemanly behavior the other day. You remember, when I was lost in my own thoughts?" He leaned down, his breath warm against her cheek.

Briana's heart sped with the beat of the music.

"Am I forgiven?" he asked huskily.

She pulled back, clearing her throat. "Of course, my lord."

Was she imagining things? Or was he trying to play with her mind?

"A little air, Miss Garland? You look a bit warm."

Out of breath, she nodded. "Yes . . . please." It was the heat of the room doing things to her brain. Yes, that's what it was.

Before she knew it, the man had her out the ballroom doors and down a secluded trail of the Elbourne gardens. During those innocent summers so long ago, there had been a few times when Briana and Emily had hid in the bushes and spied on the Clearbrook brothers, and now as Briana passed a certain stone bench, she immediately recalled every single detail of Clayton's past encounters.

She halted, digging her feet into the ground.

Clayton turned to her, his hand still curled about her elbow. "Feeling better?"

"Yes," she said, trying to keep her voice calm as she looked around. "I, er, if you would be so kind as to return me to the ballroom, I will be forever in your debt, my lord."

Bright white teeth flashed in the pale moonlight, and she felt light-headed. He took hold of her shoulders and gently pulled her closer to him, so close in fact that she could study the little scar at the corner of his eye. "Forever in my debt is a long time, Miss Garland. However, may I point out that you have barely had a chance to catch your breath?"

He was right about that. She could hardly breathe at all. He was so compelling, she found she could not move. "I would, um, like to return to the dance floor," she said faintly.

He ran a finger over her ear. "You are a Fairy Lady. Gabrielle was right." His hand traced her cheekbone, moving to the freckles on her nose.

"Magic," he said, his voice lowering along with his lips. She froze as his mouth covered hers in a slow, drugging kiss.

"A magic Fairy Lady." His comment was a mere whisper in the wind, and—horror of horrors—he was staring at her as if he had never seen her before.

Shocked, Briana stepped back, raising a hand to her lips. Heat filled every inch of her. He looked as confused as she felt.

"Why did you do that?" she asked rather sharply.

"Why did I kiss the most beautiful girl at the ball?"

Her mouth was burning from his touch, yet she remembered Clarice, she remembered her father, and most of all, she remembered her lieutenant and all his fancy words before he left and got himself killed. But Alistair had never kissed her like that!

The man seemed to be studying her. "You didn't like it?"

Of course she liked it. "No," she said a little too prudishly.

His eyes twinkled. "Maybe I should try again. I seem to be losing my touch."

She took another step back, her knees bumping against the stone bench. With a wicked smile, he pressed a gentle finger to her shoulder and she lost her balance. He caught her, pulling her against the bench as his body sprung beside her.

"There. That's much better."

Briana blushed. "That was not very gentlemanly," she said, keenly aware of his scrutiny.

"Briana, may I call you by your Christian name?"

Stunned, she stared at him, wondering if he had stopped at the club and had too much wine before the ball.

"Certainly not," she said, trying to pull away, feeling her heart softening under his steady gaze. No, she could not let him do this to her.

He chuckled and held tight to her hands. She tried to ignore the wild beating of her heart, but it was impossible. Dappled moonlight spread over the bench and she glanced toward the ballroom. He tilted her head toward his. "I'm over here."

"I know that," she said coolly. "I do have a brain."

"I noticed that." His voice held a certain degree of admiration that surprised her. A moonbeam brushed across his face, making his glittering eyes appear more powerful.

"Do you know, Miss Garland, I believe you have more life in you than all the women I have ever known." He turned his head toward the ballroom, smiling. "Except for my sister, that is."

Briana took that as a compliment, but she had no idea why the man was doing this to her.

He brought her hand to his lips. "So beautiful, yet so scared."

A hot ache grew in her chest. She tried to ignore her body's reaction to him. She owed Clarice and every woman like her sister a place to stay, a place to feel safe. A man like Lord Clayton could ruin her plans. He could ruin her life if she let him. Her heart could be easily swept away by this man and all her plans easily forgotten.

"I have no fear of you, my lord," she said calmly.

"Clayton. My name is Clayton."

"My lord," she repeated firmly.

His eyes darkened. "You smell of roses. Sweet and innocent. And yet there is a hint of vanilla about you. I find it fascinating."

Though she knew she should return to the ballroom, Briana felt a tiny glow of excitement inside her.

The man wrapped his arms around her waist and pulled her closer.

"Briana."

She shivered. "My lord—"

He kissed her ear. She almost fell off the bench.

"Briana, sweetheart." His lips moved to her neck. "Marry me."

She froze. "Wh-what did you say?"

He smiled, taking her hands in a gentle but firm grasp. "I asked you to marry me."

Her tongue grew thick. Was this some kind of joke?

"This may come as a surprise, but I truly want to marry you."

She swallowed, still in shock.

"It would be an agreeable arrangement for both of us."

He didn't wait for her response, but continued his little speech as if they were having tea with Gabrielle.

"You would live in the country with your mother. And I, on the other hand, would spend most of my time in Town."

Her chest throbbed with pain. It spread throughout her entire body until her hands began to ache.

"Of course, I would make certain you had a life of luxury, reading all the books you love."

Beneath the glow of the moon his eyes sparkled with pride. She would like to box his ears! "You would have access to the most fashionable dressmakers in England. Servants would be at your beck and call. It would be a simple marriage of convenience."

His face seemed to beam at that last comment. *A simple marriage of convenience?* That was the last thing she had expected from the man.

She blinked in awe as he continued to explain their marriage and all the wonderful aspects of her becoming his wife. Her pain soon turned to a cool numbness and then to a scorching fury.

Good grief! He was acting like some gallant prince sent on a journey to save her from a life of doom.

"We can obtain a special license and marry next week." He went to kiss her again and she turned so his lips fell upon her cheek. *The arrogant oaf!*

He smiled, seeming to presume her jerk of the head was due to her innocence. *The man was amazingly ignorant!*

He rose from the bench, taking her with him. "No need for a long engagement. Why don't we make our announcement tonight?"

Briana's mouth opened and shut like that of a codfish caught on a hook. She could hardly think of what to say.

"I have chosen a perfect place for you to live. It's within a day's ride from London." He swung his gaze toward the music drifting from the ballroom, then back to her.

"I can be by your side for family functions and such, but beyond that we can both live our separate lives."

"No," she said calmly.

His lids fell halfway over his eyes. It took him a moment to answer. "Very well. If you would like to be closer to London, I can see to that. Perhaps Lord Henshield's mansion. It's for sale, they say. A prime piece of land it is, too."

"No."

His brows gathered in thought. "Something near Dover, then? If I recall, your mother's family resides near there—"

Holding back from slapping him, she started for the ballroom. It was odd that her refusal never seemed to register in his brain. "No, thank you. I really don't think we would suit at all."

He grasped her elbow, stopping her. "What?"

She spun around, her veins bubbling with rage. This man

was almost as spoiled as the prince. He was acting as if he had never heard the word "no" before. And that was probably true, at least from the women he knew.

"I will not marry you, my lord. I will not live in a house in the country. I will not play party to your frivolous notions of marriage. I *cannot, will not, never, ever* be your wife."

The man stared back at her in confused silence. Then to her astonishment, his shoulders shook with laughter. "Ah, I see. You are quite the little mind worker. Very well, you win. I will give you twice the pin money any wife in the *ton* is allowed. You may travel at your convenience to and from the Continent whenever it amuses you. Unless, of course, you are with child."

With child! The man was insane!

"And to let you know what a kind husband I shall make, I will give you two homes, one in Bath and one of your choosing." He puffed out his chest, making her want to plant him a facer.

She opened her mouth to object, but his strong hands drew her into a locking embrace and he kissed her, thoroughly, expertly, and with all the intimacy of a man wooing his intended. She couldn't gather her wits quickly enough to protest. Finally he let her go, and she stepped away from him, her body badly shaken.

She blinked rapidly and curled her hands into fists. "You seem to have everything figured out, my lord."

"Trust me."

He sounded so arrogantly pleased she wished she were a man so she could call him out! And *trust* him! What did he think she was? Some dull-witted female? "I am overwhelmed, my lord."

There was an edge of sarcasm to her voice that he obviously missed. A smile tipped the corners of his mouth, sealing his fate. "We should get along nicely . . . *Briana.*"

He whispered her name with such gentleness and charm she had to pause to throw the shield back over her heart.

He peered at her, waiting for her to speak.

Planting her hands on her hips, she lifted her chin another inch to glare at him. "Do you know, I believe you are the most overbearing, egotistical, arrogant man of my acquaintance, sir.

would never marry you. Not if you came to me on hands and knees."

She flung her hands toward the ballroom. "Go buy yourself another wife, my lord, for it will not be me."

He stared at her as if she had rocks in her head.

Humiliation welled up inside her, and she knew she was on the verge of tears. But she would finish this out if it killed her.

He raised his hand to touch her, and she quickly fell back a step. His eyes narrowed. "Perhaps you misunderstood—"

She didn't let him finish. "How dare you! How dare you assume I would fall over you like some ignorant female bent on marriage to anyone who would take her."

She regarded his stiff profile as a subtle warning, but her anger had elevated to such a boiling fury, nothing would stop her now. "How dare you," she whispered with such venom it made her own toes curl. "You, sir, are no gentleman."

Clayton watched in shock as the lady swept him a disgusting glance, spun on her heel, and returned down the trail toward the dance floor. With mixed emotions, he followed her, his gaze attached to the sway of her body. When she disappeared into the ballroom, a strange numbness enveloped him. What the devil had just happened?

He was a few steps from the dance floor when Marcus walked into his path. "What did you do to Miss Garland?"

That's exactly what he wanted to know. "Nothing."

"Oh? The lady looked quite upset. She slipped behind the large urn."

Guilt filled Clayton as his gaze searched the room.

With a stern brow, Marcus crossed his hands over his chest. "I do believe there were tears in her eyes."

Clayton rubbed his chin. The little bluestocking had dressed him down like some holiday goose. "Yes, well, we all know females are fidgety creatures."

"I don't like what you're doing, Clay. That lady has an innocence about her that makes a gentleman want to defend her. From what Em's said, Miss Garland has gone through hell the past few years. Go find one of those ladies on the amended list."

Clayton's jaw stiffened, recalling the snapping green eyes sweeping over him as if he were some villain. "I intend to."

What the devil had he been thinking? He didn't need a termagant for a wife. He needed a biddable bride, not some green-eyed spitfire who would lash out at his every word, making him feel like some boy reprimanded by his governess. He should have followed his first instincts. Oh, the lady might love children, and she might have adorable freckles, but by heaven, he needed a convenient wife, not some lady who made him feel vulnerable!

For that very reason he was not ready to pursue this scholarly chit who could jerk his heart from his chest with just one kiss. Devil take it, not even Lady Serena could do that.

He slipped his hand to his inside pocket and drew out the list, slapping it into Marcus's hand. "Lead me to them."

Marcus pushed the list back. "Are you serious?"

"You just told me to use it," Clayton insisted.

"I've reconsidered the entire situation. Let Gerald have the deuced castle. It isn't worth your future."

"It *is* my future," Clayton growled. "It's all I have."

His eyes narrowed into two irritated slits as he stole a glance across the floor. "And what the devil is Kingsdale doing here?"

Marcus followed his brother's gaze. "Think he returned from Egypt a while ago. Haven't seen much of him lately, though."

Clayton didn't answer. His total concentration was on Lord Kingsdale, hovering over Miss Garland like some lapdog. "Gad, I believe the man is infatuated with her brain."

A light of comprehension came to Marcus's eye. "The lady in question has spent time studying ancient Egypt, has she not? But if you ask me, it's more than her brain he's infatuated with."

A strong sense to shield the woman from harm swept through Clayton. His gaze took in the delicate nature of her body, and he instantly recalled holding her in his arms. A blow from Kingsdale could kill her. "She may not want me, but I will dangle from a rope before that man has her."

Marcus held back his smile. "Now, this I want to see."

Chapter Nine

The music swelled in volume along with the disturbing feeling enveloping Briana as Lord Kingsdale bowed over her hand.

"Miss Garland, it has been so long since we have been together. Would you do me the honor of the next dance?"

Agatha stood two feet away, caught in deep conversation with Lady Hatton. Disappointed and a little uneasy, Briana realized she was not going to gain any help from her godmother.

She looked up at Lord Kingsdale, who was awaiting her answer. He was a handsome man with jet-black hair and a distinguished gray lock above his temple. His jacket fit him to perfection, needing no padding to add to his athletic form. If she hadn't known his true nature, she might have been impressed.

"It has been ages, my lord," she said, puzzled by the man's appearance at her side.

Lord Kingsdale loved Egyptian artifacts almost as much as she did. Two years ago he had believed they could share a life together based on their love for Egyptology. His ideas were a bit frightening, and she had humored him, hoping he would not pursue their relationship any further than mere acquaintance. However, his interest had grown to obsessive proportions, and she finally had to sever their friendship.

"Ages," he said with a twitch of amusement about his lips.

It was the strange gleam in his dark eyes that told her he was still attracted to her. But in spite of his interest in her as a woman, it did nothing to heal Lord Clayton's blow to her heart.

She had seen Lord Kingsdale only once since he had asked her to marry him, and that had been at a distance.

"You must forgive me, my lord. A headache prevents me from joining the dancing."

"Why, Miss Garland, ever the more reason for me to take you for a walk about the room."

Suddenly Agatha's keen gaze took in the scene. "Briana, my dear, why don't you take a walk, then fetch me some punch?"

Did Agatha have any inkling to this man's character? Was she trying to make Lord Clayton jealous? One never knew about her godmother or her tactics.

Briana's cool gaze met the man's smiling face. Lord Kingsdale never liked to lose at anything, even if it was a trivial matter of asking a lady for a turn about the room.

She instantly recalled the scene when she had rejected his marriage proposal. He had grabbed hold of her shoulders, and at the time she had believed if Clarice had not walked into the room the man might have smacked her.

Later she speculated that his firm hold on her had been pure disappointment at her response. However, looking at him now, she had no idea what to believe anymore.

Trying to stall for time, she peered across the room and locked gazes with Lord Clayton. Even from where she stood, she could detect his violet blue eyes narrowing on the man beside her.

Good grief, was *he* jealous?

She thought of the difference between Lord Kingsdale and Lord Clayton and inwardly frowned. Although both men were handsome and arrogant, the similarities stopped there.

Where Kingsdale was quick to anger, Clayton possessed a stoic calmness, reaching a rage only when pushed beyond his limits. Where Kingsdale was impatient to get his way and did not tolerate limitations, Clayton possessed a certain charm that allowed him to maneuver around his obstacles in a polite and gentlemanly manner.

Clayton. Oh, Clayton, why did you have to treat me so shabbily?

"Miss Garland?" Kingsdale put out his arm, deliberately forcing her to either take it or cause a scene.

She gave him a stiff smile. "Very well, my lord. A short walk and then some punch for my godmother."

The man's gaze gleamed with approval, and a minute after circling the floor he turned to face her. They were standing near the doors to the garden and a warm breeze caressed her cheek. Behind them couples began to gather for a country dance.

"Do you still hate me, my dear?"

The question surprised her. "I don't hate you, my lord. But you were rather forceful when I turned down your marriage proposal." There it was, that swift shadow of anger in his eyes. It disappeared as suddenly as it had come.

"I loved you." He said it so softly she almost missed it.

Uncomfortable now, she concealed her frown. He had never mentioned love. Even Lord Clayton had never mentioned love.

He glanced toward the sea of dancers, then shifted a regretful gaze back to her. "Can you forgive and forget?"

She clasped her hands tightly. She had no wish to give this man any hope they would be together. "I can forgive, my lord. But I will never forget. I am only human."

His smile didn't quite reach his eyes. "At least that's a start. Now, I think it wise we fetch that punch for Miss Appleby."

He took hold of Briana's elbow, escorting her into the hall. "I was hoping to see you here, wondering if I could make amends."

She glanced at him. "I said I already forgave you."

"Yes, but there is something else I wanted to say." He ushered her along the marbled floor, hastily pulling her into a room off the hall. It was the duchess's private sitting room.

Briana was taken completely by surprise when the door shut behind him. "My lord—"

"My dear, you must know I adore you."

"Adore me?" Something about his expression frightened her.

"Yes, adore you. There is something that draws me to you. It did years ago; it does now." His brows dipped considerably. "You are not running from me, are you?"

Briana stumbled against the back of a chair and halted. He strode closer and the distinct scent of musk and cloves filled the air. It was making her ill. With a pang of regret she wished for the sweet fragrance of bayberry soap. Lord Clayton might have his weaknesses, but he would never frighten her like this.

She blinked and skirted the chair, finding herself backed up against the wall, his tall body towering over her. She boldly met his gaze. His eyes glittered ominously, and a sudden chill bumped down her spine.

"This is most inappropriate, my lord. Someone will be looking for me." The back of her throat had gone dry. "You had best open the door."

He pressed a hand against the wall, leaning toward her. "You were always full of surprises. I remember the day I met you at the lending library and you were taking out a book on Egyptian death. Do you remember?"

Egyptian death? Her apprehension grew.

"Yes, I remember. You were interested in the same thing."

His hand dropped and circled her waist. "I was interested. You had something most women of the *ton* did not."

"Please, don't do this." She gripped his arm, but it was like a steel band about her gown.

Ignoring her plea, he continued, "You had brains, my dear. You knew more about Egypt than I did." He gave a little chuckle. "In fact, when it comes right down to it, you know more about the world than anyone I know. You have captivated me for years. I tried to stay away, even looked for other women with your qualities, but it always came down to you."

Her anxiety increased at the smoldering look in his eye. "I need someone like you, Miss Garland. Someone I can talk to. Someone who isn't going on about what gown to wear or what color she wishes to match her wrap."

"You need me?" she asked calmly, her mind struggling for a way out of his arms that would not make him angry.

"Yes," he answered, the challenge in his voice undeniable. "And I think you need me. We would do well together. I see things in you, secret things, hidden things you are not about to share with any man, and that intrigues me."

"I want to return to the ballroom."

"Not yet." His hands moved to her shoulders. "I have watched you. Did you know that?"

Her heart pounded wildly as she played for time. "What do you mean?"

His eyes softened, and he slowly loosened his grip. "Oh, I

have my ways. But I see in you unique qualities, like the secret places found in the pyramids of the great pharaohs."

"Secret places?" she asked, slipping from his hold.

He laughed, shaking his head. "Yes, like now. You are planning to make your escape."

Her cheeks flamed, not with embarrassment but with stupidity for allowing this man to maneuver her into a room alone. He was good at that. He always had a way of sneaking past her defenses.

"I won't hurt you." He pulled her into his arms. "But you fascinate me. Always have. You hide away, fading into the background, hoping no one is looking. But I see you. I have always seen you." She wondered how often he had watched her from afar.

His smile seemed genuine as he regarded her. "You remind me of my uncle's bureau. It had a secret compartment that held all his treasures. When I was a boy, I watched him open it one day. There was a small button in the back of one of the drawers and if pushed at the same time when you pulled open the bottom drawer, the secret compartment opened, too. It was a hard feat for a ten-year-old, but I did it."

Briana felt his hands on her tighten. What in the world was he talking about? "My godmother will be wondering about the punch."

Dark eyes ran over her. "I think it will take me some time to find all the hidden compartments in you, Briana, but I intend to keep searching."

"I have no interest in your search, my lord. And I did not give you leave to call me by my Christian name."

"Ah, ever the lady," he said softly.

To her surprise, his hands dropped from her side.

He bowed. "Soon, you will see. Soon, you will understand. I have faith in you, my dear. We are of the same blood, you and I. Passion runs deep in our veins. Egyptology is a fascinating subject, and side by side we can delve into the minds of the pharaohs and the slaves, determine how the pyramids were built and where the treasures are hidden. There is no end to what we can accomplish together."

Her blood ran cold. The man wasn't just mad, he was dangerous. Knowing he was letting her go, she walked hurriedly across the room. Without a word, she wrenched open the door, her insides shaking. Closing her eyes in relief, she stepped out of the room and dashed around the corner, afraid Kingsdale would follow.

He was obsessed with her and Egypt. Somehow she would have to make him understand she wanted nothing to do with him.

She wasn't paying attention to where she was going when two strong hands took hold of her shoulders.

"I can see why you turned me down, Miss Garland." Lord Clayton glared over her shoulder at Kingsdale, who had suddenly stepped behind her. "A better offer, I presume?"

A deep, familiar pain lodged in her breast. He was the same as the rest of them. He was no different from Kingsdale, or her father, or the man who had seduced her sister. They thought only of themselves.

"I believe you owe the lady an apology." Kingsdale's voice was soft, but alarmingly angry.

"Do I?" Clayton asked, his eyes locking on Miss Garland's white face as she jerked from his grasp.

Anger sliced through him. Anger that this woman had brushed his proposal aside as if it were nothing but a roll at breakfast. Anger that she was in the room with Kingsdale and not him. Anger that Kingsdale was looking at her as if he were a sailor on leave who had not seen a woman for months or even years.

"I need no apology from you or anyone, my lord," the lady said, lifting her chin. "Now, if you will excuse me."

Kingsdale reached out and grasped her wrist. "Briana."

Briana? "I would suggest you keep your hands to yourself," Clayton said, jerking Kingsdale's hand off her person.

Kingsdale's eyes darkened. "You have insulted my future wife and you owe her an apology."

The lady gasped. "Y-your future wife?"

Clayton's blood turned to stone. "My apologies, madam. I had no idea."

Miss Garland's green eyes flashed with contempt as she glanced from Clayton to Kingsdale.

"I never agreed to be your wife," she said to Kingsdale, her tone frosty. "In fact, I have no idea why you assumed otherwise. Good night, gentlemen." And with that, the lady turned on her kid slippers and headed toward the ballroom.

Kingsdale let out a small chuckle. "The lady's temper is as fiery as her hair."

Clayton's hands stiffened. "I don't think she cares for you any more than I do."

"Old memories die hard, do they not?"

"Old memories?" Clayton scoffed. "You know, Gregory, as childhood friends, we really never addressed our differences. You were a liar and a cheat. Something I forgave because of our youth. But I have seen you in action, and if you dare harm one hair on that lady's head, I will come after you. Do I make myself clear?"

A twisted grin spread across Kingsdale's face. "So, you finally see her as a gem, do you? It took you long enough. The girl has been in love with you since we were schoolboys."

Kingsdale's remark took Clayton off guard.

"Do we understand each other?" Clayton asked in a dangerously low voice.

Kingsdale stared at his fingernails, rubbing his thumb against his third finger. "When we were children, I never saw anything in the freckled-face redhead either."

The man looked up, his eyes glittering with determination. "But I have come to see that the lady has more brains than Wellington. I need a wife. I want a wife. The lady has qualities I admire."

"You mean she enjoys studying Egyptian culture?"

Kingsdale smiled. "You know me well, my friend."

"I don't think the lady's interested."

The man's obsession with Egypt had made the rounds at White's. Everyone had something they held dear to their heart. But now it was Kingsdale's strange obsession with Miss Garland that truly troubled Clayton.

"Did I tell you she fell in love with me a few years ago?" Kingsdale replied proudly.

It wasn't true. The man was lying.

Kingsdale pursed his lips in triumph. "Yes, well, it would be a surprise to you, wouldn't it? Anyway, I did a stupid thing. I left her. Had some business on the Continent. By the time I returned, she refused to see me. Bad timing, I suppose."

Clayton barely checked himself from taking the man apart. "It seems you have had bad timing with all the ladies of your acquaintance."

Kingsdale laughed again. "None of them sparked my interest. The devil of it is, Clay, there is something about Miss Briana Garland that stirs my blood. I want her, and it's time I wed."

Clayton's lips thinned. "Well, she doesn't want you."

"You were always the gentleman. But I will tell you something, being a gentleman does not always win the ladies. One has to be a bit forceful, if you get my meaning."

Clayton took a step toward the man. "By God, if you force—"

"Clayton!"

The two men turned to see Lady Emily coming toward them.

Kingsdale lowered his voice. "Don't interfere, Clay. You were like a brother to me growing up. I haven't forgotten that."

Clayton's jaw tightened. "A brother? Yes, I found that out soon enough when you stole Maria from under my very nose. Oh, I admit she was not the type one would marry, only a simple girl from the country, but innocent all the same. However, when you were done with her, the girl was sent to live in America with her long-lost aunt. Yes, I know your ways, and I don't like them."

Kingsdale let out a sardonic laugh. "All is fair in love and war, eh? Like that time at Vauxhall Gardens?"

The question didn't deserve an answer. Clayton turned to his sister. For an unguarded moment, he saw the cool glance Emily sent the man. Had Kingsdale approached his sister without his knowing? The thought infuriated him. Of course the man would not dare take a step in that direction now, not with Stonebridge as her husband. But Miss Briana Garland was another matter.

Clayton thought of the lady at Vauxhall. She had been lucky he had come along when he did. What if it had been Miss Garland?

The thought didn't sit well with him. Not at all.

Chapter Ten

"*B*riana, child, did you hear a word I said?"

Briana was staring out the window of the carriage as it rolled over the cobblestone streets toward the outskirts of London. The steady *clip-clop* of hooves had distracted her from Agatha's words, but it did nothing to divert her mind from the events of the previous evening with Lord Clayton and Lord Kingsdale.

"I'm sorry, Agatha." She gathered the shawl about her shoulders and turned toward her godmother. "I was woolgathering."

The older lady lifted a keen brow. "Does it perchance have something to do with Lord Kingsdale and Lord Clayton? Or why I did not receive my punch last night?"

Briana was helpless to stop the blush from working its way across her cheeks. How much did Agatha know?

"Never knew Kingsdale well," the lady went on. "Heard he had an eye for Egyptian art. Handsome gentleman. Well educated. His father died five years ago." The parasol thumped. "Never liked the old badger. Emily's mother never liked him either. La, if it is a choice between those two gentlemen, my dear, I would definitely choose Lord Clayton."

Briana peered out the window and picked up the small bouquet of daisies resting on her seat. "I am not choosing anyone. I already told you my plans."

Agatha frowned as the carriage came to a sudden halt in front of a small church. "Your sister would not want you to devote your entire life to a cause that keeps you from having a family. I made that choice and have regretted it ever since."

Briana's throat constricted at the sight of the small cemetery in the distance. "Today was Clarice's birthday. She would have been nineteen. I cannot go back and save her from the past, but I can help other women in the same predicament."

Her grip tightened on the flowers. "Society throws these women aside like crumbs. It isn't fair, Agatha. Women have no rights. It just isn't fair."

The older lady gave Briana's knee a motherly pat. "Life isn't fair, child. But you must not let the choices of some men ruin your entire life. Your father was wrong, and I believe he died with the burden of your sister's death weighing heavily on his heart."

Briana looked away, tears clogging her throat. "Wh-what about the man who put Clarice in that predicament in the first place? What about him?"

Agatha sighed. "I wish I knew, child. I would have the man clapped in irons for what he did to your sister. But that is neither here nor there. Go to her grave and say your prayers. Tomorrow we leave for Grimstoke Hall."

Briana took hold of the door, wishing Agatha would walk to Clarice's grave with her. But the emotional toll on her godmother was too much.

Briana leaned over and kissed the elderly lady on the cheek. "I love you."

Agatha sniffed, gently batting her away. "Go on with you now. Two sobbing females might scare James into driving away without us. I don't like to hurry you, child, but it looks like a storm is brewing in the west."

Briana glanced at the angry clouds closing in on them and gave her godmother a weak smile, then made her way toward the graveyard. She stopped in front of a small flat stone etched with Clarice's name. About a hundred feet away stood the church, an ancient-looking building of red stone, decorated with stained glass windows depicting Christ's birth.

Kneeling, Briana placed the flowers on the gravestone. Tears stung her eyes as she remembered her sister's sweet face.

"I'm sorry, Clarice. I'm sorry you could not be here on your birthday."

She raised her gloved hands and brushed back the tears trickling down her cheeks. *Oh, Clarice, I miss you so.* A crisp wind blew through the trees, and she let out a shuddering sigh.

"I'll make things right, though. There are four women staying in the vicar's old cottage not far from here. I intend to find them a better home soon. I have positions set up for three of them after they give birth. I hope to give them a chance for a better life, a better life than they would have had on their own."

A chance you were never given.

The clatter of wheels and jangle of reins brought her head around. Dust billowed in the air. A shiny black carriage was stopping in front of the church. A young woman dressed in a simple ivory gown descended, followed by an older couple. Another coach appeared and halted behind the first.

Of course. A wedding.

Briana's lips trembled as she bent toward the gravestone, brushing away the dirt lodged in the crevices of her sister's name. "It should have been you, Clarice. I hope the bride will be happy. I hope you're happy where you are now."

She let out a shaky breath as she rose. "You're probably laughing at me now, knowing my plans for Grimstoke's party."

Thunder boomed above her, and Briana gathered her shawl tighter about her shoulders. "Yes, I know, it's something you would insist on being part of. You were always so impulsive. And you probably cannot believe Whitehall has asked me to investigate the silly rumor. But being Violet's friend certainly helps."

Fat raindrops plopped against her face, quickly increasing in intensity. She shuddered, raising her gaze to the black clouds hovering over the church.

"Agatha is livid, as you can well imagine."

A streak of lightning pierced the sky and she frowned as the daisies began to droop beneath the driving rain. "I'm sorry I wasn't there to help you. I'm so very sorry."

"Briana!" Agatha called worriedly.

Briana gave a short wave to the older lady as she took one last glance at her sister's grave. "I miss you, Clarice."

Wrapping her shawl over her head, Briana hurried toward the carriage and almost slipped as the footman assisted her inside.

Agatha clucked her tongue as the door snapped shut. "Should have used my parasol."

Briana looked up, her green eyes twinkling with mischief as the rain trickled down her face, mingling with her tears. "I would never do such a thing. What would you do without it?"

Her godmother managed a smile as the carriage jerked forward. "Don't play me the fool, young lady," she said, wiping her eyes. "I have not forgotten about Lord Grimstoke's. Depend upon it, you will let me do the snooping."

Briana wasn't going to agree to that. Whitehall had asked her to go, not just Agatha. "I know his daughter, Violet. My cover is perfect. Besides, I don't believe I am in any danger. We are, after all, only investigating a rumor."

"Oh, there is always a danger, child." Agatha frowned, her grip on the parasol tightening.

Not a good sign, Briana thought. "Is there something I should know?"

Steel gray eyes locked on Briana's face. "We were correct. Whitehall has very good reason to believe Lord Grimstoke holds a grudge against the Regent. It seems the man lost a great deal in some card game with Prinny."

Briana's eyes widened. "And so now we have motivation. Do you truly think there is a possibility his lordship may be passing on information about the Regent?"

"It is only speculation. A slender thread at best. Whitehall has the most powerful agents investigating more significant leads. Ours is only one of them."

"But I cannot believe Lord Grimstoke would do such a thing."

Agatha peered out the window. Rain beat against the carriage, blurring the countryside. "Revenge is quite a motivation. Good friends can make the best of enemies. Never forget that. Besides, everyone in the *ton* knows Lord Grimstoke is a fickle creature. Seems solid as a rock one moment, then caves in to drink and vices that could spin your head the very next."

Vices that could spin her head? Briana waited anxiously, eager to expand her education.

Agatha gave her a stern gaze. "No, I am not telling you anything about that! But you must see that this entire mission puts you in way too much danger. As I mentioned, we have other agents working other places where the threat is thought to be much greater, but—"

"No buts, Agatha. This is perfect. Don't you see? As a friend to Violet, I can fade into the crowd like I usually do. Snooping will come naturally."

"Fade?" Agatha looked appalled. "My dear girl, if you were fading at last night's ball, then I am going blind indeed."

Briana fidgeted with her shawl. "An isolated incident, to be sure. Lord Kingsdale and Lord Clayton were only playing against each other. I am nothing to them at all."

Agatha let out an annoyed sigh. "If you did not notice Lord Clayton's eyes following you the entire night, I daresay you were the one who was blind."

Briana studied the floor of the carriage. All her life she had wanted Lord Clayton to notice her, and now that he had, she wanted nothing to do with him. A marriage of convenience? It was insufferable. "I saw his attention on two other ladies."

"Aha! So you noticed, did you?"

Briana's head snapped up. "And what does that mean?"

"It means you have a fondness for the gentleman."

"I do not."

"Well, he won't be your problem at Grimstoke's anyway. Didn't see him on the list of guests."

"The man's a nuisance."

Agatha eyed her thoughtfully. "Perhaps you should take a look at the list." The lady pulled a paper from her reticule and handed it to Briana.

Briana's gaze traveled over the paper and her heart stopped. She looked up at Agatha.

Agatha's eyelids fell as she let out an aggravated sigh. "La, there was nothing I could do about that. Seems Lord Kingsdale was invited at the last minute. Always happens, you know. People are added and dropped at a moment's notice. Never really know until one gets there."

Briana handed back the paper. "I don't like him."

Agatha sighed. "Knew that after the ball. Should have told me before I gave you permission to take a turn about the room with the man and fetch me some punch—that I never received, by the way."

Briana dropped her head back against the leather seat. "Oh, it's such a mess. A few years ago he asked me to marry him. He wasn't happy when I turned him down, but it seems he wants to try his hand again. I have heard stories of his riotous behavior in Town. I don't know what's true. But I don't like him."

"Not all men are like Kingsdale, my dear."

"No, but it seems the men I know are concerned only about their own welfare. My papa was. The man who got Clarice with child was. Alistair was. Even Lord Clayton—"

She stopped herself before divulging to her godmother what had transpired in the garden during the ball.

"Oh? And what about Lord Clayton?"

"Nothing."

Nothing at all, except he broke my heart. He was like the rest of them. He didn't a care a whit about her or her feelings.

"We are to journey to Grimstoke's tomorrow, then." Agatha pulled out another, larger piece of paper that was folded in her reticule. "Here is a rough map of the house."

"I was there once," Briana said, "but it was years ago."

"If our thread of information is true and Grimstoke Hall is the location, Whitehall's mysterious source has identified the drop-off point as the library, as I told you already."

Briana looked up at her godmother. "A secret hiding place? It sounds, well, rather formulated, does it not? Could we be decoys?"

"Possibly. Sometimes agents are set up as decoys, but I cannot tell you the truth, because I honestly don't know. I was delivered this information only days ago."

"But a drop-off point given by some unknown source sounds so absurd."

Agatha laid the house plans on the seat opposite her. "Absurd-sounding, yes. But many absurd things have led to dangerous consequences. Look at Napoleon. Who would have thought the little Corsican could conquer as much as he did?"

Briana knew Agatha was right. Absurd as it sounded, they had to take this seriously. Dropping her gaze to the map, she studied the house. "A drop-off point could be in any of the books, for all we know. There must be a thousand of them."

"Yes, a daunting task." Agatha's eyes began to gleam. "However, we do have other clues. There is, as you know, the specific area of Grimstoke's desk."

Briana laughed. "Can it be so easy?"

"If there are any missives at all, Headquarters believes they will be in that very area."

"I take it *the source* conveyed this information?" Briana replied sarcastically. "How very convenient and utterly silly."

"Indeed," Agatha said. "Nevertheless, it is the information we have been given. And having you fade into the walls will be impossible with Kingsdale there."

Briana frowned. "I bid him farewell last night."

Agatha folded the papers and stuffed them back into her reticule. "You are young. You will eventually find that men do not take rejection well. They sulk and simmer, planning their next move. But never fear, I will be with you as your chaperone."

The lady raised her parasol and whacked it against the seat. "La, my dear! If the brute does not leave you alone, I will bop him over the head with this!"

Briana's lips quivered with mirth. "It will take a few good whacks. I have heard he has a very hard head."

Agatha smiled. "You have yet to see me in true form. Ask Lord Stonebridge."

Chapter Eleven

"*T*he lady whacked me with that deuced parasol!" Clayton threw his sister a dazed glare. "I can only say I am glad the old bat is out of the house right now."

Emily was pouring tea and looked up, calmly setting the teapot onto its tray. "Why in the world would Agatha do that?"

Clayton shrugged. "Don't know. It happened when I walked past her in the ballroom the other night. It was so swift, no one saw it. Afterward, she acted as if she were the sweetest woman on earth. And d—dash it all, Em, she knew exactly where to hit me." Frowning, he sat back in his chair.

Clayton had come here this morning in hopes of catching Miss Garland alone. He needed to warn her about Kingsdale. But upon his arrival he discovered the lady and her godmother had already left for the country. Staying with friends, Emily had said.

Clayton had wanted to smile. It would be hard for Kingsdale to follow them there. Still, he would have to warn Miss Garland sooner or later about the man. But not for a while. Today he was leaving for Grimstoke Hall, with this being his last stop before he rode out of London.

"Oh, come now, Clay. Agatha does not use that parasol without cause."

"I cannot agree with you, dearest."

Clayton looked up to see Lord Stonebridge standing by the door. The earl's eyes were dancing with mirth.

"Did you have any idea your aunt almost killed me the other day?" Clayton asked with a scowl.

Jared laughed as he strolled into the room to kiss his wife on the cheek. He angled his head toward Clayton. "You must have come too close to one of her puppies."

Emily frowned. "Agatha has no puppies, Jared. There is only Nigel here."

The dog gave a loud bark.

Clayton gave Jared a cool stare. Emily watched the exchange of male glances and jumped from her seat.

"Oh, you didn't, Clay!"

Clayton stood, pulling his waistcoat tight. "What?"

Jared smiled and took a step back, his hands in the air. "I never said a word."

Clayton growled. "Depend upon it. You said plenty."

Emily clutched her teacup. "If you did what I think you did, I will be furious."

Clayton lifted a defensive brow. "What do you think I did?"

"You asked Briana to marry you."

"And what if I did?"

"You oaf!" The teacup went flying toward him.

Clayton jumped back, but not before his breeches were soaked with tea. Nigel barked. Jared laughed. Emily scowled.

"You know," Clayton said with a grimace as he strode hastily toward the hall, "there is something about tea parties in this house that doesn't appeal to me." He glared at Emily. "I thought you had outgrown your tempers. Evidently not."

Emily slapped the sofa. "How *could* you ask Briana to marry you? After all she has gone through! I cannot believe this!"

His face hardened. "I am not an ogre, Em. There are many women who would want to marry me."

"Ha! Then marry those women!"

Clayton glanced at Jared, who was standing with his hands behind his back, his brows creased in disapproval. The man wasn't going to be any help at all. "I want a marriage of convenience. I want someone who will—"

"What?" Emily shouted, finishing for him. "Understand your lifestyle? Live in the country most of the year? Have a marriage with no love? Do you want Briana to live like Mother did?"

He groaned. "It would be nothing like Mother's situation. She loved Father. Father didn't reciprocate. I am only asking for a marriage of convenience. Both of us can go our separate ways. The emotions will be plain from the start."

Emily started toward him. "You want that castle and money so much you would hurt Briana like that? I never thought you were that kind of person."

He stiffened. "I would never hurt her."

"You already did!" She cuffed him on the shoulder. "She loves you!"

Clayton turned. "What?"

Emily glared at him. "She loves you, Clay. Since we were children. You were just too stupid to notice."

"But she . . . you . . . that was years ago. You were children."

"Were. We aren't anymore."

He combed a hand through his hair, knowing in his heart that Miss Garland had had a fondness for him, had even adored him at one time. But love? "How the devil was I supposed to know?"

Nigel gave a soulful whine.

Emily took an agitated turn about the room. "How could you do this to her? This will only make her go through with her plans."

"What are you talking about?"

Emily whirled on him. "Briana has plans to provide a women's home for females in, well, let's just say delicate situations."

Clayton's expression turned suspicious. "How delicate?"

Emily sank onto the sofa, her hand flying in the air. "You know, women in delicate situations . . . without a husband."

Clayton looked at Jared, who was now frowning.

"And why was I never told of this?" the earl asked.

Emily's head snapped up. "Why? Because you're a man."

Clayton wasn't even going to respond to that comment. But the *ton* would surely shun Miss Garland if she dared try to follow through with her plan as an unmarried woman. "Why the devil would she take this project upon herself?"

"Because her sister was in such a delicate position and Sir

Garland threw the poor girl out of the house. We all know Clarice drowned, but I believe she killed herself, and deep down, I believe, Briana thinks the same."

Emily shook her head in frustration. "She doesn't trust men, Clay. And now you have given her another reason not to trust them. She always thought you a wonderful man, kind and considerate. I told you she adored you when we were young. And lately I see how she looks at you when you play with Gabrielle. Her face simply glows when you are around."

• "Why the deuce didn't you tell me?"

Emily swallowed. "I never said a thing to her or you. I thought eventually . . ." She shrugged. "Well, it doesn't signify. You wanted to have a marriage of convenience, and the poor girl never wanted to marry after what happened with her and the lieutenant."

Clayton's expression froze and his voice rose. "What lieutenant?"

"I should not be telling you any of this, but I don't want you to hurt her any more. Briana was once in love with a lieutenant who pledged to leave the army, but the man went back on his promise and was eventually killed at Waterloo."

Clayton's lips thinned. For some selfish, idiotic reason, he didn't like to think of the lady in love with anyone but himself. "And her trust in men came to a new low when her father threw Clarice out of the house? Needless to say, the man responsible for Clarice's situation never came forward either. Am I correct?"

Emily nodded. "She vows never to marry and instead intends to take care of these women—"

"In delicate situations," he finished for her. It was a noble cause, but it was not for a young lady to carry out alone. "I take it Miss Appleby knows her goddaughter's plans?"

"She loves her, Clayton, and so do I." Emily set her chin. "And I believe you hurt her. I am sure of it. It will take me a long time before I forgive you!" •

She hurried from the room, her silk gown rustling against Nigel's fur as the dog marched alongside her, his nose in the air.

Disgusted, Clayton glanced at Jared.

"I assume the lady rejected your offer," the earl said calmly. "So what's your next step?"

"I intend to find a wife. When next I see Miss Garland, I will apologize for my behavior."

Jared's eyes darkened. "I warned you, and I am not happy."

"You are not her family."

"And you are?"

Clayton threw up his hands. "I have no wish to argue with you. Emily is quite enough, thank you."

Jared crossed his arms over his chest. "Marcus told me you intend to seek out a bride in the country. Some house party, I believe. Grimstoke's, is it?"

"Hell and thunderation! Is there anything else you know?"

The earl scowled. "Don't do it, Clay. A marriage of convenience will haunt you the rest of your life."

"I am without funds. It's easy for you to say. You have a wife and children who love you. You have plenty of money. I have nothing."

"You have a family. Brothers, a sister, a mother, a stepfather." Jared smiled. "Why, you even have me."

Clayton's lips twitched at the earl's attempt at humor, but it didn't change his mind. "As a gentleman, I will see to my needs as I see fit. I have a few weeks to secure my destiny. A castle full of money sounds rather inviting, especially to a man who does not want to ride on his family's coattails the rest of his life."

Jared stuffed his hands in his pockets. "Emily is furious."

Clayton threw a booted foot upon the hearth. "Very well. I admit it. I didn't know everything about the lady before I approached her."

"Didn't you?"

A dark thundercloud seemed to hover over them as they glared at each other. Clayton knew the earl was referring to Clayton's knowledge of Miss Garland's partiality toward him. And to tell the truth, it had surprised the hell out of him that she had rejected his offer. Now, at least he knew why.

The mantel clock chimed twelve, and he realized he was running behind schedule. Because of the little tea incident, he would need to change clothes before he started for Grimstoke

Hall. If he rode long and hard, however, he could make it there tonight. His trunks had been sent on ahead of him. He also had his list of ladies that would suit his needs.

Miss Cherrie Black was a bit young, but she was pretty and had a quiet disposition, not at all like the auburn-haired Fairy Lady from the other day. Miss Black would not care a whit if he lived in Town and she was to reside in the country. Yes, Miss Black was at the top of his list.

"Uncle Clay, did you have another ackident?"

Gabrielle's concerned voice made Clayton cringe. The little girl had walked into the room and was staring directly at the wet spot on his breeches.

"Yes, Gabby," Jared said, his shoulders shaking with laughter. "Poor Uncle Clay had another accident."

"Oh," she said, tipping her head. "Is that why Mama is mad?"

Jared chuckled. "Well, poppet, I think Uncle Clay wasn't very nice."

Clayton gritted his teeth and stalked from the room.

Gabrielle ran after him. "Uncle Clay."

He looked over his shoulder, trying to smile. "Yes?"

"Mama still loves you."

He bent down and flung his arms wide.

Gabrielle jumped into his arms and kissed his cheek. "I love you, too. Don't be sad."

His heart constricted as her tiny hand patted his cheek.

"Everything will be all right. Ackidents happen."

Jared lounged in the hall. "That's what it's all about, Clay. A castle and a dungeon full of money can't buy that."

Clayton put Gabrielle down, sending her off to play. "Don't play with my mind, Jared. A woman ran away on me once. I am not about to put myself in that place again."

"Oh, I understand now. You are a coward. You won't try love again. Is that it? Or is it that you don't understand love at all and you feel stupid?"

Anger simmered in Clayton's veins. "I want a marriage of convenience."

Jared leaned against the doorjamb, his arms crossed over his chest, his amber eyes regarding Clayton with a steady gaze.

"So, you really did ask the lady to marry you? Or was it more you telling her the two of you would make an agreeable couple?"

Clayton felt a stab of guilt. "I think you've made your point. Now, if you will excuse me, I have a house party to attend. The next time you see me, I *will* be married." The challenge in his words wiped the smile off the earl's face.

"You have it all figured out, except the bride, is that it?"

Clayton pulled out his list. "I have the lady right here."

Jared walked toward him and grabbed the paper from his hands. "Miss Cherrie Black?" He looked up at Clayton. "And pray tell, where is Miss Garland's name? Or is she out of the running?"

"I said I think you have made your point." Clayton snatched the paper from the man's hands and turned to leave.

"Clay."

Clayton kept walking.

"You might want to prepare for that apology."

Clayton halted. "Why the devil would I want to do that?"

Jared turned his back on his brother-in-law and started down the hall. "Oh, didn't you know? Miss Appleby and Miss Garland will be at Grimstoke's party, watching you search for a bride."

Briana sat across from Agatha as the carriage rolled toward Grimstoke Hall. They had spent part of the afternoon at a posting inn due to trouble with one of the horses. Two hours later they had started out again in hopes of reaching the mansion by nightfall.

However, Briana's mind was not on the mission. It was on Lord Clayton Clearbrook. She had been blinded by his good looks and sweet-talking ways. He had tricked her into thinking he was a true gentleman. But at the ball the other night he had degraded her, killed the last feelings of love she ever had for him.

He was looking for a marriage of convenience, nothing more. It didn't matter to him whom he married, just so the lady would bow to his requests. It was an arrangement many gentlemen of the *ton* preferred. It was an arrangement her own parents had had.

"You know, dear, I have been thinking it over," Agatha said, turning her gaze from the window and tapping her fingers along her parasol, "and I believe that someone may have caught wind of our little escapade. Mind you, it might be nothing at all."

Briana gave her godmother a look of surprise. "You mean someone knows we are on to them?"

"To be a bit more precise, someone may be on to me. Some papers were stolen at Whitehall with my name on them. I obtained this information just before we left."

"Then we must go back! You must go back!"

"La, I have always been a target. More than you will ever be. Whitehall has tried to keep my name from everything. But precautions are only that—precautions, not reality."

The lady shrugged. "Sometimes these things leak out. It may be nothing at all. I really don't think the enemy has a notion of my interest in their doings, but since it is your life on the line, I must be frank. You must keep your distance from me if things get, well, let's just say suspicious. Actually, the more I think about it, the more I realize you should keep an eye out for anything out of the ordinary and that's all. I can take it from there."

Briana's brows fell int a disconcerting frown. The reality of their mission was quickly beginning to sink in. And Agatha's cavalier attitude was too calm. The lady was trying to shield Briana with an unemotional, straightforward attitude when in fact the mission was getting more dangerous by the minute. Agatha obviously didn't want Briana snooping into anything beyond her own bedchambers. But Briana wasn't going to fall for Agatha's ploy at all. "I don't like the entire arrangement."

"I know, child. But we are talking about the assassination of the Prince Regent. And although we must follow through with our mission, I must tell you that many at Whitehall believe there is a strong possibility the perpetrators are in Bath."

But did Agatha believe that? Briana wondered. Or did the lady believe the enemy was at Grimstoke Hall?

Agatha was becoming so good at this acting game, Briana

wasn't sure what she was thinking anymore. In truth, the only thing Briana did know was that Agatha would step between her and the enemy if she had to, and that horrid thought sent an icy finger of dread down Briana's spine. This previously exciting mission was swiftly turning into a dangerous game of life and death, where Agatha's calm demeanor only worried her more.

A light rain began to fall, and the *clip-clop* of the horses' hooves slowed. "Has the Regent been told?" Briana asked.

"He's told what he wants to hear, and he definitely doesn't want to hear about an attempt on his life. He is not the most popular man in England these days, squandering money as if it were printed for the sake of him and him alone."

"I see." An unwelcome tension enveloped the carriage as Briana stared out the window. Though Agatha didn't care for the Prince Regent, Briana knew the lady would do what was necessary for the stability of her country. A country she loved.

"And for goodness' sake, keep Kingsdale at a distance, child. You will have to be firm, and perhaps a bit unpleasant. It is not in your character to give someone the cut-direct, but it must be done if he keeps bothering you."

Briana didn't like the thought of Lord Kingsdale's being at the party, but she would do what she had to do.

She turned back to Agatha. "I can handle Lord K—"

The vehicle jolted sideways, cutting off her speech. Her heart jumped to her throat at the sound of screaming horses.

Agatha threw out her hand. "Hold on, child!"

Briana reached for her godmother just as the carriage tipped onto two wheels. "Dear Lord!" she shrieked. Her gaze shot to the door as the ground came up to meet her. Then her world went black.

Chapter Twelve

*I*t was raining heavily as Clayton pulled back on the leather reins of his horse, coming to a halt. He noted what looked like an abandoned cottage in the distance. Weeds and brush surrounded the small dwelling, but it would do. He could wait out the storm there.

Spurring his horse into a gallop, he turned the bend just as another blast of thunder boomed above him. His horse reared back.

"Easy, Belle." The animal whinnied and he patted her mane. "That's it. Easy now."

Something caught his attention and he squinted past the sheets of rain. Gad, what the devil? An overturned carriage?

Belle snorted as if sensing the distressed cries of the downed horses farther along the road. Clayton gripped his reins tighter. Some idiot driver nipping at the spirits, he thought with a scowl. By heaven, he would like to whip the man.

Setting his teeth, Clayton hurried toward the accident. A man stood beside the vehicle waving to him.

"What the devil happened?" Clayton shouted, dismounting.

"My lord!" the man cried, bending toward the carriage. "It's a miracle you appeared. . . . Broken axle . . . threw us sideways . . . horses tumbled. Harry here got caught beneath the wheel."

Clayton started forward and his heart stumbled. God help him, it was old James talking to him. His gaze jerked to the Earl of Stonebridge's crest. Emily? Gabrielle? No, he had just left them this morning.

He had a sinking sensation in his belly as he recalled Jared's words. *Oh, didn't you know? Miss Appleby and Miss Garland will be at Grimstoke's party, watching you search for a bride.*

Rain continued to pour from the sky as Clayton grabbed the overturned wheel and helped lift it a couple of inches, giving Harry enough clearance to climb out from beneath the carriage. The man hadn't suffered any terrible injuries, only a bruised leg.

Clayton turned to James. "The ladies?" he asked hurriedly. *Certainly they were not in the carriage.*

"Inside, my lord. Haven't heard a peep since we tipped. Scared, I think. Had to get to Harry. Horses are lame, though. Whinnying like babies. We'll have to shoot them. Pistols are in the box over there."

"Forget the deuced horses! Follow me!"

Clayton had already moved around the carriage. James was still in shock and shaking from the accident, but devil a bit, Clayton needed him.

"Miss Appleby? Miss Garland?" Clayton's voice roared over the hammering rain.

No answer. He climbed on top of the tilted carriage and peered inside. He gripped the frame, his fingers digging into the opening. "Briana," he said breathlessly.

He hadn't meant to say her name, but sheer terror swept through him at the sight of her limp body. Her face was as white as his neckcloth and her forehead was streaked with blood. Agatha was beneath her, looking like a corpse.

The horses began to wiggle, shaking the vehicle. He glanced up. "James!"

"The horses, my lord?" the man asked, his body shivering.

"Shoot the poor devils! Then help me get these women out!"

Clayton carefully slipped inside the carriage, making his way to Briana first. He felt for a pulse. "Briana, sweetheart, speak to me."

His heart gave a little kick. She was alive. He lifted Agatha's hand and felt a pulse as well. He dropped his head against his chest and took a deep, agonizing breath. "Thank God."

There was a boom and then another. The horses were dead.

"Can you lift them?" James asked.

Clayton nodded. "It will be tricky, but we can do it."

The two women were pulled carefully from the carriage and placed on the grassy knoll beside the vehicle, where a carriage blanket had been thrown to keep them partially dry.

With some rope, Clayton secured another blanket over the tilted carriage and tied the other end to a nearby tree. He told James to take his horse and ride on ahead to obtain a doctor and another mode of transportation for the ladies and Harry, who was resting in the shelter of some trees.

Inwardly thanking the earl for his emergency thinking, Clayton found a small medicine box in the carriage, which he used to attend to the ladies' injuries. He had seen worse in the war, but the sight of their blood had terrified him.

Miss Garland had a head wound, a small gash behind her ear. Agatha had a large bump on the back of her head and some small cuts. Both of the women were still unconscious. Clayton knew he had done all he could for the ladies. He had finished cleaning Miss Garland's injury when she started coming around.

As those beautiful green eyes gazed up at his face, a tidal wave of relief swept through him. What was it about this woman that tied his stomach into knots whenever he saw her?

He took hold of her hand. "It's all right, sweetheart. You've had an accident." He managed a smile. "It was a good thing I came along when I did."

"Agatha," she whispered hoarsely.

"She's had a good whack to her head, but she'll be fine once we get her to Grimstoke Hall."

"Must . . . stay with her."

Clayton ran a hand over Briana's pale skin. "Don't worry."

"M-must be with her."

Clayton's brow creased at the fear he saw in the lady's eyes. "I'll stay with her. I promise. Now rest."

A tear rolled down the lady's cheek as she closed her fairy eyes. "Th-thank you."

He frowned and placed a kiss upon her forehead as if she were his. He didn't want to leave her side. What kind of spell had she cast upon him?

The entourage arrived at Grimstoke Hall late that night, and Clayton was sorely regretting his promise to Miss Garland, who was resting comfortably in the adjacent bedchamber. She had not complained once during the journey in the dilapidated carriage they had obtained from a nearby vicar a few miles from the accident. Though the bumps had made her wince, she had been alert, avoiding any glances his way.

He knew she had been remembering his offer of marriage, but her only concern had been for her godmother. Clayton had assured Miss Garland—who needed sleep herself—that he would personally look after the older lady.

Miss Appleby, on the other hand, had awakened inside the vehicle and had told him exactly how she felt with a lump the size of three eggs on the back of her head.

Although Miss Appleby was now abed, the doctor had told Clayton that the lady also had a badly sprained ankle and should not be up and about for days, and because of her head injury, she was not to sleep during the night. Though it seemed an unusual demand, Clayton had heard of similar requests regarding such head injuries during the war.

Yet it was devilish hard trying to keep Miss Appleby up most the night. She was in excruciating pain, but Clayton soon realized that telling her stories of the war—something she seemed most interested in—seemed to work. She knew she had to stay awake, but she didn't like it.

Lord Grimstoke had been all assistance, even providing a personal maid outside Agatha's door. The door was left open an inch for propriety's sake, Grimstoke had announced, giving Clayton a curt glance. It was the first time Agatha had smiled since the accident. Clearly embarrassed, Clayton wasn't about to go back on his promise, so he endured Agatha's laughing gray eyes and settled in a chair beside her bed for the night.

If Jared and his brothers could see him now.

With a frown, Clayton regarded Miss Appleby's plump, pale form swallowed up by a mound of pillows and covers. Her lids were slowly sliding over her eyes while he was in the middle of one of his battles. "Miss Appleby," he said a little louder than usual, "am I boring you?"

Her eyes flickered open. "Yes . . . yes, you are."

His eyes twinkled. "Good. It's the least I could do after that attack with your parasol."

For a second her lips twitched, and then her eyes closed.

Clayton cleared his throat, trying to wake her. Nothing. A branch of candles flickered at the end of the bed, providing more than enough light for the room, but obviously not enough to keep the lady awake. He glanced at the door. What to do? Should he lean over the bed and shake her?

"I am still awake, my lord. Don't look so scared. No one is going to demand that you marry me."

Clayton flinched, his gaze shooting back to the lady. "Miss Appleby, you do enjoy torturing me, do you not?"

"No, not really." She yawned and winced. "I'm too tired to torture you. But if you want me to stay awake, why don't you tell me something interesting?"

His brows lifted in surprise. "Madam, I thought I was telling you something interesting." There was an amusing edge to his voice that cut through the formality of the situation.

A smile lifted the corners of her mouth. "Well," she drawled, "since we are on such good terms and only a good story will keep my mind conscious, why don't you tell me about Lady Serena?"

For a full minute he could only stare at her.

"Don't sit there like some widemouth bass with your jaw hanging on every word I say," she said unapologetically. "Entertain me, my lord."

"I fail to see what my past has to do with anything."

"You told me about the war. Now tell me about your heart." Her gaze was firm, making him feel about six years old.

Who the devil had she been talking to? Emily? "I don't think it wise," he said stiffly.

"Pffff. Hearts are made to love, my lord. And before you open your mouth again, let me tell *you* a story."

A chubby hand rose from beneath the linens. "No, not a word. This is my story, my lord. A story of how I found love, lost love, and never loved again."

The sun had begun to peek through the sides of the curtains when Clayton realized the lady had kept him captive for a rather long time herself.

Wordlessly, he had sat glued to his chair, listening to this extraordinary woman tell her story of how she had met a handsome naval officer, had fallen in love, and had lost him at Trafalgar. He was younger than she, and feeling pressure from Society, she had refused his proposal of marriage. She regretted it as soon as he had left, but it was too late. He had died during the battle.

"I have never told anyone the true story," she said, her eyes misty, "but it seemed appropriate, since you had the gallantry to sit by an old maid and succumb to the embarrassment of Lord Grimstoke's servant guarding my virtue."

He chuckled. "I can see why a man would want you, Miss Appleby. I give Grimstoke credit for guarding you."

The lady gave him a light swat on his wrist. "What the ladies say is true, then. You are a charmer. I have been warned, and so has my godchild."

At the mention of Miss Garland, all playfulness fell from his face. Had Miss Appleby been told about his proposal? "I see."

"You had better see, my lord, or another whack from my parasol will be the least I do."

Clayton sank back in his seat and gaped at the older lady. Devil take it. There had always been a certain mystery about Miss Agatha Appleby, and he didn't doubt her in the least.

"And another thing," Agatha said. "If I ever catch you proposing to that wonderful girl again without some feeling behind your words, I will—well, I will send word to the duke himself."

Clayton's face went grim. *More the reason for me to marry and gain that deuced castle!* He loved his brother Roderick, but he didn't need the duke's interference in his life.

There was a knock on the door. The maid entered, crossing the room to drawn open the curtains, and mentioning something about an early breakfast. It took all Clayton's willpower not to follow the servant out the door. The duke was one of the very reasons he wanted that castle. To him it meant freedom from Roderick, who thought to run everyone's life, including Clayton's.

Clayton poured a drink of water for Agatha and handed it to her. "My brother has no say in what I do, madam."

The lady's gray eyes peered over the cup as she sipped. "I declare, you do get your back up. But depend upon it, one word from my mouth on your conduct toward my godchild, and the duke will cut off your quarterly payments."

Would he indeed? Clayton stared at the lady as an adversary would study his opponent. Undeniably, Miss Agatha Appleby was more than she appeared. He took her cup and set it down on the table. "I have other means of supporting myself."

Her sharp gaze narrowed. "Do you now? Since you lost everything in that ridiculous tobacco venture, I suppose you mean that old goat's castle."

Clayton had started to rise, the chair scraping against the floor, and he caught himself midway. Who the devil had told her about that?

"I am not as blind as you think," she said, waving her hand toward the door. "But that is neither here nor there. Since I cannot be by my godchild's side, I want you to do it for me."

Clayton stood and adjusted his jacket, halting at her words.

He leaned against the bedpost, struggling to maintain a serene appearance. "First you tell me to stay away from the lady, and now you want me to stick to her like a paid companion. I believe that lump on your head has done more damage than the doctor thought."

She rose on her elbows, her sleepy gaze searching the room. "I am as sane as you are, if that is any measure."

He laughed, but the wheels starting turning in his mind. Was she mad? Why would she want him to keep an eye on Miss Garland, the very person he had been warned to stay away from?

Was it because of the carriage accident? He intended to investigate that entire incident. The footman had mentioned a broken axle. Had it been sheared on purpose? Or had it purely been worn and Stonebridge's servants missed it? What the devil was going on here?

"Where in the blue blazes is my parasol?" she snapped.

"The last time I saw your weapon, madam, it was squished between the door and the seat of the tipped carriage. Broken like Napoleon's blasted empire."

She huffed. "Never compare any of my effects to that man, if you please."

It was hard for Clayton not to laugh. He pulled out his pocket watch. Five o'clock. The lady's eyes were starting to droop. The doctor had said that if she stayed awake until five in the morning, it would be quite all right to let her sleep the day away.

Clayton had already decided that he would leave when the maid brought in the breakfast tray. It was odd, but he was beginning to feel a strange urge to look after Miss Appleby, and it had nothing to do with duty or his sister's attachment to the lady, let alone that she was Stonebridge's aunt.

"You need your rest, Miss Appleby. I made a promise to your precious goddaughter that I would stay by your side during the night. I believe I have done my duty."

The lady's head sank into her pillow. "I thank you for that, my lord. But a maid would have sufficed."

"Forgive me for being blunt, madam, but you would have had the maid in tears and running from the room in thirty minutes. And besides Miss Garland, my sister would never have forgiven me if something had happened to you, and neither would my brother-in-law. So sleep the day away and rest that sore head and injured ankle. Oh, and be secure in the thought that nothing will happen to your goddaughter, for I have no intention of proposing to her again."

Steel gray eyes captured his, but there was a weariness in Miss Appleby's expression that told him she was losing her edge. "That isn't what I meant."

They both turned their heads as the maid entered again with the breakfast tray. "I know it's early, but his lordship wanted a tray sent to your chambers as well, my lord," the girl said, setting the food beside Agatha.

It seemed Grimstoke had insisted on sending the servant to be at Miss Appleby's side by the appointed time. Clayton needed his sleep, and now that he knew the older lady would be fine, he had to address his own problems, namely finding a bride.

Miss Appleby looked drained, but she managed to raise her forefinger and curl it, summoning Clayton to her side.

He nodded for the maid to wait outside the door, then he leaned his ear toward the lady, his lips twitching. "I am at your command, madam."

"Do not leave her alone."

Clayton's brows creased. Before he could answer, she grabbed hold of his sleeve. "Kingsdale . . . "

Clayton stiffened. Kingsdale here?

"Promise me . . . my lord." The lady was fighting with everything she had to stay awake. "Keep her away from him. Don't . . . like the man."

"I will give her fair warning about the man, Miss Appleby. But Miss Garland will have to make up her mind about him, not me."

Another frown flitted across the lady's face. "Other things . . . danger . . . must watch her."

The lady started to rise, and Clayton put a gentle hand to her shoulder. "Upon my word, you are going to kill yourself if you think to get up with that cursed ankle."

"Must warn her." The lady's eyes were mere slits.

"I believe your godchild is resting comfortably. No need to concern yourself."

The lady fell against her pillow, thoroughly exhausted. The next moment a deep sigh passed her lips and she was fast asleep. Clayton walked to the door and called for the maid. He took a step into the hall.

"Keep her in bed. You can send another tray to her room when she awakens. I as well as the doctor will be checking on her. As long as she passed the night without complications, the doctor mentioned a few drops of laudanum in her drink or her food. Once she opens those eyes, she'll demand to get up. She must stay immobile until she heals."

"I have seen to many ladies, your lordship. She be like my own mum."

Clayton left, feeling quite satisfied that Miss Appleby was in the best of hands. He would have a little food and then rest. But as soon as he entered his bedchambers and discarded his jacket, the image of Miss Garland and Kingsdale stood out in his mind. Did she know anything about the man's past and his treatment of women?

His conscience would not let it go. He would have to warn her. He told himself it was his duty as a gentleman and as a friend of the family. After that task was done, he would search for a bride.

Frowning, he pulled out his list. Instead of Miss Cherrie

Black, all he could see was a head of rich auburn hair, two sensuous green eyes, and a pert little nose sprinkled with adorable freckles. No, he thought, smiling. Not freckles. *Feckles!*

He raised his hand to the bridge of his nose and gave it a pinch. Hell and spitfire. For the life of him he couldn't remember what Miss Cherrie Black looked like at all. He blamed it on his loss of sleep. That was it. It had nothing to do with feelings for Miss Garland. Nothing at all.

In her chamber down the hall, Briana peeked through a crack in her door and overheard Clayton spouting orders to the maid outside Agatha's room. His voice was low but still audible to her ears. The man was an enigma. He cared for Agatha as if she were his own mother.

When they had arrived at Grimstoke Hall, Briana had wanted to stay at her godmother's side, but both the doctor and Lord Clayton had insisted she rest. Lord Clayton had promised to stay with Agatha during the night. Knowing the stubborn man was probably the only one who could stand up to the headstrong lady, Briana had agreed, and it seemed he had kept his promise to the last detail.

His coldness toward marriage bothered her, yet when he thought others were not looking, he showed a heart of gold. Oh, for a few short minutes during the night, Briana had tiptoed down the hall and spied on him and Agatha, listening to their conversation—not that they ever knew she was there. The two were so wrapped up in Lord Clayton's war stories, they didn't even flinch at the snores coming from the maid posted in the hall.

Frowning, Briana slowly closed her door and went back to bed. She pulled the covers up to her neck and stared at the ceiling. While it was true that Grimstoke's servant was certainly no guard dog, Briana wished with all her might that someone or something existed in this grand house that would guard her against Lord Clayton's charms.

She couldn't deny that the man's kindness was beginning to penetrate even the hardest part of her heart.

Chapter Thirteen

*L*ater that morning Briana situated herself on the window seat in Lord Grimstoke's guest chamber, examining Agatha's papers that she had extracted from the lady's reticule the night before.

Once Lord Clayton had descended from the vicar's carriage, shouting orders for Grimstoke's servants to send for a doctor, Agatha, though still in pain, had used the time to warn Briana that perhaps their sudden stop had not been an accident after all.

Minutes later Briana heard Lord Clayton mention something to their host about the axle on the Stonebridge carriage being sheared; whether it was worn or done on purpose he wasn't certain. At that point Briana could no longer dismiss her godmother's warning.

Briana had had a breakfast tray sent up to her chambers, and after eating she had stopped in to see how her godmother was doing. The lady was sleeping, looking fragile and pale, like a small child lost in a sea of pillows and satin covers.

Immediately after visiting Agatha, Briana met up with the doctor, who praised Lord Clayton to the highest heavens. It seemed his lordship had been a miracle worker. Well, Briana didn't need the doctor to tell her that. She had seen it for herself. The man was quickly breaking through her defenses.

"Bree, may I come in?"

The young voice belonged to Grimstoke's only daughter, Violet, taking Briana completely by surprise. They were to meet later in the day. Stuffing the papers back into her reticule, Briana stood and walked toward the door. "Come in."

Violet hurried into the room and greeted Briana with a hug. The young lady stepped back, clasping Briana's hands.

"Oh, Bree, last time I saw you, you were in mourning, and now here you are, coming to our house party and you have an accident along the way. Papa told me all about it this morning at breakfast. It must have been dreadful."

Violet was a small replica of her father. Short and plump, with curly brown hair. But what she didn't have in looks, she had in heart.

Briana gave a reassuring smile, but her head still ached from the accident. For reasons she didn't want to admit, she made no mention of Lord Clayton's attending her wound.

"As you can see, I am quite fine indeed," she said to Violet. "Only a small cut behind the ear. But it is dear Agatha I am worried about."

"Papa has sent Chloe to watch over her. She is the best of maids. She took care of me when I had the inflammation of the lungs last year. Oh! I must say I adore your gown."

Briana dropped her gaze to her green gown trimmed in white ribbon and lace. Besides everything else going wrong, it seemed Emily had made a switch of Briana's dresses—actually her entire wardrobe. All her gowns were of the latest fashion, including her sleepwear. It amazed Briana how Emily could get away with something like this, but she had. She must have made plans for the extensive wardrobe weeks ago.

Emily had probably thought she was doing Briana a favor— her friend had even hinted as much—but the beautiful clothing would make it extremely difficult for Briana to fade into the walls, especially with the low-cut necklines and fancy laced bodices. Briana had never thought Emily would truly do something like this, but then again, Emily's plans were never commonplace at all.

"Thank you. I believe this is the latest creation of Madame LaPorte. But I must say that your father has been exceedingly generous. I cannot thank him enough for his wonderful care of my godmother. She is more fragile than she looks, you know."

Lord Grimstoke had indeed been most gracious, insisting on the very best for both his female guests.

Violet smiled, giving Briana's hand a squeeze. "I vow that woman is more robust than Prinny himself."

Prinny himself? Thoughts of the mission assaulted Briana's conscience. What about the assassination plot? And Lord Grimstoke? Would she find some damaging evidence that would convict Violet's father? The very idea sickened her. Grimstoke could not be involved. He could not.

Briana managed a chuckle. "You know my godmother. She thinks she can do anything. But she must be kept in bed for the next few days, and I daresay that will be the real challenge."

"Oh, I know. Chloe informed me that Lord Clayton was at her bedside all night. How lucky you were he came along when he did. Along with the doctor's orders, his lordship has agreed that keeping the lady abed with laudanum is the wisest choice if she becomes disagreeable. I believe Lord Clayton is very concerned about Miss Appleby. He is quite the honorable gentleman."

"Yes, quite honorable," Briana said, her memory of Clayton kissing her still clear in her mind. "We were fortunate indeed. I had no idea he was invited to your house party."

Briana distinctly recalled his name not being on Agatha's list. Was he pursuing her? Did he even know she was attending Grimstoke's party? No, of course not. Her mind was running away with her. She meant nothing to him. He only wanted a convenient and biddable bride. Had he not told her so the night of the ball?

Still, she wondered what reason had pressed him to seek a bride now? Was the duke pushing him to marry?

"Let's sit down, Bree. These new slippers are hurting my feet. I think the ribbons are cutting off my circulation."

Briana laughed as they made their way to the window seat.

"Now," Violet said, smiling, "back to Lord Clayton. He was invited at the last minute. Mama was surprised at his wish for an invite, but one cannot slight the son of a duke."

I did, Briana wanted to say. Yet she could not deny the hint of disappointment she felt at the thought of Lord Clayton looking for a convenient bride at Grimstoke Hall. She was not certain of his reasons for wanting to marry so quickly, but she had to admit his help the past twenty-four hours had been nothing but wonderful. He had been an angel throughout their entire or deal.

Why, the man had apparently even charmed Agatha during the night. This was the Lord Clayton Clearbrook most people knew, the man most people adored, especially women. This was the man Briana had fallen in love with when she had been sixteen.

Violet pressed a hand against the windowpane. "Oh, look There he is now."

Briana tried not to show her surprise as she peered out the window. Lord Clayton was standing in the gardens below speaking to Violet's father. When Lord Grimstoke looked away, Lord Clayton quickly lifted his gaze. Briana blushed and leaned away.

It seemed Violet had missed the exchange, for her eyes were glued to another gentleman walking toward the two men.

Briana noticed Lord Clayton stiffen. It was only slight, but he had done it all the same. The man joining the circle was Lord Kingsdale.

Violet rested her brow against the pane. "Is he not hand some?" Her voice was filled with awe.

"Very handsome."

Too handsome for his own good, Briana thought with a frown. Lord Clayton was worming his way into her hear whether she liked it or not. A wink, a word, a smile—anything he did affected her.

Violet tilted her head toward Briana. "You had a fondness for him a while back, did you not?"

Briana felt her color rise. She had never told Violet about her feelings for him, had she?

"Oh, I know he is a rogue," Violet said with an embarrasse chuckle, "and that is why you finally broke your liaison, but vow the man is simply too dashing to dismiss."

A small lump of jealousy coiled in Briana's breast. "Y-you are in love with him?"

Violet frowned. "Would you mind if I were?"

Briana shook her head, turning her gaze back to the thre

men. "Why should I mind?" Violet would probably fit into Lord Clayton's plans quite nicely. He would be able to go about London without his wife's interference, and Violet would gladly stay in the country, where she felt more at home. Lord Clayton's obligation as the son of a duke would be fulfilled.

Violet sat back. "Well, with Lord Kingsdale one never knows what he will do next. And whether you agree with me or not, I fear the man still has a liking for you. You were ever the intellectual and he seems to like women with brains."

Briana could not hold back her surprise. She had thought her friend was speaking of Lord Clayton. For a reason she didn't want to identify, her heart swelled with relief.

"I am not interested in Lord Kingsdale, Violet. And for your sake, I would stay away from the man. He is, well, not what the ladies would call gentle."

Violet turned toward the window with a sigh. "How very puzzling. And I thought him such an agreeable man. I think Papa likes him."

Briana leaned forward as Violet's father left the gardens. The remaining two men were still exchanging words. Lord Clayton glanced up at her, his expression hard as he looked back at Kingsdale.

Violet put a hand to her mouth, a mischievous smile springing to her lips. "Mercy me! Lord Clayton seems to know we are watching him."

Briana turned away, quite embarrassed to be caught staring. Why did she have a feeling the men were arguing about her?

Violet's eyes gleamed with adventure as she rose from her seat. "Papa thinks he is looking for a wife."

"A gentleman from such a fine family must marry sometime," Briana said, trying not to show the anxiety growing in her breast.

"Oh!" Violet exclaimed, clapping her hands. "Speaking of family, did you know his cousin, Sir Gerald, is attending the house party? He is a friend of Papa's and arrived only yesterday."

"Is he?" Briana remembered Emily mentioning the man's name a few times, but for the life of her she couldn't recall what her friend had said about him. She had also seen his name on the list of attendees, but she had not known he was Lord Grimstoke's good friend. Agatha had been planning to go over the list in the carriage before the accident.

"They met at one of Prinny's parties last year," Violet said, lowering her voice. "I am shamed to admit it, but Papa likes to gamble and it seems Sir Gerald has the same vice. But I cannot lie, Bree. I rather like the man."

A hint of a smile touched Briana's lips. Violet's tastes in gentlemen changed like the rain in spring. "Ah, now we are getting somewhere. Does your father agree to the suit?"

"Oh, it's nothing like that. Papa thinks I need an older gentleman. But Sir Gerald wears the latest fashions. His neckcloth is tied to perfection, with just the right amount of starch. Some would say he's a bit arrogant, but I believe they are only jealous because he enjoys the finer things in life."

Briana listened intently to Violet talk about the man. If Grimstoke were involved in the plot against Prinny, could Sir Gerald be involved as well? She battled against the very thought of Violet's father's being embroiled in the horrid scheme.

"If you are feeling better, Bree, there will be a little soirée tonight. Nothing as formal as a ball, but Papa has hired some strings for the evening. I vow if any of the three gentlemen we talked about asks me to waltz, I will just swoon."

Briana broke into a smile. "You will not."

Violet sighed dreamily. "I suppose not. But Papa said Lord Clayton was very concerned about you last night. Maybe that's why he kept looking at you from the gardens. Don't deny it, Bree."

Briana slid her finger over the nightstand. "The man found my carriage overturned, and he sees me as an obligation, nothing more."

"If that's the way you see it, I cannot change your mind. But it could be that the man has eyes for only you. I heard when he arrived last night, he asked for a bedchamber near Miss Appleby and you. He made it abundantly clear to Papa he was going to take full responsibility for both of you while you were here. And I can tell you that Papa didn't like that at all."

Briana felt an inexplicable tenderness toward Lord Clayton for his gallantry. "Why would your papa object?"

Violet giggled. "'There will be no impropriety in my house,' he said. Meaning you and Lord Clayton."

"Ah, I see." Briana's eyes crinkled with amusement. That, of course, was never going to happen.

"But Papa is quite strict with things like that. He will demand satisfaction if any of his guests are compromised. I hate to say it, but he has done so many times before."

"Compromised?" Briana squeaked. "Really, Violet, what do you think of me?"

Violet rushed to her friend's side. "Oh, no, I am not accusing you, Bree. I am only warning you. Last year, Lady Farrow and Lord Commings were stuck in a cottage for a few hours during a snowstorm. Papa insisted they marry, and there was nothing for it but for them to do as he said. It was unfortunate for them that the archbishop has good friends in the area and visits many times during the year. A special license was easily obtained and the couple was forced to marry."

"I knew they were married under strange circumstances," Briana said, frowning, "and they are never seen together . . . "

"Indeed, they are not. Lady Farrow believes Lord Commings had it planned all along. He wanted her father's money, you see. Well, that's what she thinks anyway."

"I feel sorry for both of them."

"I don't believe things are as bad as they appear, but I only told you the story because rumors have it Lord Clayton is searching for a wife. Papa is becoming ever so stuffy lately. He wants no scandal attached to his name. He was quite upset when Lord Clayton insisted on watching over your godmother."

Briana could not hold back her laughter. "Yes, I know. A maid was posted outside during the night. And speaking of your papa, I have heard he has an excellent book collection about the ancient pyramids of Egypt. I was wondering if I could see it."

Briana contemplated how a man who was so afraid of scandal could ever be involved in an assassination plot against the

Prince Regent. It just could not be so. This mission would probably turn out to be nothing at all.

"Of course you can see them," Violet said as she walked toward the door. "Truly, Bree, reading is one thing, but a lady must be careful. Being labeled a bluestocking is quite another."

Briana felt sorry for her friend. How could a woman not be curious? "I don't intend to marry like you do, Violet."

Violet's hand fell from the door. "Goodness' sakes, why not?"

"I have my reasons." Briana didn't want to explain herself. Instead she reached out to her friend. "If you wish to make me happy, you will lead me to that collection, and I promise I will make it to the dance tonight."

"Oh, Bree! That would be wonderful! I would be in your debt if you stood by my side for a bit. But I will not push you if you are still nursing your injury."

"Consider yourself in my debt."

Violet gave Briana a hug. "I am so glad you came."

Briana smiled as they left the room. She needed to make her way to the library without anyone the wiser. She hated to use her friendship with Violet, but the Regent's life was at stake. And if Whitehall's source was to be believed, and Grimstoke was involved, Briana had to search for evidence. Whoever had forwarded the information about Grimstoke must have had good reason. Revenge, perhaps? That was always a good motivator, truth or not.

Of course, there was a slim chance the information was true. Agatha had mentioned other agents with more significant leads, searching Bath. But it didn't undermine the fact that the Prince Regent had been booed by the crowds when he had opened Parliament earlier this year. Many people were not happy with him. There were a number of people that could be plotting against him.

Questions danced around in Briana's head as if she had downed two bottles of champagne. Was Lord Grimstoke merely a pawn in a game of revenge? Was this investigation at the house party a total waste of Whitehall's time? Briana didn't know what to think, but since Agatha was still in bed dosed with laudanum, she would have to make the investigations by herself.

Drink in hand, Lord Grimstoke sat in his chair and lifted his head as the maid walked into his private sitting room.

"There be nothing in her reticule or her belongings, my lord," Chloe said. "I looked everywhere."

"Dash it, Chloe. She has ties to Whitehall. We cannot let her out of our sight."

"And what about us? When will we be leaving this place?"

"As soon as I get my money. The Regent played me for the fool last year at the tables and I intend to see the right of it."

"Your wife?"

"She don't know a thing. Sits in bed eating rolls all day. It's Violet I'm worried about. Got herself set on marriage to a gentleman of the *ton*. Won't work. No one will be the wiser, but when I leave, well, by Jove, we must take her with us."

"Oh, love, she won't want to come along. Why not send her to that cousin in India? Seems like a fine gent. Wanted to marry the girl for years. He won't mind if there's talk."

Grimstoke steepled his hands against his chin. "Simon always had a liking for her. He may be twenty years older, but I can count on him. Owes me a favor, too. He will see I did the right thing with Prinny and all this. Violet won't like it, but it will be the best thing I can do for her. Never liked scandals, you know. But once I run off with you . . ."

He shook his head. "No, no. Have to have her settled. That's what I'll do. Simon it is. He'll take care of her like a queen. Violet needs pampering, you know. After we are settled in America, well, who knows, Simon might take it upon himself to move there too. In fact, I'll make it worth his while."

His gaze was tired. "Good thing I have you, Chloe."

Chloe snuggled against his chest. "Good thing, Grimmy."

"You'd best get back to Miss Appleby. That goddaughter of hers is my daughter's friend. Quiet little thing. Don't want her involved in any of this. Might upset Violet, you know. If we can keep Miss Appleby in bed, all will be good. Add a little more laudanum, enough to have her sleep the day away. Can't have her dead, won't look good. Magistrates and all that."

Chloe pulled away, her eyes wide with curiosity. "Did you have something to do with the carriage yesterday?"

"No, by Jove, not my style. Don't know what happened there. Meant to take care of Miss Appleby when she arrived. You know, put the laudanum in her drink. Make her too tired to follow up on us. Well, it worked out nice and tight for us, did it not?"

The maid gave him a saucy smile. "What about your contact? Won't he be leaving you a message about the money?"

"Yes, well, can't have him knowing we have trouble. Won't be any good to us at all. And to tell you the truth, don't know if the contact is male or female. But all I have to do is pass on the exact schedule Prinny will be taking when he visits Bath again. The Regent always lets me know his plans in case I want to join him. He don't tell many people."

He sent a concerned look toward the door and lowered his voice. "They plan to take the Regent on the road. Scare him a bit, you know. He's been very careful since the crowd turned on him a while ago. Keeps his itinerary private."

Chloe's fingers moved seductively over his cravat. "It ain't right that old Prinny took your money at that game down in Brighton. Ain't right at all."

Grimstoke wrapped his hand about her waist. "That's right. Cheated me, he did. Took almost everything I had in one roll of the dice. Ain't going to let that go, no matter who he is. Let them kidnap the fat old goat. Should wake the country up a bit, I daresay. It will give the old boy a good scare, too. They'll let him go, of course. They ain't going to kill him, you know."

The maid frowned. "But what if they do kill him?"

"They ain't going to. Be a blasted mess. They only want to scare him. Let him know they ain't fond of his excessive living. Some fanatical group, don't you know. Knew we were old friends."

Grimstoke tapped angrily against the side of the chair. "We still keep in touch, though it pains me every time I put my hand to the pen. My blasted luck never holds up when I've been out drinking all day. But that's neither here nor there. Whoever wants the exact route and time is willing to give me money so I can leave this country for good."

"But I thought you said the Prince cheated you."

"Yes, well . . . indeed he did. He should have known I wasn't up to snuff that night. Could have let me slide a bit, don't you know. Never you fear, Chloe, we will sail off into the moonlight together."

Chloe's brows knitted into a frown. "And you have the information?"

"I'll be leaving the message in that secret chamber. And why should he or she not have it? Received a missive to leave the information there at a specific time during the house party. With over fifty guests, I don't know who it is, and I don't care. It ain't every day the Prince Regent is kidnapped, and the less information I know the better."

"Ah, there you are, Cousin. Thought you might be up for a ride. 'Depend upon it,' I said to myself, 'the old boy will be in the stables saddling his own horse.'"

Clayton's nerves cringed at the sound of the haughty but familiar voice. He slanted his gaze toward the stable door and narrowed his eyes. What the deuce was his cousin doing here?

"Never knew you were one for house parties, Gerald." His cousin was a good-looking man—a bit too broad in the face, but the ladies seemed to like him, even if he was a conceited oaf.

"Come now, cuz, let's not play games. I know why you're here." The man dropped his gaze to brush a speck of dirt off his waistcoat.

Contempt flashed in Clayton's eyes. Gerald was a selfish prig. The meticulous pains he took with his dress made Clayton dislike him all the more. "And may I guess why *you* are here?"

"No need to guess, cuz. You want Cathaven's treasure. Nothing surprising about that."

"And you are here for the very same reason, I presume?"

"The devil, you don't think I aim to let you have it all, do you?" Gerald singled out a piece of straw on the door beside him and flicked it to the ground. "The thing is, cuz, as a gentleman, I aim to be fair about this. Let you know I'm here and all that nonsense."

Clayton dropped the reins in his hands and stepped back from the stall. "You followed me here?"

"Not exactly, but I ain't an idiot. Had it set a month ago to attend Grimstoke's. But after that deuced will, I made other plans, parties and whatnot. Leaned heavily on your character, cuz. Figured you would be looking for a bride at some gathering or other. Suitable wife. Biddable. From a good family. All that rubbish."

Gerald laughed. "A case of mere chance you ended up here. Not that I didn't have the other major events covered. Unfortunately, I could do nothing about an intimate gathering you attended in Town or at one of Elbourne's stuffy balls. Lucky for me you found nothing there. And this is one of the last grand house parties of the Season."

With a smug smile on his lips, Gerald leaned against the stable door. "Sent my regrets to all the other parties the minute I heard you were coming here. My valet is friend of your valet's sister, don't you know."

Clayton barely stopped himself from strangling the man.

"Well, cuz, don't look at me like that. Old Cathaven was a cantankerous old fellow, but Zeus, never thought he had all that money. To tell you the truth, almost popped a button on my brand-new waistcoat when I found out."

Clayton returned to his horse, pulling it from the stall. The man was a deuced nuisance. "I fail to see how you following me will affect my choice. And if by some chance you do meddle in my affairs, you will pay dearly."

"Dueling is illegal, you know," the man sputtered. "Upon my word, cuz, you can't do anything about me being here."

Clayton glanced over his shoulder. "I never liked you, *cuz*. You're a conceited, arrogant old fellow yourself, and for the goodness of your health I would advise you to return to London."

Sir Gerald stiffened. "Listen here. I ain't about to take orders from you. And just so we can be fair about this, I will tell you now that I will do anything within the law to keep you from marrying before the allotted time."

He sneezed vigorously. "Dratted stables. Don't like them at all. Dirty. Look at that. Straw on my new boots. Won't do at all.

Well, good day, cuz. See you tonight. Grimstoke hired a quartet. Dancing and all that. Think I'll take a turn at the red-haired chit you brought in last night."

Clayton's hand froze on his saddle. "She won't be dancing."

"Won't she? I don't think that carriage accident will stop her. Saw her stepping into the library only minutes ago." He rubbed his nose with his handkerchief. "Blasted stables."

He sneezed again, then looked up. "Saw Kingsdale walking into the library, too. Chit gets around, don't she?" He shook his head. "Well, *au revoir* and all that." Flipping a hand in the air, the man disappeared around the door.

Clayton stepped back from his horse and slammed his riding whip against the stall. "What the devil am I going to do with her, Belle?" The horse neighed.

Clayton didn't know what he was more furious about, his cousin's presence, Kingsdale's interest in Miss Garland, Miss Garland's gallivanting about the mansion when she should be resting, or Kingsdale's meeting with the lady in the library.

He had seen the lady staring out the window earlier. Even from the distance he had seen her green eyes glittering with anger at how he had treated her the night of the Elbourne ball. But he had seen the frank admiration in her eyes as well.

He had never expected her to deny him anything. In fact, no woman had ever refused him even one kiss. But in the past twenty-four hours he'd realized he was attracted to the red-haired Fairy Lady. And dash it all, he had decided it was Miss Garland or nobody.

Miss Cherrie Black had not made it to Grimstoke's party. She was still in London, recovering from a cold. He had barely been interested in her anyway. No one seemed to fit into his plans like Miss Garland did. Devil take it, there was just something about her. She might not be the perfect wife, and she might want more than he was willing to give, but they could find a compromise. He was sure of it. And besides, he would lose his right arm before he'd let the lady marry Kingsdale.

He strode from the stables toward Grimstoke Hall. Where was that blasted library?

Chapter Fourteen

*W*orrying her bottom lip, Briana glanced at the library
door through which Violet had happily departed only
minutes ago. She set aside the books her friend had pulled from
her father's Egyptian collection and rose from her chair. How
long did she have? Five minutes? Ten? An hour at most?

After a long pause she walked toward Lord Grimstoke's
desk. A small fire crackled in the hearth, reminding her very
much of the sparks that would fly if she were caught snooping.
As quickly as she could, she rifled through the desk drawers.
All of them were unlocked. Her heart sank. She knew that any
important missives would not be neatly folded in an unlocked
drawer for anyone to grab.

Her eyes kept moving warily back to the door. She turned
full circle, then glanced at the brick fireplace behind her. She
let go a deep sigh, wondering if it was wise for her to continue
her search without Agatha's direction.

Where could the missive be? Had it been dispatched or was
the courier waiting for a certain time to place the document?
Did Agatha know about the timing or was she waiting for more
information? Or was this all for nothing?

Her brow wrinkled in thought and her eyes narrowed. The
mantel? Was there a secret hiding place there? A movable panel
from years ago?

She walked forward and pressed her hand against the cool
brick, feeling for any sign of movement. The orange flames of
the fire flickered in the corner of her eye.

The door clicked and with the quickness of a cat, she dropped her hands to her sides and spun around.

"Ah, Miss Garland, what a pleasant surprise."

Her heart thumped at the sight of Lord Kingsdale standing on the threshold. "Good afternoon, my lord."

His gaze traveled from her face to the stack of books on the nearby table. A wicked smile tipped the corners of his mouth.

"Reading again? You never were one to sit idle, were you, my dear? Hmmm, last time we met it was in the duchess's private sitting room, was it not? And here we are, alone again." His eyes moved over her. "How very fortunate. You look lovelier than ever."

Briana's warning to Violet rang in her ears. It was as if Kingsdale were stalking her. Pushing him away would be harder than she'd thought. Ignoring his intense assessment of her person, she made her way to the chair, picking up the book she had been reading earlier.

"I would rather forget about the last time we met, if you please, my lord. You see, I am fortunate Lord Grimstoke has such a wonderful library. His collection on Egyptian architecture is fascinating."

She hated to give him the cut-direct, but he was beginning to grate on her nerves. She opened the book and pretended to read. "If you would excuse me."

The man walked closer, his intimate chuckle sending a ripple of uneasiness down her back.

"Come now, Miss Garland, don't play games with me. I know you adore the pyramids, but you are not reading about them now. You are waiting for someone in particular, are you not?"

Her head snapped up. "What?"

"Lord Clayton Clearbrook, perhaps? I hear he was your knight in shining armor on your little journey here. And of course the man did seem a bit protective of you the last time we met."

"I don't need protection from anybody," she said coolly. "And Lord Clayton has no say over what I do."

"Is that so? Heard he was in a rare fit when they brought you in with that wound to your head. You are well?"

A trace of worry lit the man's eyes, and she wondered if she had misjudged him.

"A bump behind the ear. A mere scratch. Nothing significant."

"From what I hear, Miss Appleby is in worse shape."

Briana started. Could he be hoping she would be without a chaperone for the next few days?

She lifted her chin. "A blow to her head and a sprained ankle have left her in bed for the next few days."

"I see. And does your injury preclude your attendance at tonight's little soirée?"

"I don't believe I will be dancing, my lord. However, I may watch from the side."

He strolled across the room, his eyes never leaving her face.

She was determined not to flinch. What did this man want from her? She had refused his offer of marriage years ago, and friendship with him was out of the question.

He came within a foot of her, his dark eyes studying her face. Without another word, he brought her hand to his lips. "Then *I* will watch from beside *you*."

She tried to pull free of his hold, but his grip on her hand was too strong. "My lord—"

Her words were cut short when the door flew open. Heat flooded her at the sight of Lord Clayton walking into the room. His violet blue eyes glittered with such contempt she wanted to fall through the floor. How was it that he always caught her with Kingsdale? Was someone feeding him information?

Kingsdale glanced over his shoulder, his hand still holding hers. Briana gave a slight tug, but the man stood firm.

"Ah, Lord Clayton. I was hoping the lady would give me a dance tonight. You don't mind, do you?"

"Mind?" Clayton responded stiffly. "The lady is not my wife."

Briana felt the slight of his words as if he had slapped her. Tears burned the back of her throat, but she refused to show him how much he had hurt her. Instead she gave him a brilliant smile. "Indeed, I am not your wife, my lord."

"How very fortunate for you," he said, his words carrying a warning of disapproval as he glared at Kingsdale.

Briana pressed her lips together in anger. It took her a moment to respond. "I have promised the first dance to Gregory."

She was so furious, she blurted out Kingsdale's Christian name before she could think. Now she had done it! Agatha would skin her alive. How dim-witted could she be? Lord Clayton seemed to bring out the worst in her. •

The intimacy of the announcement brought a smile to Kingsdale's lips. He couldn't have planned it any better. He released her hand and gave her a curt bow. "Until tonight."

Clayton stood perfectly still as Kingsdale strode from the room. He waited for the man's heels to click down the hall, then he shifted his gaze back to Miss Garland, who had turned her back on him. The lady seemed to be studying the fire as if some great secret were tucked inside its flames.

And when the devil did she start wearing such expensive, low-cut gowns? Thunderation, she was sending him to Bedlam!

With a decided turn, he snapped the door closed. He saw her jump and almost smiled. "Gregory?" he inquired harshly.

Two green eyes peeped through thick lashes as she turned her head to look at him. "Did you say something, my lord?"

He marched farther into the room, deliberately placing the desk between them. Jupiter and Zeus, he wanted to wring her neck. "I came to warn you about Lord Kingsdale."

"Who?" she said innocently.

A muscle twitched in his jaw. "I am speaking of Kingsdale, Miss Garland. The man who just left here."

She made a full turn to stare at him. "Oh, Gregory?"

He slapped his hand to the desk. "You should stay away from the man."

"Why?"

Heaven help him! *Why?* Did the chit want him to spell it out for her? "Because."

"I see. Well, I appreciate the information, my lord, but I believe I can make my own choices, thank you."

Without another word, she returned to her reading material, dismissing him as if he were some lowly servant.

Shocked at her indifference, Clayton mentally counted to

ten as she turned the pages of her book. Pacing around the desk, he struck a hand against the mantel and stood a few feet away from her. He stared at the auburn curls framing her face, remembering the time he had caught her sleeping in the duke's library. She had been enchanting . . .

"Miss Garland."

She said nothing and turned another page.

His gaze shifted to the graceful turn of her ankle where her gown had pulled up a few inches. Devil take it, he wanted to take her in his arms and—and what?

He started pacing again, staring at the back of her head. She was the most obstinate woman he had ever encountered.

He stopped and spun on his heel. "He is a rake!"

Surprised at the outburst, Miss Garland shot out of her chair and turned to glare at him. Her small hand fisted at her side. "He wants to marry me!"

"Well, he cannot marry you!"

"Oh? I fail to see why you have any say in the matter!"

"I have a say because your chaperone put you in my care!"

"I don't need a chaperone," she snapped back, her face coloring.

His lips spread into a devilish grin, and he felt a certain calmness begin to overtake him. When the lady was angry, she seemed to lose all control. He should have noticed that little fact sooner. "In truth, I don't care what you want, Miss Garland," he said softly.

She brought a hand to the back of her head and rubbed it. There was a flicker of pain in her expression that reminded him all too well of yesterday's accident.

His calm demeanor instantly fled. "And why the devil are you not in your chambers? You should be resting."

She grabbed the back of the chair, her face turning redder, from embarrassment or anger he wasn't certain. "This is silly. You? My chaperone?"

"Nevertheless"—his voice was dangerously low—"you will do as I say."

Every muscle in her body seemed to turn to stone. "I won't. You have no say over me."

His hand sliced through the air as he strode closer. "Oh, yes,

I do! Kingsdale has done things I cannot even begin to explain. But I vow, if I see you alone with the man again—"

She poked her finger in the air and started walking toward him. "You'll what? Have tea with him and spill it all over your breeches? A fine laugh he will have then. Or will you tell him how you proposed to me in such a kind and decent way?"

In one swift move he grabbed hold of her wrist. She pulled away, backing up against the desk, where her hand accidentally knocked Grimstoke's writing box to the floor. Her gaze jerked to his. "Now, see what you made me do!"

He instantly released her as she bent down to pick up the box. A small container of wax fell beside it, along with Grimstoke's seal.

Ashamed at his childish actions, Clayton knelt and picked up an ivory letter opener that had fallen out of the box.

What the devil was wrong with him? She wasn't his sister, and yet the urge to protect this female had consumed him. Or was it something more because he wanted her for his bride? The idea of a marriage of convenience began to vex him.

He shook his head and accidentally brushed her shoulder. Her hair shimmered like a sparkling stream running over red stone. She smelled of sweet vanilla. Her skin was smooth and white—

Hell's bells! The sudden realization that love could be part of his problem sobered him instantly.

"Let me help you," he said, more harshly than he intended.

She cast him a look of disdain, then dropped her gaze. "I don't need any help from you."

He tipped her chin, noting the tears glistening in her eyes, wondering if a kiss would shed his tumultuous feelings. "Forgive me. That was not gentlemanly."

She sniffed and settled the box back onto the desk.

He wiped a tear from her cheek. "The last time I did this . . . I kissed you."

Her expression was thunderous. "The last time—"

He wrapped an arm around her waist and pulled her against him, pressing his lips to hers. She was soft and pliable in his arms, an innocent flower crushed beneath his grip. To his surprise she returned his kiss.

"Bree!"

The kiss ended abruptly as they both stared at the intruder.

"Violet! I, uh, didn't see you," Miss Garland replied shakily.

Her friend giggled. "Evidently not. I came to see how you were doing with the books."

Clayton watched in amusement as both ladies turned pink with embarrassment. He bid the ladies a good day, but as he retreated from the room, the taste of Miss Garland still lingered on his lips. Was he mad? He wanted the lady as a bride, but he certainly didn't need to form any deep emotional attachment to her, like love. Love would thoroughly destroy his plans.

"I've searched the area around the desk and everywhere in between," Briana confided to Agatha later that evening. "I don't know where else to look."

Briana held tight to her godmother's hand as the woman lay in bed. Agatha looked pale and worn, much older than her years.

"Wish I could help," the lady murmured. "So tired . . . wasn't given any more orders . . . could be nothing . . . nothing at all." Her tired eyes regarded Briana in a new light. "New gown? Mustn't wear that . . . too much attention . . . won't fade at all . . . "

Briana rested a cool hand against her godmother's forehead. At least the woman noticed the gown was not Briana's usual attire. Agatha's senses were still acute. "You'll be better soon. Don't hate me, dearest, but I must tell you that your drinks have been laced with laudanum."

Agatha's lids opened wider, though Briana could tell she was fighting sleep. "Thought it was my head wound," she mumbled.

"Now, now," Briana said in a defensive tone as the lady tried to sit up. "We did it for your own good. You mustn't try to stand. That ankle of yours is still quite swollen."

Briana knew that if they hadn't laced Agatha's drinks with laudanum, she would have tried to get out of bed and would have further injured her ankle. Still, Briana wondered if the laudanum should never have been given. She frowned. She knew as much about head wounds as she did about cooking a pig. To-morrow she would have the laudanum stopped.

She gently stroked her godmother's brow as the lady's lids drooped. "And you mustn't worry about our mission. I will keep looking. If there is something in the library, I will find it. Perhaps one of the guests—"

Agatha's hand reached for hers. "No . . ." She was struggling to stay awake. "Must . . . tell . . . his lordship . . ."

Briana smiled and nodded, trying to comfort the lady. She could easily believe her godmother had put Lord Clayton in charge of her. "Yes, yes, we can talk later."

With a sigh, the lady drifted off to sleep before she could say another word. Briana didn't like the ashen color of Agatha's skin or the circles beneath her eyes. But it was the frightened look in her godmother's gaze that truly bothered her.

Briana departed from the room, leaving the maid to return to Agatha's side. There was no doubt in Briana's mind that Agatha had planned to keep her from the hunt. The lady would have devised some way to keep her busy while she herself did the real snooping. But now everything had changed. And it was not the first time Briana wondered if the carriage accident could have been planned.

Suddenly the sweet scent of bayberry drifted toward her, reminding her of summers at Elbourne Hall and Clayton.

"How is she?"

Briana glanced up to see him waiting in the hall. Something flickered in the back of his eyes. Worry? Or was he still angry over her stupid remark this afternoon? Or was it that kiss? Why had he done it? But the real question was why had she not stopped him? She should have. Whitehall's assignment was much more important than her ambivalent feelings toward some handsome gentleman who could charm her with nothing but a look.

"She's a bit drowsy, but I think she's on the mend."

His violet eyes softened. "She's tough. But I was afraid without that blasted parasol by her side, she might wither away."

Briana's lips quivered as she struggled to look at him. They had said nothing about the kiss earlier. Yet there was an awk-

wardness between them now, more so than when he had proposed marriage.

"What is it?" he asked.

She shook her head. He seemed to truly care for Agatha, and
that touched her deeply. "Nothing. I'm just worried about her."

"I'll make certain she has the best of care."

"Well," she said, trying to end the conversation, "perhaps I
will see you tonight."

"You should rest." His eyes darkened and slid over her in a
critical manner, as if she looked like some ragged doll left in
the gutter. The air about them sizzled.

She was furious at the way he could play her emotions. Why
was he doing this to her? "Perhaps you should see to your
bride. Word has it that you are searching for one."

His lips curled into a charming smile. "Jealous?"

He infuriated her. "Why would I be jealous?"

He took one step forward, she took one step back. He chuckled, causing the skin to crinkle about his beautiful eyes.

"Not so sure of yourself?" he asked, capturing her gaze.

She stiffened. "You think this a game? Well, it isn't. That—
that kiss this afternoon meant nothing. I have better things to do
than humor you, my lord. Go find a wife who will live in the
country and bow to your commands, for it surely won't be me."
Lifting her chin a bit higher, she turned and started for the
stairs.

"Best strike her off your list, cuz. Don't think she takes
kindly to your wooing efforts."

Clayton swung around to look toward the end of the hall,
where Sir Gerald was lounging against the wall, his face half
hidden behind a pair of potted palms.

"Oh," his cousin said, stepping out of his hiding place,
"don't you know? I requested a chamber close to yours."

"No," Clayton said coolly, "I didn't know."

"Must say, was terribly convenient having my bedchamber
beside these palms." His cousin tilted his head toward the
stairs. "By Jove, have to give her credit, though. Somehow the
chit found out about your plan and threw it back in your face."

He flicked a piece of lint off the sleeve of his jacket. "She
the first female to tell you no?" He looked up, his eyes gleam-

ing with pleasure. "The thing of it is, cuz, it gives me devilish satisfaction to think so."

"You were always a sneak, Gerald," Clayton said in a clipped voice. "But on my honor, I vow you will not have the castle."

"On your honor?" Gerald's gaze traveled over Clayton from his well-polished boots to his neat-fitting riding jacket. "I say, this is indeed a surprise. Honor for a man who would wed for the sake of money?" The man adjusted his neckcloth. "Don't flatter yourself. It's not honor, it's plain greed. I have no doubt about that."

He laughed, pulling out his watch. "Heard you have been paying mind to Miss Cherrie Black. Word has it she will arrive today. Her mama is determined to marry her off, cold or not. Perhaps I shall make it known that you want to wed her for the sake of that dingy old castle. What say you to that, old boy?"

Gerald narrowed his eyes on his breeches, brushing a hand across them. "Come to think of it, you might have another *no* from a woman. Won't that be a record? Perhaps we should take bets at White's. Upon my word, cuz, I may take it up to inform everyone here about your little bride hunt."

Clayton treated the man to one of his most condescending glares. "Even if the story comes out, I won't have far to look for a ready female. In fact, I have ones on my list who would marry me tomorrow. But you know my character so well, don't you? I do so like to look over my prospects before I make a choice."

His cousin scowled. "Depend upon it, cuz. I'm going to make it deuced hard for you to marry anyone."

Clayton wished to throw the man out the window. Instead he hit him where it hurt. "Do as you like, but . . ."

Gerald lifted a proud brow. "But what?"

"Pray, do not wear the maroon-colored waistcoat. Makes you look like a puffed-up bird who ate too many prunes."

Two spots of crimson dotted Gerald's cheeks as he snapped a hand to his perfectly fitted waistcoat. "Well, I never."

Clayton started down the stairs, laughing. "Oh, you can depend upon it, *cuz*. I never would either."

Chapter Fifteen

"*I* think Lord Clayton is in love with you," Violet said, twirling a finger about her curls as she sat on Briana's bed. "And I daresay all the gentlemen will adore that beautiful gown you are wearing, especially what's in it."

Inwardly Briana frowned. She was seated at the writing desk, finishing a letter to her mother. Darn Emily and her plans. The silver green gown she wore was the highest-cut dress she could find for this evening, but it set off her features perfectly, making it impossible for her to become invisible.

Briana had found a note from Emily tucked inside her fan. Her friend wished Briana a successful house party and hoped she wasn't angry for Emily's intervening in such a delicate matter. The dear lady had no idea she had wreaked havoc on Briana's cover.

Although Briana was flattered by Violet's comments, she knew that in a few minutes the soirée would begin downstairs and she would probably run into Lord Clayton. She didn't want to think about him or the way he made her feel. She had to set her sights on her mission, not on some spoiled lord who didn't care for rejection. But hiding from anybody in this gown, or any of the gowns in her wardrobe, was nearly impossible.

Folding her letter, Briana looked across the room. She was becoming increasingly uneasy about using her relationship with Violet to further the mission. If her friend were to gain any inkling of what Briana was doing, she would be hurt beyond repair.

"Lord Clayton is concerned about himself, like many of the

lords I know." But as she said the words, she knew it wasn't totally true. He had cared for Agatha. He loved Gabrielle. He had invaded her heart, whether she wanted it or not.

"He didn't seem as if he was concerned about himself in the library." Violet squinted. "Is he a hateful rogue, then?"

Briana sealed the letter, her mouth quivering with mirth. "No."

Violet giggled and jumped off the bed. "I knew it. He is divine." She clapped her hands against her cheeks. "Oh, if Papa had caught you today, you would be married in no time."

Briana was certainly glad it had been Violet and not Lord Grimstoke who had walked in on her. She had heard the stories. Her host could be persistent when he wanted to be.

"I am not marrying him."

"Then what were you doing kissing him in the library?"

"He caught me in a weak moment. In fact, the man took me off guard when I accidentally knocked your father's writing box onto the floor."

Violet gasped. "Is it broken?"

"No, I put it back on the desk. There might be a scratch or two, though. I really didn't mean to damage it. Is it an heirloom of sorts?"

"Father received it two years ago from his aunt who traveled all over the world. He says it's made of Brazilian rosewood. It was her last gift to him before she died."

"Oh, Violet, I feel dreadful."

"We won't tell him what happened. I do it all the time."

Briana's stomach turned at the thought of Lord Grimstoke knowing she was hovering about his desk. Being in his library was one thing; handling his personal effects was quite another. "But what if he sees the scratch?"

Violet's brows knitted into a frown. "I can tell him I was looking for those secret drawers he told me about and I dropped it by accident."

Briana tried to keep her voice calm. "Secret drawers?"

"Yes. When one opens the box, there is a writing surface and another drawer for pens and whatnot. But below that are two secret drawers."

"Have you seen them?"

Violet shook her head. "I read my aunt's letter and Papa said something about them in passing. But I have tried everything to disengage whatever springs my aunt mentioned. One never knows what you could find in a secret drawer."

Briana put a hand to her pearl necklace at her throat and peered into the looking glass. "Yes, one never knows."

"Do you know, my lord, I adore Northern England. My mother's family is from there."

Clayton gazed down at Miss Cherrie Black as they paired up for the country dance. "I take it you have been speaking to my cousin, Sir Gerald?"

She gave him a sly glance and sniffed. Her nose was still pink from her cold. "I am not without a heart, my lord. But I would prefer a marriage of convenience, too, if you must know the truth. I was rather relieved when your cousin told me about your quest for a fitting bride. Love is such nonsense, you know. My parents go their separate ways and are quite content in their relationship."

Clayton knew her parents. Though a gentleman of High Society, Sir John Black was a red-nosed drunk who made visits to the opera quite frequently, and not for the singing entertainment. His wife was a flighty female who gossiped about everyone in the *ton*.

Clayton wondered about the lady in his arms. Though her parents were not perfect, they were from a decent family line and the lady seemed well adjusted. But now he wondered. Her thoughts on marriage were beginning to trouble him.

He might want a marriage of convenience, but her point that love was nonsense was just not true. It might not be for him, but his siblings had marriages based on love, and they were doing quite fine indeed.

"I knew the moment Sir Gerald spoke to me that he has other plans than to see you married," she said boldly. "Does he?"

Clayton's lips thinned as he parted from the lady, then returned to her side. Was this the kind of marriage he actually wanted? A marriage without love, without respect? And who was to say his wife wouldn't turn to another man? The thought of Miss Garland and Kingsdale made him grit his teeth.

"You are quite perceptive, Miss Black. My cousin will inherit the castle if I do not marry by the allotted time."

"And you need a wife before then," Miss Black said, smiling.

"You would not mind?"

Was that greed he saw in her eyes? Miss Garland's sparkling green gaze filled his thoughts, and he frowned at the difference between the two women.

"Is this a proposal, my lord?"

"No, but as long as we are being frank with each other, it seems the next logical question."

"I would not at all mind being a convenient bride. As I said before, my parents have a similar arrangement. Mama visits her friend in the country and Papa his friends in Town."

Clayton's brows arched as they parted again. She had just confirmed his very thoughts. "Your mother has *friends*?" he asked when they reunited. "Or should I say *friend*?"

The lady blushed as the music ended. "My lord, you know what I mean."

Clayton bowed and handed her to her next partner. "Indeed, I do, Miss Black. Indeed, I do."

Hoping Lord Kingsdale had forgotten her stupid remark earlier this afternoon, Briana shifted her gaze from the dance floor to the dandy making his way to her side.

Violet made the introductions. Ah, Sir Gerald. So this was Lord Clayton's cousin. They certainly didn't look alike.

The slightly built man standing before her was clothed so neatly, so exactly, she wondered how long it took him to dress. His stiff collar points seemed to be touching his ears. Some would call him handsome, but to Briana he had an annoying habit of flicking imaginary pieces of lint off his clothes when he thought no one was watching.

"I heard you had quite a journey to Grimstoke Hall," Sir Gerald said, taking Violet's seat as she walked onto the dance floor with another gentleman.

Briana regarded the man with a thoughtful stare. Anyone here could be involved in the plot against the Regent, even this gentleman sitting beside her. For all she knew, he could have planned their accident. "Yes, it was quite a turn of events."

"Terrible. Terrible. You were quite fortunate Lord Clayton

came along when he did." He picked a speck of fuzz off the chair. "Quite fortunate indeed."

Briana turned her eyes upon the dancers. Clayton was coupled with a pretty blonde who seemed rather attached to him. Her heart constricted. It was Miss Cherrie Black. A marriage of convenience was exactly what the woman was looking for.

"Heard you had a slight injury to the head, Miss Garland."

"Nothing significant."

"And did I hear Grimstoke's daughter correctly? You are not dancing?"

"No, I am not, sir."

He sat meticulously straight in his chair, careful not to wrinkle his jacket. "I see. And Miss Appleby's injuries?"

Briana clasped her fan tightly in her hand. She needed an excuse to venture to the library to take a look at that writing box one more time. And she didn't like this man asking questions. He was bold, obnoxious, and beginning to vex her.

"My godmother is mending slowly."

He leaned toward her, his breath smelling of mints and brandy. "How very dreadful for you. May I take this moment to express my deepest sympathies. If you need anything at all, please do not hesitate to ask. I happened to acquire the chamber a few doors down from yours."

Briana snapped her fan shut and glared at him. "Sir!"

He shrugged. "Upon my word, you have no reason to act the prude with me, my girl."

"And what do you mean by that?" she hissed through her teeth.

"You gave your kisses freely to Lord Clayton—why not me?"

The hungry gleam in his eye only enraged her more. "I think you should leave."

He bent over to rub a scuff off his shiny black shoes. "I heard you speaking to him in the hall, Miss Garland. Passing up marriage to a Clearbrook is not at all the thing, you know. A son of a duke. My word. What were you thinking?"

He shook his head regretfully. "Perhaps you find marriage offensive. Can't say I blame you. That family is a bit stuffy. I came to Elbourne Hall once and was never invited back. That's how it is with *those* people."

He flicked a piece of hair off his knee and rubbed his nose. "Of course, Lord Clayton's immediate situation may appall you. I, on the other hand, have no pressure to marry. Ever."

Briana gritted her teeth, her patience with this man quickly thinning.

Finally he rose, took her hand and bowed over it. "Think about that, my dear girl." His eyes devoured her. "Perhaps we could get along nicely."

Briana yanked her hand from his. She had never been so insulted in her life. Perhaps having Agatha by her side had added a little to her reputation after all.

"Miss Garland, I believe you promised me a dance."

Briana looked up and decided Lord Kingsdale was the lesser of the two evils. She had stupidly agreed to a dance with the man, had she not? Besides, he could do nothing to her on the dance floor. He wasn't a fool.

"She ain't dancing, Kingsdale," Sir Gerald said in a pompous tone. "Had a head injury the other day, don't you know."

Briana rose swiftly, managing a brittle smile. "My lord," she said, putting out a stiff hand toward Kingsdale, "you're late."

Kingsdale took her hand. "Detained by business, my dear. Forgive me."

"But you said you did not dance, Miss Garland," Sir Gerald sputtered. "Y-your injury."

Briana gazed at him with a look of reproach. "I never said such a thing, my lord. You only assumed it to be so."

Sir Gerald rambled on about injuries and fatalities as Kingsdale swept Briana into his arms for a waltz. Her head still ached, but she was not about to sit out the evening with nincompoops like Sir Gerald hounding her. And what did he mean by fatalities?

"He's an idiot," Kingsdale said with a scowl.

"Indeed, but I don't think he knows it." Briana didn't like being in Kingsdale's arms, and she immediately wondered if she would have been safer with Sir Gerald. That knock to her head must have scrambled her brain. Nevertheless, she had to temper her anger or she would never rid herself of this man.

"What made you change your mind about dancing with me? Was it Lord Clayton? Or that peabrain we left behind?"

"I said I would dance with you and I am doing so."

"You were never a good liar, my dear. In fact, that is one thing I liked about you."

His eyes darkened as he tightened his hold on her. "Afraid?"

"This is just a dance between two people, my lord, nothing more."

Irritated, Briana avoided his gaze by looking over his shoulder, only to catch sight of Clayton staring directly at her. She faltered a step.

"Tired?" Kingsdale said, still holding on to her elbow when the music ended.

"Yes. Perhaps I should call it a night."

Kingsdale smiled as he escorted her off the dance floor. "So you are not afraid of me, then? I thought perhaps you wanted to rid yourself of my presence as soon as possible."

"No, but you must understand there is nothing between us, now or in the future."

He was directing her toward the terrace, and she went with him, knowing in the back of her mind that it was a bit reckless, but she really didn't have time to dawdle. She had a mission to accomplish. She had to set this man straight before things got out of hand. They would not go far. The terrace was within sight of the ballroom, after all.

"I think you are wrong, Miss Garland. We have always had a connection of some kind. You cannot deny it."

His arrogance was unbelievable. A warm breeze caressed her cheeks as she stepped outside. She stopped a little ways from the terrace and turned to him, her chin set.

"A connection for you is a stepping-stone to marriage, my lord. I don't love you and I never will."

"You did once." His tone had become chilly.

The man was living in another world. "No, you only thought I did. We had some things in common, but nothing significant."

"I disagree. You know more about Egypt than most lecturers on the subject. You have a great understanding, Miss Garland. We could do well together."

Briana realized they were close enough for other people to hear their conversation. She moved down the steps, beneath the trees but still in sight of the ballroom. "I have to make this perfectly clear, my lord," she whispered. "I don't want to marry you or anyone, ever."

His entire body seemed to change. "Why, because of your sister?"

His words stunned her. "How—how dare you speak of my sister. You know nothing about her."

"I know she was with child when she died."

Briana felt the color leave her face. "Do you know the man?"

"Perhaps I do."

He took hold of her arm and escorted her beyond the sight of the dancers. She let him because she wanted to know the truth. He would not dare lay a finger on her at Grimstoke's party.

"Would you marry me if I told you?" He stopped and glanced down at her, his lips twisting into a cynical smile.

She shook her head, realizing she had been a fool to let him draw her away from the party. "I want to return."

He grabbed her hand. "Think about it, my dear. I could take you to Egypt. We could travel to all those places you've seen in your books. I know people who enjoy what you can only dream of doing. We could explore pyramids and tombs. Delve into life and death. This English Society is such a bore. We could live like the pharaohs. I will have money soon. More money than you could ever imagine."

Briana slipped easily from his grip, glancing over her shoulder. She had to return to the ballroom. He was so engrossed in ancient Egyptian lore, he didn't know reality anymore. "I wanted to know about my sister. But it seems you lured me here without intending to tell me anything, because you don't know any facts at all. And to set matters straight, I don't want your money."

"But I want you." The pain that flickered in his eyes touched her. "My baby brother was killed in that hateful war. The Regent should have stopped Boney long ago. I don't have anyone anymore. Don't you see? You could make my life complete."

His eyes pleaded with her, and for a moment she almost reached out to him. "You would make me whole again, my dear. I have a few things in England I have to consider, but after that I will be free to travel."

The man was playing with her emotions as if they were toys

to be discarded at a moment's notice. "I appreciate your offer, my lord, but I cannot accept."

His jaw hardened and he jerked her toward him, grabbing her pearls in his fist. "Cannot or will not?"

She gasped, aware of the dangerous glint in his eye. She tore herself away, slightly ripping the delicate outer bodice of her gown.

"Is it someone else, Miss Garland? Or have I not been forgiven for leaving you those years ago?"

Gulping, she grasped the small tear in her gown. He was in his own demented world. Him leave her? She was the one who had rejected his offer. "I have no need to marry, my lord," she said as calmly as she could. "No need at all."

He took hold of her chin, tilting her face toward his. "You will. I hear our host is quite the champion of innocent maidens. If he finds us alone and you with that small tear in your gown, for which, my dear, I am heartily sorry, he may demand a wedding. The archbishop visits the neighboring village this time of year."

The blood drained from her face. Violet had said as much.

He laughed then, patted her cheek and dropped his hand. "Never fear, I won't force you. What are a few more weeks to change your mind?"

She glared at him, refusing to cower.

"Ah, still the prim and proper miss? But I like that. Indeed, I do. You have the royal blood of the pharaohs, my dear. I can see it in your eyes, green as the calmest sea yet glinting with a cool radiance that can bend a man to your will."

Realizing he was letting her go, she fled from his side, skirting the terrace and hurrying through another door into the hall. No excuse could ever cover the tear in her gown.

Fighting back the fear that Lord Kingsdale was following her, she rushed up the stairs. She heard a voice and hurried into the library, closing the door behind her. The man was insane. If he hadn't mentioned Clarice, she would never have fallen into his trap.

She gazed about the room, her hands shaking. Fingers of moonlight fanned through the slight opening in the curtains, while a tiny glow of dying embers illuminated the hearth.

Taking a deep breath, she tried to calm herself.

If he were following her, she would stay here until she felt safe. Her bedchambers were another flight up. She swallowed tightly. Perhaps she could continue her search for the missive.

She crossed the room and picked up a candlestick, lighting it from the smoldering remains of the fire. She noticed the writing box had been moved since her encounter with Lord Clayton. Could that be a sign?

Hope spiraled within her. Could this hold what she was looking for? Heart hammering wildly, she sank into the chair and dragged the writing box toward her. She frantically searched about for the release mechanism Violet had mentioned. The lonely flame beside her wasn't enough. She couldn't see the details—

"Writing secret letters, Miss Garland?"

Briana inhaled sharply, letting the writing box fall to her lap. She slowly turned toward the tall shadow looming near the curtains. In the dim candlelight she had missed him, but she couldn't mistake the deep voice that she had known since childhood. "You should have made yourself known, my lord."

Lord Clayton moved swiftly toward her, his eyes gleaming like sapphires in the glow of the candle. "Did your rendezvous with Kingsdale end early?"

She froze, her senses going numb.

He took another step and stopped, clasping his hands behind his back. "Come now, Miss Garland, we both know the man is more than fond of you. Why have you run from him? I saw you on the terrace and then the two of you disappeared."

A deep silence blanketed the room, increasing the tension between them. She couldn't think of a response. Her tongue felt like the down of her pillow. Could he be part of the assassination plot? No, it was impossible.

She nervously fingered the writing box while swinging her gaze toward the door. The walls of the library seemed to be closing in on her. What could she do? What should she do?

"Why are you here, I ask myself," he said, breaking into her reverie. "I wonder, could it be the same reason as I?"

Merciful heavens! Could Clayton be part of the conspiracy? Or was he taking Agatha's chaperone suggestion to heart?

She peered up at him, noting the light shadows dancing

along his jaw. The lines around his mouth were harsh and un-forgiving.

He had taken her completely by surprise more than once, but this was the outside of enough. Why was he here? What was going through his head? "I had a headache, my lord, and needed some time alone. So, if you don't mind leaving—"

He let out a sardonic laugh that prickled her skin. "I needed some time alone, too, you see. I have been in this room only a few minutes. I left the soirée as soon as I saw you with Kingsdale." His voice seemed strained, but there was a hint of his usual arrogance in it that irked her.

The embers from the fireplace glowed eerily throughout the room. She stood, setting the box in front of her. He was watching her intently. He moved to sit on the corner of the desk.

Her throat tightened, and she felt a blush work its way up her neck.

"I like books just as much as you do, Miss Garland. In fact, the Elbourne library became my second home. I remember when you were staying there one summer and you confiscated all my books on planetary movement. I was livid to discover they were gone."

She remembered that, too. A small smile lifted the corner of her mouth. "If I recall correctly, I was studying Galileo's theory of gravity."

"You always had a fertile mind. I think that's what I liked most about you"—he paused and leaned toward her—"among other things."

Among other things. The aroma of bayberry broke her defenses and her heart leapt to her throat. He was too close. She moved away and accidentally bumped the candle, killing the flame and sending the wax spilling onto the floor.

The silence of the room engulfed them as their outlines danced against the tiny glow of the fireplace. He seemed to be waiting for her to speak.

"I was going to write a letter," she blurted, colliding with the chair. *What a pitiful excuse!*

"Really?" he said, rising, coming around the desk, blocking the fireplace. "How very unusual. In the middle of the night? While there is dancing going on downstairs?"

His voice lacked the usual charm, and again she wondered why he was walking the library at such a strange hour. What did he want from her?

"I said I had a headache, my lord." She tried to move, but the chair blocked her way. She needed to get away from him.

"I don't believe you. Tell me the truth. Was Kingsdale the reason you fled?"

She leaned into the chair. "I should be leaving. If you want to stand here all night—"

Before she knew it, he had wrapped a strong arm around her waist, pushing the chair away and pulling her toward him.

The red embers abruptly illuminated his face. His expression was hard, his eyes fixed. "Were you going to meet Kingsdale here?"

She shoved at him, hurt by his accusation. "I don't know what you're talking about. And I don't know why you are interested in my affairs at all, unless you are jealous."

"Jealous? Of Kingsdale? The man is not the marrying type, no matter what he says." He glared at her and fingered the rip in her gown. His jaw stiffened.

"Did he hurt you?" His hold on her slackened, and he seemed genuinely concerned.

Puzzled by his change in mood, she lowered her gaze. There was so much about this man that was kind and decent, she was afraid she might fall in love with him and be unhappy the rest of her life. But he wanted a convenient bride, someone who would look the other way, and Briana could never do that.

She looked up. "Lord Kingsdale wants to marry me."

His hand slipped down her wrist while eerie shadows played across his sharp features. He seemed to be smiling. "But you won't marry the man because you love me."

She blinked, thinking she had heard incorrectly. "I what?"

"You love me." He said the words with such utter conviction, she wanted to box his ears.

"I certainly do not." Or at least she wasn't about to tell him she did.

"You do. You don't want to admit it because I hurt you."

She spun away, giving him her back. "You want a wife to satisfy your family. I won't be a party to that kind of marriage."

"You're wrong." She could almost feel the tenderness of his consuming gaze. "I want you."

He came from behind her, circling her waist with his strong hands. His palm spread across her stomach and his breath was a warm puff against her neck. "I want you."

The words twisted her heart. "No," she said softly.

When he said nothing, she turned in his arms. A knot rose in her throat as she faced him. "I made a vow. I won't marry, my lord."

His hands moved to hers, holding them. The gentle strength of his touch stirred her. She wanted to fall into his arms, tell him her worries, trust him. But it wouldn't work. Her past had taught her not to put her life in any man's hands, mentally or physically.

"Emily told me about your house for women. I can help."

She stiffened. He would ruin everything. "She should never have told you. I don't want any help."

"I want to help."

She was imprisoned between him and the desk. "I don't need your help. I don't need anyone's help."

"I won't hurt you. I'm not like Kingsdale—or your father."

What did he know about her father? Yet his voice was soothing, breaking down the barriers around her heart.

"You must know I adore freckles." His finger trailed along her nose. "Especially Fairy Lady *feckles*."

There was a hint of humor in his voice that made her giggle. "You are very wicked, my lord."

"I know," he whispered. In one swift move, his hand pressed gently on her neck and he kissed her.

Without warning, the pearls—accidentally loosened from Lord Kingsdale's grip during their earlier encounter—fell off the string and clattered to the desk. At that exact moment the door swung open, letting the light from the hall sconces shine into the room. To her horror, Lord Grimstoke stood on the threshold, his expression cold and quite determined.

"What the devil is going on in here?"

Briana drew in a sharp breath, and Lord Clayton pushed her behind him. "Nothing," Lord Clayton replied coolly.

"I am not addlebrained," Grimstoke replied, stalking into the room and lighting a small lantern he pulled from the shelf.

Briana hadn't moved, but from this angle Grimstoke's dark eyes traveled over the small tear in her gown and the scattered pearls. He shot a disgusted glance toward Lord Clayton. "I will not be subject to any of that in my home!"

Lord Clayton stiffened beside her. A burning embarrassment swept through Briana as she stepped forward. Clayton caught her elbow. "Don't say a thing," he commanded in a low tone.

"You have compromised a lady, my lord," Grimstoke declared.

"But, Papa—"

Briana's gaze shifted to the door, where Violet stood, wringing her hands nervously.

"You should not have had to see this, Violet. But now that you have, I will demand satisfaction." Grimstoke placed the lantern on the desk, scattering the pearls even more. "And since Miss Appleby is ill and this is my home, I take full responsibility for Miss Garland."

Briana shrugged out of Clayton's grip. "But my lord—"

Grimstoke cut her off. "I thought better of you, child. You will marry this man before you leave here. Do you understand?"

Briana opened and closed her mouth as she stared at Violet's white face. It was a compromising situation, but marriage?

"I'll see to the matters," Clayton replied stiffly. "The archbishop is staying in the nearby village. I can obtain the special license tomorrow."

"Then you will marry tomorrow," Grimstoke replied hotly. "There are some who were already mentioning your disappearance at the dance, my girl."

Briana's throat started to close. If only she had not worn this gown, she could have easily blended into the crowd. If only Emily had not interfered with her wardrobe. Oh, this was such a mess. "I can explain—"

"It matters not, Miss Garland. Some of my guests have noted Lord Clayton's departure as well. Explanations will do nothing."

He gave her a critical look. "Especially after this! It would do well for you to stay in your chambers until this situation is taken care of. I will act as your father on this. In fact, depend upon it, I am determined to keep this secret until you are wed."

A vile heat shot through Briana as she tried to explain. "But this is all a silly misunderstanding."

Clayton snatched her wrist. "It must be done," he hissed, turning his back to Grimstoke, "or your reputation will be ruined."

Briana stood in stunned silence. The reality of what was happening finally dawned on her. "You planned this."

Clayton's face hardened.

Briana flushed. "Of course," she whispered. "Silence is always the best defense, is it not, my lord?"

"Violet, fetch a shawl for Miss Garland," Grimstoke interrupted. "Can't have the lady walking the halls with a torn gown. Looks like a ladybird from Vauxhall Gardens."

Clayton spun around. "You are speaking to my future wife. I will not fail to set you straight if you utter one more word in that direction, Grimstoke, your home or not."

Grimstoke's lips tightened. "I have plans for Violet. Guilt by association, don't you know?"

Briana thought her host absurd. This entire situation was absurd! "Violet wasn't compromised in the least, my lord—"

Lord Clayton grabbed her arm, stopping her. "You may explain to your guests that we had this planned from the very start," he commanded Grimstoke. "Do we have an understanding?"

Grimstoke looked appeased. "Indeed. Now it would be best if you took your leave, my lord. I will wait for Violet to bring the shawl and then Miss Garland may return to her bedchambers."

Clayton gave Briana a curt bow. "Until tomorrow, Miss Garland."

With a throbbing pain in her breast, Briana watched in shock as her intended left her alone with their angry host, alone with her tumultuous feelings, alone with her broken heart.

Chapter Sixteen

*B*riana wanted to tell Agatha everything that had transpired with Lord Kingsdale and Lord Clayton, but when she sat by her godmother's side early the following morning, she saw how weary the lady looked and thought better of it.

"You should never have given me laudanum," Agatha said groggily.

Briana brushed a gray lock from the elderly lady's forehead.

Agatha's lips pinched into a scowl. "You knew they were doing this to me, child. How could you?"

Briana lifted a brow. "I wanted you to heal. I know that you would have tried to move around the first day we came here. As long as your head injury was not grave, laudanum was the only solution. I did tell you about it yesterday, but I don't think you remembered."

"This is a dangerous mission, Briana. You cannot follow leads by yourself. If I had my way—"

Briana gave her a wry smile. "I know. I know. You would have me home with Mama. But I did discover that Lord Grimstoke has a favorite writing box he keeps in the library. Violet told me it has some kind of secret drawers. I believe this may be the lead we have been looking for."

Agatha shook her head. "I have a writing box back at Hemmingly. Was given to me by my father. Has a secret compartment as well. It's unlikely something is hidden there. Too easy by far. And there is something else."

Briana waited. "What?"

"That gown, child. It looks like one of Emily's."

Briana frowned. She was wearing a gown of pale blue silk, with white ribbon along the edges. It was the plainest of what was left in her wardrobe and still it was lovely. "I think it is Emily's. Or at least it's from the same dressmaker. Emily didn't like my drab colors, so she switched my clothing before we left, hoping I could attract some interesting gentlemen."

Gray eyes twinkled. "Couldn't very well tell her why you wanted to blend in, now, could we?"

Briana smiled. "No, I guess not. She meant well."

Agatha yawned, and Briana knew the lady was desperately trying to focus her thoughts. "You know, dear, the more I think about it, the more I believe the source is someone in Grimstoke's family. Could very well be Violet. The specifics about this case are too exact."

"Violet? Why would she give her father away? I cannot imagine her doing that, and in such a secretive way. I admit the source is providing Whitehall with rather detailed information, but Violet? It just isn't something she would do."

"Well, child, I could say the same about you in this instance."

Briana sighed. Agatha was right. No one was exempt from doing something unusual or out of character. Anyone could be the enemy, even someone as innocent as Violet.

Heartsick about the previous evening, Briana realized now she had to disclose everything to Agatha. "I probably should have spoken to you first about the writing box. I tried to open the drawers, but . . ."

Agatha straightened. "Someone suspects you?"

Briana threw a frustrated hand over her eyes. "No, it's just . . . well, it was all so innocent, you see. It happened so fast . . . I mean, we were alone . . . and then he kissed me . . . and then Grimstoke demanded we marry."

"Grimstoke? The cad! The man's already married. Why, I'll have the scoundrel in chains by the time this is done!"

Briana lifted her head and gave the lady a hesitant smile. *Dear, sweet Agatha.* "Not Grimstoke. Lord Clayton."

Agatha eyes froze on her face. "What?"

Briana could feel her cheeks turning pink. "Lord Grimstoke found us together. While I was in the library examining the writing box, Lord Clayton happened to be lounging in the shadows. He was there before I entered. I didn't see him until it was too late."

"Too late for what?" Agatha snapped fiercely. "And what about that kiss you mentioned?"

Briana stared at the bedpost. "I . . . well, you see . . . after I danced with Lord Kingsdale—"

"What in the blue blazes does that man have to do with this?"

Briana's eyes shifted back to Agatha. She had never seen her godmother so agitated.

"He lured me into the gardens and we argued. I knew he was not right in the mind and I fled. My bodice was slightly ripped during our altercation and my pearls were loosened. The necklace gave way while I was in the library. So when our host saw Lord Clayton and me together, um, kissing, the man assumed the worst."

Agatha's eyebrow shot up. "Indeed."

"But marriage, Agatha! He demanded I marry Lord Clayton."

Agatha paused. "And so you must. Lord Clayton can ride out the storm, but you will be ruined. Grimstoke will not let this pass. He is an eccentric. One never knows which way he will turn, but once he announces his intent, he rarely backs down. I don't like saying it, but this can jeopardize everything you have worked for, even that women's shelter."

Tears filled Briana's eyes. "Oh, Agatha. What shall I do?"

"What? Does that scoundrel refuse to marry you?"

"No, and that is the problem. He has been looking for a convenient bride for some time, and he stupidly asked me to marry him when I attended the Elbourne ball."

Agatha pursed her lips but said nothing.

"I told him no, yet last night I believe he compromised me on purpose."

"Oh, child. Lord Clayton may be a bit of arrogant, but he is a gentleman. I would never believe him or any of his brothers of forcing a woman to marry him."

Briana shot out of her chair. "But I don't want to marry him! I don't want to marry anyone!"

"Where is he now?"

"I don't know. Maybe on his way to obtain a special license. Maybe he did it already. I just don't know."

"All the way to London?"

She shrugged. "All I know is that the archbishop is staying in the nearby village. If Clayton can't obtain the license there, I'm sure he would ride to London. Either way I'm sunk."

Feeling miserable, Briana paced about the room, too restless to sit. "Don't you see? It's all too easy. He is only following what duty dictates. He wants a convenient wife to place in the country while he gallivants about Town. I won't have it."

"Who said you had to listen to him, my dear? Why cater to a man's whims? If he has a fondness for you, the world is yours to command."

Briana stared at her godmother. Did Lord Clayton care for her a little? Could he love her just a bit? Or was her heart wishing for things that could never be? "You think he has a certain fondness for me?"

Agatha swept the covers aside and swung her legs over the side of the bed, swaying a bit. "Does a king have a crown?"

Briana hurried toward her. "Don't get up. I beg you."

Agatha scowled. "And when is this wedding to take place?"

"If Lord Clayton obtains the license, Grimstoke is determined we marry today."

Agatha opened her eyes wider. "To satisfy our host's sense of propriety and to stem the gossip, I suppose. Not that marrying by special license will do that, but I vow your fiancé will have something to say about that."

"He wants it known that we had planned our wedding a long time ago."

Agatha gave a nod of approval. "Good thinking. An affair of the heart. You were swept away with passion and wanted to get married without the fuss of all the parties and whatnot. Your families will be thrilled."

"My mother will be overjoyed. Except for our mourning period, she has pursued Lord Clayton ever since I can remember." Briana raised her fists to her cheeks. "It is all so humiliating. I cannot go through with it."

"Yes, you can. You love him, do you not?"

"I don't want to marry him."

"That doesn't answer my question, young lady."

Briana's fists fell to her sides. "Yes, yes, I love him! Is that what you want to hear? But what does that matter? He will let me down like all the other men in my life. Papa turned on Clarice and let her die. The man who got my sister with child let her die. Even Alistair was a disappointment. I have learned my lesson, Agatha. I cannot marry Clayton. I cannot."

"Because you are afraid," Agatha blurted out. "Do you want to end up like me, child? Do you want to be an old maid because you were afraid to love? Is that what you want?"

Hot tears flowed from Briana's eyes. "I didn't mean—"

Agatha waved her hand. "I made my mistakes years ago. I vowed never to love a man again, and you know I stayed true to my promise. But I never tried, Briana. I never gave myself another chance. It was a mistake I will not let you make. Besides, the lieutenant left you for war and duty; that is a different matter entirely.

"He may have promised you something, but that is only human to choose between two goods. You must trust again. You must. And if you won't look at this for yourself, look at it as serving your country."

"What do you mean?"

"If you marry Lord Clayton, all suspicion that you were in the library searching for clues will be lifted. You were meeting your fiancé in a clandestine place, planning your nuptials. If the enemy is about, all presumption you are involved with the mission, or me, will be behind you. You will be safe."

Briana sank onto the bed, knowing Agatha's words held some truth. "This is not something I wished for. If I have to marry him, I will, but not on his terms. I will not be kept in the country like some forgotten relative. I will stay in Town when I want and where I want."

Agatha hid her smile. "You might get away with that. But when you are married to the man, he will have a say in what you do with your future plans, especially with your women's shelter."

Frowning, Briana looked up, intending to speak, but Agatha raised her hands, stopping her. "I have seen him with Gabrielle.

He is not unreasonable. The man has a gentle side. If he did not, I would never allow this to go through."

A deep heaviness centered in Briana's chest. "I will have the stipulations of our marriage written up before we marry."

Agatha's brows lifted. "Usually a relative does that for you. Perhaps if I stepped in—"

"No, all I want is his promise in writing that I may do what I wish—or I will not wed him."

"But if he refuses, not only will the mission suffer but so will your reputation, child. Think of your mother."

Briana rose from her chair, frustration clawing at her brain. "Well, what can I do? He doesn't love me!"

Agatha closed her eyes. "You must make him love you, Briana. I know he has a fondness for you. It will take time, but I believe you two will get along quite nicely if you try."

Briana blinked back her tears. "A marriage of convenience based on fondness. What a horrid future."

Agatha gave her a pitying look. "There are many paths you can choose, child. There is the path of least resistance, where you allow your relationship to flounder until you cannot stand to look at each other anymore, or the path of action, where you make a decision to gain your husband's love and make a good life for yourself. Some women will never have a chance with a husband like Lord Clayton. The man has a heart. He just needs a little prodding from you to find it."

Briana pulled a pillow from the bed and pressed it against her chest. "You think so?"

"Am I ever wrong?"

Briana laughed, watching her godmother's eyes gleam with mischief. "I am not about to answer that."

"I hate to bring up our true reason for being here, my dear, but we must address the facts."

Briana sobered, her thoughts flying back to the Prince Regent. "I will marry today, if that is what I must do."

"I think it for the best. If only I had been with you—but that is neither here nor there. I am able to hobble around a little bit. So the next chance we have, you can return to the library with me. We will search for the missing piece of this puzzle together."

"No. If we have to make a quick escape, it will be too dangerous for you. I am thinking perhaps the carriage incident was not an accident after all."

The lady patted Briana's hand. "Perhaps. But I do not think anyone believes you are involved."

"You may still be in danger."

"Maybe, but it might be nothing at all. Only our imagination. I do not think anyone intended to kill me. If they did, I would be dead by now."

Goose bumps popped out on Briana's skin. "If anything should happen to you . . . "

"Fustian, child! I will beat the enemy senseless. That is, if I find another parasol worthy of my efforts."

Briana's laugh became a stream of steady tears. "Oh, Agatha," she said, giving the woman a heartfelt hug. "I do love you so."

Clayton found himself pacing the gardens behind the ancient gazebo, waiting for Briana to respond to his summons. He hated meeting in secret, as if they had done something wrong, but he wanted some privacy. Their crazed host had been hounding him like he was some unruly schoolboy about to bolt, and it took every ounce of willpower for Clayton not to hang the man by his toes on the nearest chandelier.

Confound Grimstoke! The man had visited Clayton in his chambers, making certain the special license had been obtained and that Clayton was going to fulfill his part of the bargain by marrying the lady in question.

In addition, the odious man had stopped Clayton in the hall only minutes ago, verifying the time everyone would be at the church. However, Clayton knew the man was only double-checking to make certain Clayton was still in the vicinity.

Clayton lifted his gaze to the blue of the afternoon sky and closed his eyes. Dear God, he would rather Miss Garland consent to marriage than force her into it. But their host had made it abundantly clear he would not back down. Lord Grimstoke would not tolerate a scandal under his roof.

Clayton stared at the back of the aged gazebo and grimaced. What a pompous ass. A few months ago he'd seen Grimstoke at a masquerade with a lady who was definitely not his wife. But that was the way of the *ton*—as long as one played along with Society's rules, it was all right.

Clayton seemed to recall that it was last year when Grimstoke had been so foxed he'd lost a grand sum of money to the Prince Regent. But the devil of it was, Society didn't look down upon that either. Men won and lost at gaming tables all the time.

Yet why was it that Society still made women suffer most in times of disgrace? Clayton's fingers curled into his palm. Dash it all, he was not about to let a woman suffer because of him.

From the look Miss Garland had given him yesterday, he wondered if he would have to drag her to her wedding. Nevertheless, he had obtained the special license, and in less than an hour he was to set out for the tiny church two miles away.

It didn't help matters that stories were already circulating about Miss Garland's disappearance last evening. She had stood out like a princess in her fashionable gowns of silk and lace.

Though she wasn't a conventional beauty, she was a pretty little thing. But to Clayton, it was more than what she wore that fascinated him. Perhaps it was the way her eyes laughed when she played with Gabrielle. Or maybe it was the way she carried herself when no one seemed to be looking. Or was it the way she cared for the people she loved, like that mother of hers? Or was it partly her desire to help those poor women in need?

He wasn't sure what it was, but she definitely had him hooked. And it didn't help his disposition any when she wore those striking gowns, drawing his attention and that of every other gentleman in the room like flies to porridge.

Could it be love? Yes, he thought wryly, it could be just that. He smiled. There was a chance this could work out better than he'd expected. Love wasn't so bad after all. He realized now that he had never truly loved Serena. With her, it had been a selfish kind of worship. But to love Miss Garland . . .

He almost laughed out loud. With her, it would never be a marriage of convenience, because there was nothing convenient about Briana Garland at all. He had given himself permission to love again, and by Jove, it was a wonderful feeling.

The rustle of fabric turned his head. A head of shimmering auburn curls came into view, and a grin pulled at the corners of his mouth. Miss Garland had changed from the blue silk he had caught a glimpse of this morning. She probably thought she was clothed more demurely, but the lady looked irresistible, dressed in a light green gown scooped at the neck, revealing her creamy white skin. And Gabrielle was right. The lady resembled a fairy with her luminous green eyes and freckled nose. She was adorable.

"Good afternoon, Briana."

She halted a few feet from him. Black circles surrounded her eyes, making him feel guilty as hell. "I have not given you leave to call me by my first name, my lord."

He suppressed a laugh. The woman had spirit.

"Are you laughing at me?" she snapped.

"We've known each other for years, not to mention you are my betrothed. That gives me some right to use your Christian name."

Her chin rose a notch. "If you think marrying me will give you all rights, you are sorely mistaken."

He frowned, wondering if she thought him as cruel as Kingsdale or even her father. "You think me a tyrant? Is that how you see me?"

"No," she said, dropping her head and kicking a pebble off the path. "But I don't like this. I don't like being forced."

"You think I like it?" he asked, remembering her words that she thought he had planned the entire scene. "Contrary to what you may believe, I did not plan this."

"But you wanted a wife. You already made your intentions known to me at the Elbourne ball. You are the son of a duke. It's clear to me and everyone else in Society that if your brothers do not provide an heir you must."

The pain that flickered in her eyes squeezed his chest. Did he dare tell her the truth? No; his disclosure of the will might send her flying back to London, reputation or not. "Indeed, you are correct. I needed a wife and I have my reasons."

"Why not Miss Cherrie Black, then?"

Was that jealousy in her expression? "I am not considering her or any other lady, *Miss Garland.* The fact of the matter is we were seen together in a compromising situation and we must marry."

She stared him directly in the eye, her expression cool. "I already spoke to my godmother about this."

He considered as much, but he was devilishly glad that blasted parasol had been damaged in the accident.

"And I am ready to marry you, my lord."

His eyes widened considerably. "You are?"

"I have my mother to think of, let alone Agatha and her guilt in all this. I have no wish for anyone to suffer needlessly because of something I did. And I do believe Grimstoke could make things very difficult if I did not comply."

What about love? he wanted to ask. Still, he realized they had reached a point in their relationship where some rules must be set. If she had had any love for him before, she certainly didn't show it now. He wished she would tell him what she was thinking. "I will never hurt you, Briana."

"But you already have," she said hoarsely, spinning around, dragging her fingers across the gazebo.

He placed his hands on her shoulders. The instinct to protect this woman overwhelmed him. "How have I hurt you?"

She shrugged. "I don't want to trust you, and you are making me do just that."

"I care for you, Briana. In fact, I believe I am beginning to love you."

"Love me?" she asked softly, angling her head toward him. "How could you love me?"

"Let's see. I love your freckles, for one."

She blushed. "You are too charming, my lord."

Ah, progress. "I am asking you to marry me, Briana. I will not force you. But your reputation is at stake. If Grimstoke follows through with his threat, you will be ruined. However, if you have no wish to go through with this plan, I will whisk you away to the Continent. You and your mother. The scandal will die down in time, and no one will even remember what happened here."

She shook her head. "Violet is a dear friend, but sometimes she gets carried away. I fear she has already spread the news of our upcoming marriage to Miss Black and a few other guests."

"Has she compromised your name?"

Briana shrugged, not knowing what to say. Violet could stretch the truth sometimes, not realizing the pain she inflicted. In Briana's estimation, the story would never die down.

"Then I will ask you again. Will you marry me?"

Briana thought she caught a note of vulnerability in his voice. "Yes, my lord." She lifted her face to him, and the memory of their last kiss lingered in her mind.

He seemed to read her thoughts. His touch was oddly comforting when he took her hand. "There will be no scandal. You will see. May I call you *Briana* now?"

Her lips twitched. "Yes, my lord."

"Clayton. My name is Clayton," he whispered. "Let me hear you say it."

"Clayton," she said softly.

He pulled her closer and gave her a chaste kiss on the lips. "In a few hours, you'll be mine, Briana."

"What did you say?"

"I said in a few hours."

"No, the other part."

"That you'll be mine?"

"Yes," she said in a clipped tone. "I want you to know that I will do as I wish when we marry. Is that clearly understood?"

His brows narrowed. "And what exactly do you mean by that?"

"I wish a house in Town."

"Done."

She flinched, surprised at his quick answer. "I want no words from you about how I go about my business."

His expression hardened. "Exactly what kind of business?"

She folded her hands across her chest. "I find your question irrelevant, my lord. Since we will be living apart."

"Clayton," he retorted. "I thought we covered that already."

"Clayton," she said coolly.

Instead of arguing, he had the urge to take the lady into his arms and kiss her soundly. But first, he needed to marry the termagant. "Who the devil said we would be living apart?"

"You did, of course."

"I did not."

"My lord, a word with you, if you please."

Briana turned abruptly when Agatha's voice sounded behind her. She frowned, not happy to see her godmother hobbling about on her bad ankle.

Clayton scowled. "What the deuce are you doing out here with that injured ankle, madam?"

Gray eyes snapped at him. "After what happened yesterday, the real question is, should you be out here with my godchild?"

"I am to marry the lady, Miss Appleby. I believe I am entitled to a few minutes alone with her."

"Well, my lord, by the sound of your conversation, I can see I came just in time."

Briana gasped. "Agatha!"

Clayton's brows rose in amusement. "You've made your point."

"Agatha, you should go back to bed," Briana said worriedly.

"In a minute, child. I have another point to make." The older lady took in a deep breath and rested against a knotted oak for support. "Actually"—she paused to wipe the sweat from her brow—"three points, to be exact."

"I am all ears, madam."

"But Agatha," Briana protested, "you need to stay off that ankle." Her concerned gaze swung to Clayton. "Don't just stand there. Do something!"

The man broke into a smile. "What would you like me to do? Sweep her into my arms and force her back into her chambers?"

"Yes!" Briana said impatiently.

"Listen here, you two . . . puppies!" Agatha interrupted. "I will say my piece if it's the last thing I do."

Clayton's eye glittered appreciatively in Agatha's direction. "Go on, madam."

Agatha gave him a satisfied nod. "Very well, my lord. At least one of you is listening. First, I want Briana to have full access to her planned home for women who are, hmmm, let's just say, found in delicate situations."

Clayton exchanged gazes between Briana and Agatha. "As her husband, what role do I play in this?"

Agatha sent him a pointed glare. "Nothing but your support."

Briana held her breath. Clayton looked at her with such possessiveness, the light in his eyes warmed her entire body.

"That's all?" he asked huskily.

Briana nodded uncomfortably.

His magnetic smile took her breath away. "Agreed."

"Good," Agatha said, looking very pale. "Next and probably the most important . . . "

"Yes, Miss Appleby?" Clayton's eyes gleamed with such mischief, Briana wanted to shake him. Agatha was about to fall flat on her face and he was smiling.

"You must love her," Agatha said, her finger pointing directly at his heart.

Oh, good grief! Briana wanted to sink into the ground.

Clayton clucked his tongue and regarded the two ladies for a few long seconds. "I must, must I?"

Agatha scowled, her hands fisting at her sides. "Where is a parasol when one needs one, for you certainly are in need of a good whack, my boy!"

Clayton burst out laughing. "Very well. I will love her."

A knot rose in Briana's throat. But did he mean it? Could she trust him? Was he teasing her earlier, or even now?

"Very good," Agatha said as calmly as if they were conversing over what horse they were to buy at Tattersall's. "And finally, I want this promise from both of you."

Clayton looked at Agatha, his gaze narrowing. "We are listening, but if you continue with this discussion, madam, your feet will not be able to hold up that tree."

"Listen to me, you young pup—"

Clayton growled and took a step toward her. "Madam, for the purpose of your safety, I believe we can continue our little talk in your chambers."

"Don't you lay a finger on me!" Agatha scolded, her gray eyes widening. "I can stand on my own two feet!"

Clayton let out a manly chuckle and took another step toward her. "That remains to be seen."

"Stay where you are. I'm warning you." Agatha pushed herself off the tree. "I can stand by myself, but as to my conditions,

I must demand that you will not allow Briana's mother to live with you."

Clayton's eyes danced. "That is your stipulation?"

Briana held her godmother's elbow. "Agatha, please."

Clayton gave the older lady a wink.

Agatha's gaze moved to Briana. "And what have you to say?"

Briana wanted to crawl into a hole. "Mother won't like it. She will want to live with me . . . I mean us."

"Because she has wanted you to marry Lord Clayton since you were a child?" the lady replied coolly. "Because she wants to show her friends she is living with the son of a duke? No, you will agree to this, child, or I will see to it for you."

"Agatha," Briana pleaded.

"Fustian! Your mother has her own home. She doesn't need to interfere with yours. Promise me."

Clayton turned to Briana, his eyes so full of understanding she wanted to cry. He raised Briana's hand to his lips. "If you want your mother in our home, I won't stand in the way. But she can visit as much as she wants. I promise."

The man had her heart and soul twisted into so many turns she thought she might spin on her feet. "I will see that my mother has a place in our home, but not a permanent one."

Agatha smiled. "Good, then. I will see you two at church."

Clayton kept his eyes on Briana. "And I will see you in the library after I complete a small task. It's obvious this place is not as private as I hoped. We can settle a few more things before we take our vows." Before Briana could reply, Clayton strode forward and swept Agatha into his arms.

Agatha gasped in surprise. "I have no need of your help!"

He grunted for emphasis. "Your goddaughter thinks you do."

Briana exchanged smiles with him, and her heart soared.

"You know, my boy," Agatha said, whacking him on the shoulder, "you remind me of someone I used to know."

The man's laugh held such tenderness that Briana felt her heart burst with love.

"I do?" he said mischievously. "Well, madam, you should stay off your feet, and I intend to see you do, even if it is for only thirty minutes." He juggled Agatha in his arms and gave Briana a sly wink. "Are you a gambling woman, Miss Appleby?"

"And what if I am?" she said stiffly.

"I will bet you a guinea I can make it back to your chambers within thirty seconds. Never fear—most of the guests are attending some game in the village or still in their bedchambers."

Agatha's eyes grew as wide as the knot in the tree behind her. "You will do no such thing! You arrogant puppy! Let me down!" The lady pushed against his shoulders, but it was useless.

Instead of listening to her protests, Clayton quickened his pace, dashing through the garden with Agatha in his arms. Briana smiled. This was the Clayton she knew. The Clayton she loved. And now it was the Clayton she was going to marry.

She leaned against the old gazebo and caught herself. What was she doing wasting precious time? Without anyone the wiser, she could try to open that writing box before Clayton arrived.

In truth, the transaction could already have taken place. That was, of course, if there were any communication at all. But why would Whitehall send two women to investigate? No doubt the superior agents were searching other places with more convincing evidence. The source in this case was probably a vengeful nobody bent on causing trouble for Lord Grimstoke.

Briana gave a tired sigh. For the sake of England, she had to try.

Chapter Seventeen

*B*riana's wary gaze flicked to the closed door. She wished she had the key to lock it. How long before Clayton appeared? And how many times would she find herself in a strange room alone, waiting for someone to barge in and catch her at something? This entire game was wearing on her already frayed nerves.

Her head was in such a whirl, her heart felt as if it would jump out of her chest. She was to be married within the hour and here she was, looking for a clue in a possible assassination plot against the Prince Regent.

She pulled the writing box onto her lap and lightly pressed one of the back buttons. There was a sudden click and another drawer popped open beneath her fingers.

Her breath caught in her throat. The secret drawer!

She lowered her head and peered inside, her fingers searching for anything at all. Nothing!

Had the missive already been retrieved, if there was one in the first place? Was she worrying over nothing? Was Whitehall's source trying to mislead them? She just didn't know.

Footsteps sounded outside the room, and she hurriedly snapped the drawer closed. Clayton was here sooner than she had expected. Agatha had probably whacked him a good one.

The door opened and she smiled. "You are earlier—"

Kingsdale's wicked grin unnerved her, and she quickly rose from her seat. "Ah, Miss Garland, thought I saw you walk in here a minute ago. This is the meeting place, is it not?"

Briana's body tensed. Had he been watching her in the garden? Of course he had. He was always watching her. It seemed a little too convenient for him to keep running into her, cornering her in any room where she happened to be. He was stalking her like a beast circling his prey. There was no doubt about it.

"I thought you went into the village, my lord."

"Had a bit of the headache, don't you know? Thought I would take a stroll about the gardens. And by George, you would never guess what I happened upon."

"You were eavesdropping?"

His dark eyes flashed a warning. "I never eavesdrop, Miss Garland. Women eavesdrop, my dear. Men . . . well, men hunt."

It took all Briana's effort to stay calm. "If you will excuse me—"

He flung the door closed and strode toward her. "We find ourselves alone once again. How fitting, don't you think?"

Too fitting, she realized as she ignored his silent threat and tried to make her way quickly across the room. The blood pounded in her ears as she passed him. Did he have a key? Would he dare lock her in here? Or somewhere else?

Suddenly his arm swung out, imprisoning her in his grip. He put just enough pressure on her to keep her beside him. "It's no mere coincidence that I'm here, my dear. Our meetings were never by chance. You were to marry me. Me—do you hear me?" His tone was velvety soft and edged with such anger she shivered. "All I have done up to now is for our future. Why couldn't you wait? Are you in love with the man? Do you find him better than me?"

She tossed her head back to glare at him. "My fiancé will be here any minute. You had best unhand me, sir."

A twisted smile spread across his face. "Well done, *Briana*. You have not disappointed me. You are as fiery as your hair. We will do nicely together."

The man was mad!

Kingsdale turned when the door swung open.

"Clayton," Briana said, her voice shaky. She sagged in relief as her fiancé walked into the room. But that relief was short-lived when she saw Clayton's hostile stance. It reeked of power and territorial domain. And the hardness in his gaze could not be mistaken. He was definitely angry.

"If you will please unhand my fiancée, Gregory, I will not have to shoot you." Clayton's voice cut through the eerie silence, and Briana was instantly released.

Kingsdale's gaze slid over her like a slow caress. "Only showing the lady what she lost, Clay. No harm done."

Clayton's eyes turned an icy blue. "It seems you have been trying a great deal of that lately. However, because I am to marry this lady within the hour, I would advise you not to show your face in my presence for the remainder of our stay here."

It suddenly occurred to Briana that Kingsdale had known exactly what he was doing all along. He knew Clayton was going to be here and see them together. The man was as slippery as a snake, and to her horror, his plan seemed to be working splendidly.

Kingsdale chuckled. "What a pitiful show of strength, Clayton. I thought you could do better than that. Besides, it was your fiancée who wanted me to meet with her."

He shot Briana a wink as if between lovers, kissed her hand and departed from the room.

Briana held back a gasp. "I can explain," she said, hoping Clayton would return to the same man she had known in the garden.

His expression was thunderous. "Don't even try."

Briana's heart sank.

"I will meet you at church, Miss Garland. Whatever dealings we need to go over will happen after the marriage." He didn't give her any time to defend herself before he turned on his heel and strode from the room.

Briana was married by three o'clock that afternoon by special license. Agatha, Violet, Lord Grimstoke and his wife were the only witnesses. The papers were signed and everyone returned to the mansion without further ado.

Clayton failed to mention the library incident at all. In fact, the vows were the only thing she heard him say the entire time they were at church. When they returned to Grimstoke Hall, the guests were delivered the news and an impromptu celebration took place immediately.

"I suppose we had you all fooled," Clayton said jovially, his hand on Briana's waist. "But my dear wife and I had been planning to wed for quite some time now. The archbishop's timely visit gave us the means to achieve what we thought to do at a later date."

"Why so quick about it?" one man exclaimed. "And by special license? Afraid of her mama?"

Clayton's clasp tightened. "We could not wait another day to be with each other." He turned to Briana. "Could we, dearest?"

Briana wanted to smack him. Instead she only smiled.

The crowd cheered and all were given a glass of champagne.

As the day dragged on, Briana felt trapped. She put on a happy face until late that evening when she and her new husband were standing alone in Clayton's bedchamber. The maids had quickly removed all her belongings to his room. Briana was at one corner, Clayton at the other when he turned to her, his deep violet eyes holding a glint of amusement.

Well, she didn't think this funny in the least. "You—you can sleep on the floor!"

Before she could speak another word, he crossed the room and took her shoulders in a gentle grip. "Come, Briana, I will not hurt you. But if we are to have a marriage with any hope for the future, you must trust me and I must trust you."

"Trust?" she said in a suffocating whisper. "What reason would you have not to trust me?" She blurted out the words before she thought about what she was saying. He didn't know about her work. He could never know about her work.

"Let's forget about Kingsdale. I know him for what he is. You would never seek him out as he proclaimed. I was just, well, jealous, and I do have a temper. As for me, I intend to honor my vows, as I hope you will."

Confused, Briana stared at him. "What are you saying?"

He gently tipped her chin with his finger, and she caught a trace of bayberry. Could this handsome, egotistical, wonderful man love her?

"It seems I will have to make myself plain, then. I don't want you near Kingsdale ever again. Is that clear?"

Her back instantly straightened. "You don't trust me?"

"I never said that."

"Yes, you did." She shrugged out of his grasp and started for the door.

"Where the deuce do you think you are going?"

"Out!"

"I don't think so." In a flash he was beside her, blocking her departure. The fact that he was now her husband did not help her circumstances in the least.

"Why?" she stammered, glaring up at him, intensely conscious of his powerful body next to hers. "You cannot truly think I am staying with you tonight? We—we barely know each other!"

He laughed, his violet blue eyes burning a path straight to her heart. "I have known you forever, dear wife. And yes, I am staying with you tonight."

He touched the bridge of her nose, outlining her freckles. A spark ignited between them, and she saw his self-confidence rise. "You made your vow along with me."

She looked at a spot above his shoulder, anywhere but at those compelling eyes. "Well, er, I wasn't thinking correctly."

He backed her against the wall, his hands over each side of her face. "Well, I am thinking correctly . . . for the both of us. I told you before and I'll say it again: I'm your husband and I love you. I think I began loving you when we had our first waltz back at Elbourne Hall."

The declaration sent her senses spinning. He loved her? Was it truly possible? Her knees felt weak as his mouth moved along her neck, making her shiver. It was nearly impossible to remain coherent when he did this to her. In the back of her mind she knew his declaration of love made her afraid. Afraid of her emotions. Afraid he would let her down. Afraid of her future.

"Fairy Lady." He kissed her nose. "I was wondering if I made a wish on one of those adorable freckles, would it come true?"

She closed her eyes. "I cannot think properly when you are near."

"Ah, you cannot think? That's called progress." He kissed her cheek.

Her eyes flew open. "Stop that!"

He laughed and moved his hand to the hollow of her back, fitting her against him. Her head pressed against his chest.

"Do you know what I wished for?" he whispered silkily.

She tried to ignore the way he made her feel, but she couldn't help it. The pounding of his heart echoed in her ears. She was definitely losing the battle. "You . . . you are not playing fair, my lord."

"I may be a gentleman, but I don't play fair all the time. Have you not talked to Emily about me?"

She nodded into his cravat, smiling.

He paused, his breath oddly uneven. "I own you do not play fair either, my red-haired nymph."

She peeked up at him, knowing he was as affected by her as she was by him. "Oh," she said coyly, "I always play fair."

His lips curved upward. "Indeed? And what about that time you learned to waltz?"

A smile sprang to her lips as she thought about that wonderful summer at Elbourne Hall. "It was the only way to learn the dance," she said mischievously.

He said nothing, but only stared at her with such tenderness she wanted to weep for joy.

She cleared her throat. "Depend upon it, my lord husband. You were a very good instructor. And I daresay much better than Mr. Summers."

He burst out laughing and kissed her hard. "Then come dance with me again, my love, not as a wide-eyed girl of sixteen but as my bride and as my wife in all ways." *As his bride? As his wife?*

Briana knew what he was asking of her. Her pulse quickened as the very air around them stirred with excitement and promise.

His lips seared a path to her soul. "Come. Be my wife."

Tears of happiness pooled in her eyes.

"Briana?" he asked worriedly.

A glow of warmth spread through her as she smiled, infinitely aware of the gentleness of this man. "Yes."

"Yes, what?" he asked in a husky whisper.

She reached out and touched his cheek. "I will be your wife in all ways."

His grin was overpowering. "Then let us dance together."

With a sigh, she rested her head against his shoulder. "Oh, Clayton."

He drew in a sharp, smoldering breath, and in one fluid movement whisked her off the ground and into his arms.

"Briana." Her name was smothered with a kiss as he whispered his love to her. Her lips trembled beneath his. She loved him with a power so wonderful she wanted to weep. It was as if he had turned the key to her heart, unlocking the mysteries of life.

She became lost in her husband's lovemaking, and the night passed with nary a thought about the mission or her duty to the Crown. All her thoughts were centered on her husband, Lord Clayton Clearbrook. He might not be as perfect as she recalled when she was sixteen, but he was her husband now in all ways, and in spite of everything, she would always love him.

Early the next morning, when Briana was just about to open her eyes, the door to her bedchamber banged in her ears. With a gasp, she pulled the bedcovers to her chin, immediately realizing her husband was not beside her but was marching toward her, his expression none too friendly.

She blinked. In fact, his violet eyes were dark as midnight.

"What's wrong?" she asked sweetly.

"I have recently come from a meeting with your godmother, *wife*."

"And?"

"And"—he lowered his voice, taking her in from head to toe—"what the devil do you think you're doing, acting like some kind of secret agent?"

She flinched. Drat Agatha and her meddling ways. What was she trying to do?

"Yes, that's right, sweetheart. The lady told me everything. I know all about your snooping mission, and devil take it, if you think for one blasted minute that I'm going to let my wife spy about this house like some lone soldier in battle, you had better think again."

She bolted upright. "You cannot stop me! I have a responsibility to see this through!"

He grasped her shoulders and shook her. "If anything happened to you—"

He left the words unsaid and crushed his lips against hers.

She pulled away, too afraid of how the man could worm his way into her heart and make her think of nothing but him. He had loved her to distraction last night, and she had forgotten about everything and everyone that mattered to her.

"I cannot believe Agatha told you." Annoyed, Briana slapped her hand against the pillow. "Why would she do such a thing?"

"Because I am your husband, madam. She told me she wanted to see me first thing in the morning. I accommodated the lady. Said she had something important to tell me."

It was hard to look him boldly in the face when he gazed at her as if he knew her by heart. Her soul ached for him.

"I won't pull out of my duty now," she said stubbornly.

"By heaven, you are my wife and you will do as I say."

Her eyes shot daggers at him. "I don't like you very much right now."

"Well, *wife*, whether you like me or not, you will listen to what I have to say."

She pinched her lips into a grim line. "I don't think Agatha would agree with you."

"Really? Why do you think she told me everything?"

"I-I don't know."

"Because she thinks you're an impulsive chit, and if you snoop any more by yourself, your adversaries, whoever they may be, will be on to you."

"I am not impulsive!"

He shook his head. "That doesn't even deserve an answer. But what if someone *is* watching you? Did you ever think of that?"

"Of course I did, but—"

"Hear me out." His expression softened as he sank onto the bed, cutting off her speech. "If Agatha believes there is reason to search for these letters of communication, I will be at your side, do you understand? If this mission is just another loose thread with no substance to it, then so be it."

When he took her hands in his, there was a tingling in the pit of her stomach.

"However," he continued, "I find it rather incredible that Whitehall would send two women to find an important missive regarding the assassination attempt on the Regent. It would seem more logical that your superiors are using you for a decoy and the true adversaries are making mischief somewhere else."

"But what about Grimstoke?"

"He may have some connection, but he may be a decoy as well. And who the devil knows if there is a source or not? There are just too many unanswered questions."

He had a valid point. "Very well. I don't mind if you are at my side. In fact," she smiled up at him, "that pleases me very much."

He brought her hand to his lips, his violet blue eyes never leaving her green ones. "I'm glad you are pleased."

Without a second to lose, he reached out, swept her from the bed and gave a hearty slap to her backside. "Now come down to breakfast, wench. We are to sit at the table with our host. I may not like the man's tactics"—he wiggled his eyebrows—"but I cannot dislike the end result."

She threw a pillow at him and laughed.

At breakfast, which consisted of a multitude of rolls, meat and eggs, Briana was placed next to Sir Gerald while her husband took a seat across from her alongside Violet. Clayton didn't seem pleased when they were separated, but to Briana's surprise, he complied without a word to his host.

Briana smiled, knowing he was trying his utmost to remain calm under Grimstoke's stare. She wondered if Agatha's talk had anything to do with it.

Just before coming down to breakfast, Briana had made her way to her godmother's chambers, trying to dissuade the lady from walking about for one more day. Even though Agatha had sat during the wedding, the ceremony had tired her.

Surprisingly, Agatha had agreed to stay in bed and was now enjoying a hearty breakfast in her room. However, the elderly lady had mentioned she had informed Clayton of their mission because the man, who was quite trustworthy, needed to know.

Briana didn't believe a word of it. She knew Agatha wanted

her godchild out of the line of fire. Always had. But after the mishap with the carriage, the lady had seemed extremely agitated about everything and everyone. Briana wanted to blame her behavior on the head injury, but now she wondered.

Yet what if this conspiracy theory at Grimstoke Hall were nothing at all? Did Agatha know the real truth and was she hiding it from her? Could the carriage accident have been planned by Whitehall as a decoy of sorts? No, Briana thought grimly. Agatha would never have put her in danger. But would Whitehall?

Briana's head was spinning so much from the latest turn of events that she didn't know what to believe anymore. But she did know she loved her husband. He had slowly crept into her heart and stolen it from under her very nose. Loving him was like breathing. It came naturally.

Her lips fell into an easy smile as she regarded him. She let her gaze travel along the lengthy table, which held at least fifty people. A steady stream of voices filled the room, making the meal quite informal but pleasant.

She was just about to turn her head from the other end of the table when her eyes collided with Kingsdale's. Her heart skipped a beat. She recalled Clayton's warning from yesterday and dearly hoped her husband had not noticed the man. She had not seen Kingsdale when they had returned from their wedding, and she had hoped with all her heart that he had left Grimstoke Hall.

Obviously, he had not. The twisted smile on his face made her look away. She caught sight of Miss Cherrie Black talking to another gentleman, who had come to the party only yesterday.

Briana's mind raced. Prinny's enemy could be anyone here. Or maybe no one at all. Should she return to the library and see what she could find?

She lifted her head and met her husband's dark blue gaze. Immediately his lips thinned into a commanding line, telling her no. For the love of the king, how could he read her thoughts?

Reddening, she took a sip of coffee and dropped her gaze.

"My felicitations on your marriage, Miss Garland—or is it Lady Clayton Clearbrook now?"

Briana turned a cool stare upon Sir Gerald. Clayton had not seemed happy when she was placed next to the man, but he had only tipped his head Sir Gerald's way and then ignored him completely. She, in turn, had almost forgotten about the man until he spoke and wanted to dismiss Sir Gerald without a word. Yet she had no wish to make a fuss in front of her husband, so she gave his cousin a polite nod. "Thank you. I am very happy."

Sir Gerald lifted his brow, and for a moment Briana thought she saw a flash of anger in his eyes. "Indeed, you should be. Ain't every day a lady obtains a castle and a dungeon full of money."

Briana choked on a bite of kipper she had forked into her mouth. Her husband looked up from his conversation, and she waved her hand that she was fine, smiled, and took another sip of her coffee.

"By Jove, you didn't know?" Sir Gerald said with a satirical chuckle. "Devil take it, never thought my cousin had it in him."

"I fail to see the humor in my marriage, sir."

The man's starched shirt points poked into his neck as he turned toward her. "You really don't know, do you?"

"Know what?"

He shook his head, catching Clayton's eye from across the table. Briana saw the heated exchange and felt a cold lump form in her belly. What was going on? First Clayton ignored the fellow, and now it looked as if he wanted to throttle the man.

"You think my cousin married you for love or something stupid like that?" Sir Gerald said with a small laugh, his face to his plate. "This is England, my dear girl. It ain't the Garden of Eden before the apple."

He angled his head and gave her an appreciative look. "We could have done well together, my little dove. And I would have had the castle—and the money."

"I have no idea what you're talking about." Shaken, Briana carelessly let her coffee cup clatter to the table.

Instantly she noted Clayton's gaze boring down on her.

She was startled when his chair scraped backward as he prepared to rise. Her stomach twisted in knots. Whatever information Sir Gerald was about to convey, Clayton did not want her to hear it. But hear it she would.

With a sense of dread, she saw Clayton making his excuses and starting around the table. Some people might think he was heading in the direction of the sideboard for more food, but Briana knew differently. He was coming after her.

She calmly turned to Sir Gerald. "Tell me about this castle, sir. I am most interested."

Sir Gerald brought his napkin to his lips. "Ever hear of Uncle Cathaven?"

Briana nodded, her hold on her cup tightening.

"Well, by Jove, you probably know the man was a horrid example for a human being. Was godfather to myself and Clayton."

"I didn't know," she said in surprise, watching out of the corner of her eye when Clayton was stopped by another gentleman.

"Old miser died not more than a month ago. Left his castle to Clayton, and believe it or not, the old goat had a dungeon full of money. Enough money to set Clayton up for life. I think your husband is richer now than the duke himself."

Briana felt the weight on her shoulders lift. She guessed Clayton was going to tell her later. He wasn't one to boast. "He had not told me that, but then again, perhaps he wanted to surprise me."

"Don't be stupid, girl. The only way he could have the castle was to marry within the allotted time. In essence, Lord Clayton Clearbrook needed a convenient bride in less than a month and you were it."

The food in Briana's stomach turned to dirt. *It's not true. He loves me,* her heart cried. *He loves me.*

"He don't love you," Sir Gerald sneered. "He just needed you. Thought you knew the circumstances."

"And what would have happened to the castle if he hadn't married during the specified time?" she asked coolly, peering over the rim of her coffee cup.

"I would have had it all," Sir Gerald snapped. "Those were

the conditions of the will. Why do you think I'm here? Every eligible lady knows he needed to marry for the castle. I made sure of it. And I was certain you knew, too. You little fool, do you think he would marry for love? Clayton lost his only love in the war. You are nothing to him but—"

"A convenient bride," she finished for him.

Sir Gerald's eyes gleamed with pleasure. "Indeed, my dear. Very much so."

From the look on Sir Gerald's face, Briana knew Clayton was standing directly behind her. Tears welled in her eyes, and she rapidly tried to blink them away.

"Briana, may I have a word with you?" Clayton's voice was perfectly calm.

"Perhaps the lady don't wish to leave the table, my lord," Sir Gerald said, smiling as he forked the last bit of his eggs into his mouth.

Clayton's gaze held a dangerous glint as he bent toward the table, placing his face between Briana's and Sir Gerald's.

"I will deal with you later, *cuz*," he said most sweetly.

Then he turned his gaze toward his wife. "A word, if you please, madam?"

Briana could smile just as sweetly. "I believe I will finish my breakfast, *dear*."

But inwardly her heart was bleeding. Yes, it was a marriage of convenience, but after last night she had hoped he truly did love her. He had lied to her. Led her on. Made her believe he loved her! For a dreadful moment she thought she could feel the knife-twisting pain Clarice had experienced. The only consolation for Briana was that she had married the man before she had let him take advantage of her!

Her husband regarded her in stony silence. A muscle pulsed in his neck, and for a few fearful seconds Briana thought that if she did not leave on her own accord, he was going to lift her from her seat and carry her out of the room himself.

But to her surprise he only smiled. "Very well, madam. I will meet with you in our chambers in thirty minutes."

Briana flushed, knowing this man could turn her heart to pudding with just one of his kisses.

"Not there, my lord," she murmured, looking at her food.

Sir Gerald snickered as he tipped the water glass to his lips. "Not the Romeo one has always heard about, eh?"

Briana stared at the man, aghast. Just then, the footman came from behind to place a silver pot of hot coffee upon the table. Clayton accidentally bumped the servant as the man leaned over the table and the coffee spilled onto Sir Gerald's lap.

Briana leaned back as Sir Gerald shot up in pain. Curses flew from his mouth, and the whole assembly fell deathly quiet. The entire front of the man's breeches was steaming with coffee.

Flabbergasted, Briana glanced at Clayton, who stood there, doing nothing, a grim smile dancing in his eyes.

The footman, who still held the empty coffeepot in his hands, mumbled a sincere apology. Grimstoke's face reddened as he shouted orders. Sir Gerald gritted his teeth and started for the door. A few snickers followed the man, but within minutes everyone went back to eating and conversing.

Briana glanced over her shoulder as Clayton took Sir Gerald's seat. "That was despicable," she said under her breath.

"What?" Clayton said. "I learned it from you."

Briana pressed her lips together in angry silence.

Her husband leaned closer. "As to my cousin's latest comment that sealed his fate, I am not about to take advantage of you, if that is what you think."

"You already took advantage of me," she accused, keeping her face to her plate.

"We are drawing stares, dear wife. Meet me in the library, then, if you have fear of me in our chambers. That place seems like a haven to you lately."

Briana sipped her coffee, her insides burning with grief. "I have no fear of you, my lord. I have disgust."

His hands curled by his side. "All the more reason for us to talk this out. I believe Gerald's words may have offended you."

She could no longer look at him, for she knew his cousin's accusations were true. "I will see you in the library, my lord."

"Clayton," he whispered with a hint of domination that irked Briana to no end. "Your husband's name is Clayton."

* * *

A sob escaped Briana's throat as she hurried up the stairs and hastened into Agatha's chambers, closing the door behind her.

"Whatever is the matter, child?" Agatha's arms flew out to catch her. Briana fell against her aunt's chest.

"He lied to me, Agatha! Clayton lied to me!"

Agatha patted her back. "Tell me all about it."

Briana sniffed and wiped her eyes. "He married me to gain a castle and money. He doesn't love me at all."

"That's not true. He loves you very much."

"No, he doesn't love me. A man who is in love, real love, would not lie like he did."

"Just slow down, take a few deep breaths, and tell me the entire story. I'm sure he had a reason for what he did."

Briana told her godmother everything about Sir Gerald, the castle, the money, and Clayton's meeting with her in the library in a few minutes.

"It seems he wishes to air his side of the story. As his wife, you have done him a disservice by not listening to him."

"You are in agreement with him?" she asked, the realization slicing her heart in two.

"I am not siding with anyone. I knew something about that dingy old castle and that miser who owned it. But if you ask me, I do think it childish of you to believe everything Sir Gerald has said. There are two sides to everything, you know. Even with our mission. In fact, I have received notice to leave."

Suddenly Briana became aware of her aunt's carriage dress and packed trunks. "You received notice this morning?"

"Yes. I cannot tell you how. But Whitehall believes the enemy has been in Bath all along. I am to journey there first thing. I will not be directly involved, so you need not worry."

Briana gripped the bedpost. "I am to go with you?"

"No, you are to stay here with your husband. But if you see any suspicious signs, then by all means send word to Whitehall as soon as you possibly can."

Briana turned away. They had been on a wild-goose chase after all. And because of the mission, she was now a married woman. Her bottom lip trembled. What in the world had she done? "I plan to meet him in the library. But I don't want to."

"You must. He is your husband now."

A tear slipped down her cheek. "I love him, but don't you see? He lied to me. I can never forget that."

Agatha gave her a hug. "You'll work it out. Young love is fragile, child. Now, give this old lady a kiss before I leave."

"I will miss you," Briana sobbed.

"I am not leaving England, dear. I will see you often. And do not let that mama of yours into your house for more than a week at a time. Remember, your husband is your first priority. Speak with him and I am sure everything will work out."

Confused and hurt, Briana forced a smile. Clayton was her husband now, but he had married her for reasons he had kept secret, and she would never forget that fact as long as she lived.

Chapter Eighteen

*C*layton had the writing box popped open as he examined the secret drawer. He had searched the library as soon as he had left breakfast. He believed Agatha correct. The two ladies had been sent on a pointless assignment while the players in the game were somewhere else. He had seen this type of scenario played out in the war, but blast it all, he didn't like the ladies embroiled in any kind of plot, false or otherwise.

The click of the door turned his head.

"Briana," he said calmly, closing the box.

Her chin lifted in that adorable, defiant manner and he frowned. He had not been truthful and she knew it.

"My lord," she said, taking a seat as far away from him as she could.

"Afraid of me?" The pain in her eyes turned his heart.

"Certainly not."

He sank back against the leather chair behind Grimstoke's desk. "What did that pompous idiot tell you?"

"That you needed a convenient bride."

"You knew I needed to marry."

Her face tightened. "But I didn't know why. I thought it because of your family, your responsibility as the son of a duke."

He stood, walking toward the fireplace and trailing his hand along the bricks. "What does it matter why I married you?"

"Why?" she cried, rising. "How could you ask such a thing?"

He turned quickly, realizing his words were chosen poorly.

"You deceived me," she went on. "You led me to believe

you . . . you loved me! My sister trusted a man and nothing became of it but heartache. And it seems I am to follow in her footsteps."

His expression hardened. "Pray, explain yourself."

"It means I cannot trust you," she said deliberately. "I can never trust you with my heart or anything else. You wanted money and a castle more than you ever wanted me. How can I live with that? With you?"

A long, brittle silence fell between them, and Briana felt as if a thick sheet of ice had settled over the room. The slap of his hand against the fireplace made her jump. His face was cold and unyielding as he returned her gaze. Two sapphire eyes impaled her with such fury, she knew she had pushed him too hard. He was not going to back down, but neither was she.

"Then perhaps you should live without me, madam. If you think me as loose as one of these blasted bricks, we can part and go our separate ways as I suggested the first time I proposed marriage."

"Perhaps we should," she snapped, letting her anger get the best of her. "This mission is done with anyway. Agatha received a letter telling her so."

His eyes flashed with recognition, and for a fleeting second she thought he was going to drag her into his arms and kiss her. But she was wrong. His pride had been hurt along with hers.

"Well, *wife*, all has been said, has it not? You obviously do not wish to be by your husband's side." A muscle ticked in his jaw as he skirted the desk and strode toward the door.

"Good day to you, madam. I shall take my leave of you within the hour. Rest assured that many of the guests will be departing today as well. It seems there is a better party in Brighton. But never fear, my departure will be seen as nothing more than a journey of business."

He was within a foot of the door when he turned. "As to your future, you may contact me through my solicitor and draw upon my account at the bank. You may live with your godmother, if you wish. I will send the money to her address."

"I don't want your money," Briana cried, hurt that he would not fight for their love. "I don't want anything of yours. I never want to see you again."

His eyes flicked to her stomach. "If you find yourself with child, madam, not seeing me will indeed be a wish I cannot allow. Good day."

As soon as the door snapped closed, Briana let her tears spill down her cheeks. *Oh, Clayton.*

With a heartfelt sob, she dropped her head to the arm of the sofa and squeezed her eyes shut. Why did it have to end this way?

Despair welled up inside her as her sobs turned to small hiccups of pain. She didn't know how long she sat there crying before she finally heaved a deep sigh, trying to compose herself. With her swollen eyes and red nose, she didn't want to run into anyone she knew. So she closed her eyes and tried to figure out what to do. The minutes stretched into hours as she fell fast asleep.

When she awoke, it was half past noon. Two hours after her husband had left her. He was probably gone and Agatha, too.

She looked about the room, wondering what she should do now. She was a married woman, for goodness' sake. That meant she was tied to one man, but it also meant she could venture places that a single woman was not allowed. She could travel to France, to America, to the East Indies—anywhere she wanted to go.

Assailed by a bitter sense of loneliness, she rose and wandered across the room, eyeing the writing box. How could things fall apart so swiftly? She wrapped her arms around herself and let out a shudder as she turned toward the fireplace.

The memory of Clayton slamming his hand into bricks brought tears to her eyes. She would never stop loving him. It just wasn't possible.

She sniffed and trailed her finger along the exact place his hand had touched. Had she been too harsh with him? Was it pain she had seen in his eyes when he turned to leave? Was she the one who had been too stubborn?

"Oh, Clayton," she murmured, her chest squeezing with regret. "Why couldn't it be better between us?"

She leaned her head against the mantel, trapped in her own selfishness. She hated to admit how much she needed him. How much she loved him. A crumble of mortar fell from a brick and she pushed what she could back into place. She wished she could do the same with her marriage. Make everything right again. Fill the holes and replace the emptiness in her heart.

She paused suddenly, staring at her hands. Could it be? The fireplace was old and probably needed to be redone. Many of the bricks were chipped, so it hadn't occurred to her before, but . . .

She tugged at the loose brick. Every fiber in her being tensed. A chuck of mortar fell to the floor and the brick loosened considerably. Good grief!

Her heart hammered with anticipation as she snaked her hand into the hole. When her fingers touched paper, she almost wept for joy. The secret missive! She clasped the document and yanked her hand from the hole.

"Always the little bluestocking, eh?"

Briana spun around and froze as Kingsdale clicked the door closed and turned the key.

"Searching for information wherever you can find it, my dear." A malevolent grin crossed his face as he slowly came into the room. He stretched out his hand. "I believe that is for me."

Her senses reeled as the situation finally sank in. "Y-you?"

He wrenched the paper from her hands, threw her into the chair, and sighed in exasperation. "You could have been mine, Briana. But you married the son of a duke instead. And now"—he picked up the brick and returned it to the fireplace—"you have stumbled onto a plot that may affect all of England." He frowned at her and shook his head. "I did try to warn you."

"I doubt that," she said, angry at herself for not seeing through this man.

"Really?" he said mockingly. "I told you about my brother, did I not? He died in the war."

"I fail to see why you would want to commit treason."

"Treason." His laugh was cold and lifeless. "It is retribution, my dear. Prinny killed my brother. He placed my only sibling in a regiment that was wiped out in its first battle."

"That wasn't the Regent's fault."

"My brother was all I had left of my family."

Briana was slowly beginning to see how his warped mind worked. Perhaps if she played on his emotions. "You loved your brother, then?"

Kingsdale sneered. "Loved him? I raised the pup from when he was a babe. My father didn't care, and any governesses were too wrapped up in my father. I literally begged our fat prince not to send Charles. I asked that he be given a desk job."

"And the Regent refused?" A note of false sympathy trailed on the end of her question.

Kingsdale seemed to soften. "Refused? The man laughed at me. He had promised my brother and there was nothing for it. He dismissed me as if I were a flea in his ale. Me? Can you believe it?"

Briana looked around cautiously.

"Don't even try it, my dear."

She stole a look at Kingsdale's face and regretted it instantly.

"You know," he said, "I can see the resemblance now."

"What resemblance?"

"With your sister."

Her insides chilled. "What do you know of Clarice?"

"My dear woman, I was the father of her child."

Briana felt the room tilt. "W-why?"

"Because you hurt me, Briana."

"I hurt you?"

"You wouldn't marry me. I had plans to go to Egypt. But you threw them in my face."

His confession made her speechless. If she had but known what kind of man he was she would have warned her sister.

"I have found a group that wants the Regent dead." His laugh alone betrayed his madness. "It worked so perfectly, you see. His own people booed him when Parliament was opening earlier this year. Most of them are fed up with his spending and lazy attitude anyway."

"You won't get away with this."

He shook the paper in his hand. "Grimstoke will be paid for his information. And yes, I will get away."

"Lord Grimstoke?"

"Yes, didn't you know the poor man lost at the tables? And whom do you suppose he lost to?"

Briana didn't need to answer. She knew already. Agatha had mentioned that Grimstoke had lost a good sum to the Prince Regent. It seemed revenge was a good motivator after all. But Clarice? Why would he hurt such an innocent child?

"That's right. Our dear Prinny. Fat, selfish slob that he is took almost everything Grimstoke had. Of course, our dear, devoted host thinks we're just kidnapping the old boy, scare him a bit, give him his just desserts."

"But you intend to kill the Regent?"

He put one hand on the desk, leaning toward her. "My, you have always been a clever little thing."

"What's in the papers?" she asked, meeting his glare with one of her own.

He cupped her chin in a tight hold. "Prinny's route and scheduled times when he will arrive in Bath later this month. It's a perfect ploy for a highwayman, don't you think?"

Briana was thinking furiously. She had to escape. The man was mad. Her eyes scanned the room. The window. That was her only way out. "How do you know the information you have is true?"

"True?" he smiled. "Grimstoke is still considered a loyal friend to Prinny. He knows the Regent's schedule as much as a clock knows the time." He flicked a caressing finger against her cheek. "That's how these games are played, my dear. It's always a friend. And we have found many friends in high places."

He gazed pointedly at the loose brick. "Our dear, pompous host has no idea who I am. He only wants his money returned to him with a bit of revenge against the Regent. The dropping point was to be here. The man ain't so prim and proper as one would think, is he? Greed will always have its price."

He leaned closer, his breath hot against her ear. "We have sold information to countries around the world, setting Whitehall on end. Although you, my dear, impress me. I knew Miss Appleby was involved in clandestine activities, but I had no idea about you. Of course, you must know the old woman is chasing another bad lead, is she not?"

The thought that the man might harm Agatha made Briana's stomach clench. "You'll never get away with it."

Her words seemed to amuse him. "I think you said that before. What? You intend to stop me? I really don't think so, my dear. I saw your husband leaving here two hours ago. A lovers' spat, eh?"

Briana wished with all her heart that she had never let Clayton leave in anger. "What do you intend to do with me?"

Kingsdale's gaze lingered on her face and he seemed to hesitate. "What I have done to every obstacle in my path, especially to anyone who dares to interfere in my plans. Be it royalty or women, I will not waver. But," he said regretfully, "this will be the first time I have loved the person . . ."

Briana swallowed nervously, trying to determine how fast she could make it to the window and throw it open.

"It's really a horrid shame, but alas . . ."

"You wouldn't dare!"

He rolled back on his heels. "You think your sister drowned accidentally in the Thames, do you?"

Briana felt the color leave her cheeks.

"That's right, my dear. I killed her."

Briana stiffened under his glare. *Clarice, oh, Clarice, what agony you must have suffered.* "So, my innocent sister was an obstacle?" she asked hotly.

"Indeed, my dear." With a regretful sigh, he cast a glance over her person. "It is a pity you are even a bigger obstacle, are you not?"

Clayton stared at Agatha. Agatha stared at Clayton. They were standing alone in the yard outside the posting inn on their way to Bath. "What are you doing here?" they said in unison.

"I thought you would be returning to London," Agatha snapped impatiently.

Clayton raised a brow. The lady looked a bit pale. "Why the deuce would I be doing that?"

"To show off your new bride," she said, narrowing her eyes suspiciously.

"My wife has no need of me, madam. I am off to see my brother Marcus, who has inherited a house in Bath." He peered at the posting inn, then back to Agatha. "Briana is not with you?"

Agatha scowled. "Of course not, you ninny. You left that poor child by herself? I thought you still with her."

"I believe she has a friend in Violet. I have left my wife the name of my solicitor and banker. What else does she need?"

Agatha's hands gripped her reticule and she seemed to sway. "You nincompoop!"

His jaw tensed. He should be thankful she had no parasol. "Depend upon it, Miss Appleby. I believe my wife is in agreement with you. She has no need of me at all."

"And whom do you think she needs? Kingsdale?"

His hand tightened on his riding whip. "I made certain the man had left, madam. I am not as stupid as you may think."

"Well, you are stupid," she said disgustedly. "Upon my departure I saw Lord Kingsdale lounging in the drawing room, playing chess with Mr. Wells. And it didn't seem the man was in a hurry to leave."

Clayton swung his gaze toward the road. "I was distinctly told he had left."

"Who told you, my lord?"

He looked at her and frowned. "I believe it was Grimstoke's daughter."

"Well, the chit lied."

"Why the deuce would the girl offer me such information?"

"Perhaps she is in love with Kingsdale. I don't know."

Clayton began pacing the grounds. "But why lie to me? I don't give a fig about her love life. Or Kingsdale's."

"But you never liked the man, and perhaps she knew that. Perhaps she thought she was protecting him in some way."

"It doesn't make sense." A frown flitted across his face when suddenly he looked up. "I mentioned Briana would be staying by herself while I had business away."

"And the lady mentioned Kingsdale?"

Clayton reddened. "I asked her about the man."

"Because you were jealous, no doubt." Without warning, Agatha smacked him with her reticule and stumbled back.

He winced. King George, that reticule was harder than her

deuced parasol! "Bodily harm will not move my heart, Miss Appleby."

A horse and rider came galloping toward them. Clayton noticed it was the footman who had dropped the coffee on Sir Gerald.

Agatha narrowed her gaze. "What is it, Augustus?"

Clayton's brows went up. *Augustus?*

The man handed a sealed letter to Agatha and she ripped it open. Her face turned white and Clayton caught her before she fell to the ground. Agatha's lids fluttered open. "My head. Must lie down. The blow was worse than I let on."

She returned the paper to the rider, and in no time Clayton had her in a chamber upstairs in the inn. Clayton was torn between staying with Miss Appleby and returning to his wife.

"What in the blazes is going on?" he asked Augustus.

The man looked positively morbid. "Can't say, my lord. It's Miss Appleby's business."

"My lord," Agatha whispered from the bed.

Clayton walked over to the woman. "The doctor will be here within in a few minutes, madam. Now, what have you to say to me?"

"Briana is in danger."

"What exactly do you mean by that? The mission is over."

Agatha nodded to Augustus to hand the letter to Clayton.

Clayton opened it and shot her a questioning stare. "Hell's bells!" It was from Grimstoke. The man was part of the plan against the prince and had decided to confess.

"And Lady Grimstoke was Whitehall's secret source," he replied, reading the words before him.

Agatha nodded. "It's all there in the letter. We didn't know who it was. But it's quite clear Lady Grimstoke finally divulged her dealings with Whitehall to her husband and now the man is confessing all to us. Revenge is quite nasty, you know. It seems the lady discovered Grimstoke was being unfaithful."

Agatha sighed. "And somehow Grimstoke knew I was part of all this. However, I don't think he knows about Briana."

Clayton's stomach knotted. His wife could be in more trouble than she would ever know. How could he have left her in such danger? "Then your mission is not without merit?"

"Correct." Agatha cringed and held her head. "We knew Grimstoke was a good friend of the Regent, and because of the unknown source, we thought the lord was planning something against Prinny. We had no idea who Grimstoke's contact was, and I believe Grimstoke still doesn't know."

Agatha bit back the pain. "That is why the drop-off point was so important. Grimstoke never knew if the person was a servant or even a nobleman. Yet somehow Lady Grimstoke intercepted information of her husband's dealings. She knew the drop-off point was near his desk in the library. Only someone close to Grimstoke would be able to gather that information."

"And Grimstoke would have been happy as long as he received his money," Clayton said dryly. "But since Grimstoke is a friend of the Regent's, any information that was passed along could be useful. Times, dates, meetings. All that prized information could readily lead to an assassination attempt."

"Yes," Agatha said, frowning.

Clayton gritted his teeth in frustration. "And Briana is there, alone, with nothing to do but look for evidence, even though you told her the mission was canceled?"

"I told her Whitehall was sending me to Bath." Agatha's hand shook as she reached out to him. "I fear she is in grave danger."

"You know the adversary, then?"

"No. I went over the list, but after what you said about Violet mentioning Kingsdale had left, it makes me wonder."

The disturbing thought that Kingsdale was involved in the assassination attempt sent Clayton's apprehension soaring. "If Violet is in love with the man—"

"Oh my," Agatha cried. "Do you think it could be so?"

The threat was left unsaid. "I should never have left her alone." His thoughts were going a hundred directions. If Briana died because of his departure . . .

He looked at Agatha. "I'll have need of a pistol."

Agatha nodded toward her reticule. "In there."

Clayton gave a grim chuckle. "Was it loaded when you whacked me with it?"

Agatha tried to smile. "Indeed, it was, my lord."

Chapter Nineteen

"Why didn't you tell me you were working for White-hall?"

Violet stood inside the library door, staring in horror at Briana sitting on the sofa. Briana was just as shocked to discover that Violet had fallen in love with Kingsdale. Violet had mentioned her attraction to the man, but the girl was always speaking her thoughts out loud. It never occurred to Briana that Violet would fall into Kingsdale's trap.

"You might not understand now, Bree," Violet went on, "but you will see that Lord Kingsdale wants to help England. Only he cannot help the country with the Regent being the way he is. Prinny must learn a lesson. He needs to stop all that spending and give to the poor."

Briana almost felt sorry for her friend. Almost. How could the girl be so gullible?

"She could not very well tell you she was working for the government, my love." Lord Kingsdale positioned himself on a chair opposite Briana, the pistol weighing in her direction.

Violet's eyes softened as she turned her attention toward her beloved. "You are so very smart, my lord. I admit I was surprised when I unlocked the door and saw you here with Bree. I thought—well, never mind that."

Briana wanted to shake Violet senseless. What was wrong with the girl? Kingsdale's smile was as false as his heart.

"You should never worry, my love," Kingsdale drawled. Chuckling, he returned his attention to Briana. "Worry does nothing but produce worry. We all know that life is a game of chance, is it not, my dear?"

Briana looked away, knowing she would have to work on Violet's emotions. If she were to die, at least she would die fighting. Kingsdale had said he loved her, but the next minute he said he would kill her. Would he kill Violet, too?

"You remember my sister, Violet?"

Violet shook her head, wringing her hands on her gown. "You'd best not talk to me, Bree. It won't work."

"Not another word," Kingsdale growled. "I don't want to make it hard for you."

Briana realized the man still had feelings for her. Taking a chance, she rose from her seat and started toward the desk.

"Sit down," Kingsdale said harshly.

Briana peered over her shoulder, her insides shaking. "Why should I sit down if you are going to shoot me? Why should I even listen to you?"

Violet hurried across the room. "Oh, please, sit down, Bree. He won't hurt you if you help us."

"You don't know him like I do, Violet. He intends to hurt the Regent. In fact, he intends to kill him."

"No," Violet cried. "You have it all wrong. He wouldn't do that!"

Briana looked toward the fireplace. If only she could gain control of that loose brick . . .

"Don't even think about it, my dear." Kingsdale was beside her in a flash. "A brick through a window or even to my head won't suit at all."

Briana turned and gave him her sweetest smile. "I wasn't thinking of anything like that, Gregory. I was thinking of us."

Passion lit his eyes the second his name crossed her lips. Instantly, he lowered the pistol. "Perhaps we could come to some agreement, my dear. I don't totally trust you—"

"But you love me!" Violet protested, stepping toward them. "You don't love her! You love me! You said so!"

Kingsdale's mouth thinned as he turned toward the screaming woman. Briana used the moment to her advantage. She spun around and grabbed the writing box, slamming it against the back of Kingsdale's head. The man groaned and crumpled to the ground.

"You've killed him!" Violet cried. "You've killed him!"

Briana highly doubted that. Knowing the door was locked, she ran toward the window and fumbled with the sash.

"Don't move!"

Briana froze at the sound of Kingsdale's command. She saw his reflection in the window. The gun was raised in her direction and he was stumbling to his feet.

"I don't think you want to kill me, Gregory."

"Oh, Bree," Violet wailed. "Why did you have to run? He would not have hurt you. I would have seen to that."

Briana glanced over her shoulder. Kingsdale was coming toward her.

"I loved you," he whispered harshly, the next second pressing the gun into her ribs. "You were the only woman I ever loved. I never wanted to hurt you."

Briana's heart sped. "Then let me go, Gregory. You don't want to do this."

He put a hand around her waist. "I can't do that. Now open the window." He lowered his head and whispered into her ear. "You are despondent over your husband's return to Town."

Her head snapped around so fast her nose touched his. "And I kill myself. Is that it?"

He frowned. "It didn't have to be this way. I didn't want it to be this way. But you married the man."

"What are you saying?" Violet whined from the other side of the room. "I can't hear what you're saying."

"Open it, my dear. It's not locked. The catch is unlatched."

Panic welled in Briana's throat as she followed his instructions. A cool breeze swept across her face while the window was being raised. *Forgive me, Clayton. Forgive me for not trusting you.*

"Now, my dear—"

The door burst open, halting Kingsdale's speech.

"Clayton!" Briana cried.

Her husband stood on the threshold with pistol raised. His eyes never left Kingsdale's face. "Drop it, Gregory. I don't want to shoot."

Kingsdale swung Briana around, making her a human shield. "So, you've come for your bride after all. How very sweet. And I see you have Miss Appleby's attendant. Had a suspicion about him, but, well, one never knows."

Briana was surprised to see the footman who had spilled the hot coffee on Sir Gerald standing beside Clayton.

"Please, Gregory," she begged, feeling his grip tightening. "If you ever loved me, don't do this."

The hold on her loosened. "God help me," Kingsdale whispered gruffly. "I cannot kill you. Never thought I could. You are the only woman—" He stopped, glanced at Clayton, then pressed his mouth beneath her ear. "But if you jumped with me . . ."

He left the sentence unsaid and pushed her aside. "We could have been good together, my little bluestocking." The next moment he swung the gun toward Clayton. "Good-bye, my friend."

Two shots were fired as Kingsdale leapt from the window. Violet screamed. Clayton's pistol was smoking. Briana turned away, too horrified to take in what had happened.

Clayton and Augustus hurried toward the window.

"Dead as a splattered cat, my lord," Augustus announced. "Don't know if your shot hit him or not. Didn't matter, though. Died from the fall."

Violet let out a gasp and fainted.

Clayton turned to Briana. "Are you hurt?"

"No," she said weakly. *Hold me, she wanted to say. Love me. Don't ever leave me again.*

He tucked a wayward strand of hair behind her ear, paused and walked toward Violet, sparing a glance at the writing box, fallen apart on the floor. A small grin worked its way to his lips. "I suppose those secret compartments helped after all."

Tears of frustration filled Briana's eyes and she leaned against the desk for support. "Yes, they helped. He has the papers from Grimstoke in his pocket."

"I'll get them," Clayton said coolly, glancing at Augustus. "Keep an eye on my wife and the lady."

"Very good, my lord."

Briana's heart stuck in her throat as her husband departed from the room. *Clayton!*

She dropped her lashes to hide the pain. No kiss, no hug, not even a word of love. She had lost him. She knew that now. Deep down she wondered if she had ever had him at all.

Later that evening, Briana cupped her hands around the warm tea as she sat in the drawing room of Grimstoke Hall. The authorities had already taken Lord Grimstoke and Violet away for questioning. Kingsdale's body had been removed as well.

Clayton had told Briana that Grimstoke's family would have to face the consequences of their actions, even though their host had sent the letter to Agatha, and that his wife was the unknown source, feeding Whitehall valuable information.

"The man may get off," Clayton said, sinking into the nearby wing chair. He blew out a tired breath. "I just don't know. His wife was the informant against him. It won't be easy. It's a devil of a coil."

Briana was still shaken from the ordeal. She had told Clayton about Clarice and he seemed genuinely angry over Kingsdale's despicable actions. But more than anything she wanted her husband to hold her, tell her he loved her, tell her he never planned to marry her because of his uncle's will.

"Did you plan to marry me for the castle, my lord?"

His eyes searched hers, but he wasn't asking for sympathy. "I cannot lie to you, Briana. It had crossed my mind."

She dropped her gaze to her cup. "I see."

"Do you?"

A lump formed in her throat, and she found it hard to speak.

"I love you, Briana. Doesn't that mean anything to you?"

Of course it meant something. But not everything. He said he loved her, but it wasn't enough. Not anymore. She didn't want to go to him. She shouldn't have to. He was the one who had left, not her. Tears slipped silently down her cheeks, but she said nothing.

Hold me, Clayton. Show me you love me. But the chill between them was like an icy abyss, growing each second.

"I am giving you the castle and the money."

Her heart ached with disappointment. "I don't want it."

The lines about his face tensed as he rose. "Too bad. I'm giving it to you for your women's shelter. As your husband, I do have the upper hand, whether you like it or not, madam."

"And what of your future?"

He shoved his hand in his pocket and walked toward the door. "I will have my solicitor call upon you at your convenience. Agatha will be here in an hour or so. She needed to rest. That blow to her head was more than she let on. You can return with her to London when she feels better."

The knowledge that he was leaving again seared her heart like a red-hot iron. But pride would not let her go to him.

Her spirits lifted as his violet blue eyes bored into hers and he strode forward. He bent down and lifted her hand, kissed it. "Good-bye, my Fairy Lady."

A dark shadow crossed her heart, and before she knew it he had let her fingers fall from his and he strode from the room.

Briana spread her shaking hands against her gown and swallowed a sob. She sat there for at least fifteen minutes, not knowing what to do. She had been too proud. Too arrogant. When would she learn?

"So, you think to rid yourself of me that quickly, do you?"

Her head jerked toward the drawing room's entryway. Clayton was leaning against the doorjamb, his arms crossed over his chest, his eyes searching hers.

"I thought you had left," she said.

His eyebrows rose. "Did you now?"

What was the matter with him? She wrung her hands on her gown and stood, intending to leave. She wasn't going to beg.

He took a step into the room and closed the doors, then turned to look at her again. "I think we have a few more matters to discuss."

Her chin lifted, the lump in her throat growing. "You can have your castle. I already said I don't want it."

In a few quick strides he was beside her. "Is that so?"

Her body stiffened and she spun around, giving him her back. "Yes. And if you have any sense—"

"If I have any sense?" he said softly, gripping her shoulders and leaning into her.

She swallowed. His lips were near her neck, making it difficult to think. "I, um, if you had any sense, you would . . . um . . ."

He wrapped a hand around her waist, pulling her against him. "Go on," he whispered huskily.

Her knees began to buckle. "I . . . you're confusing me."

His finger trailed along her neckline. "That's good."

She turned toward him, regaining her senses, or at least part of them. "No, that isn't good! I thought you were leaving!"

"Well, hell's bells, sweetheart, I changed my mind." His hand brushed the back of her neck, sending a warm shiver through her. "I should have told you about the castle. You have no reason to trust me again and I understand—"

It was her turn to press a finger against his lips. "Shhhh. You seem to change your mind a great deal lately." Oh, he was a charmer. But she was not going to let him go this time.

His lips turned upward. "And I can say the same about you, wife. But there is one thing that will never change." He gently tipped her chin to look at her. "When I said I loved you, that is the absolute truth and always will be."

She smiled, working her hands around his neckcloth, breathing in the scent of him. "You talk way too much." And then she kissed him, long and hard.

He swept her into his arms and started for the door. "By Jove, I am an idiot. Don't know why I didn't think of this before." His brows narrowed. "But if you think for one deuced minute that I am willing to leave you behind for all the Kingsdales of the world to fawn over you, you had best think again."

She gave him a faint smile. She didn't want to think of Kingsdale's death or the horrible day. "I love you," she said softly.

"And another thing, about this castle—" His face froze. "What did you say?"

"I said I love you, you idiot."

He pressed his lips to hers in a slow, passionate kiss. "Why didn't you say so in the first place? We could have sidestepped all this nonsense and headed to Bath for a honeymoon."

They were both laughing when the drawing room door flung open. "What in the blue blazes do you think you're doing?"

It was Agatha, and she was looking at Briana with a smiling

eye. But Clayton hadn't caught on. He was still clinging to the wife in his arms as if she would run away the minute he put her down. "My dear Miss Appleby, I am taking my wife home, if you don't mind?"

Agatha raised a discriminating brow. "It certainly looks like you are doing something else, my good man."

Clayton's cheeks colored as he let his wife slip gently to the floor. "I was—"

"Yes, just what the devil *are* you doing?"

Clayton's jaw dropped at the sight of Lord Stonebridge standing in the hall. The earl's knowing gaze switched from Clayton to Briana, then back to Clayton again.

How the earl showed up at that timely moment, Briana didn't want to know. Something to do with Whitehall, no doubt.

Clayton seemed at a loss for words, but the next moment he dragged Briana into his arms and kissed her until her knees gave way. When he was done, he held her against his side and shot a determined glance toward the earl and Agatha. "If you must know, I was sweeping my wife into my arms so I could bring her upstairs and—"

Agatha clapped her hands over her ears. "Stop! I don't want to hear it! You insolent puppy!"

Stonebridge laughed. "Go on, Clay. *I* want to hear it. I happened to be told about your new wife early this morning. Ah, don't worry, I am not going to call you out. Unless I miss my guess, you are in love."

"Of course I'm in love," Clayton said.

Blushing, Briana opened her mouth to speak when Clayton cleared her feet from the floor, moved into the hall and started carrying her up the steps.

"And for your information, Jared," he said over his shoulder, "I have a few things I need to talk over with my wife, if you don't mind."

The earl laughed. "But this is Grimstoke's house, Clay. Don't you think—"

Clayton stopped and turned. "No, I really don't think, as you can probably well testify! Miss Appleby, you can unplug your ears now."

Agatha dropped her hands. "I heard you. But listen here, you young puppy, if you ever hurt her, I will come after you!"

Briana let out a light laugh. "Clay, put me down. I think this has gone on long enough."

Clayton kept walking up the stairs. "Oh, no, madam, that is where you are wrong. This hasn't gone on long enough at all." He looked back at Agatha and gave Jared a wink. "Not at all."

Agatha gasped. "You are without a doubt the most . . . most . . . well!" She turned on her heel and marched into the drawing room.

Briana chuckled. "Clay, please. Her head injury. Let me go see her."

"Oh, no, my little bride. Jared can tend to her. You and I have some business to discuss."

Briana tightened her hold on his neck. "Oh, about the castle and all its secret hiding places?" Her words were said in such a silky caress that Clayton stumbled on the stairs.

She wanted to laugh. Merciful heavens, this man was pudding in her hands.

Clayton paused and gazed warily back at her. "You know, I think we have a problem here."

She frowned. "What is it?"

"I believe I married a woman with an intellect that exceeds my own, did I not?"

She shrugged, her eyes peeping from beneath her lashes. "Does it matter, my lord husband?"

He quickened his pace and smiled. "Not at all. Not at all."

Chapter Twenty

A month later Briana arrived at the Stonebridge townhouse to visit with her new sister-in-law. She had just returned from her honeymoon and this was the first time she had seen Emily since she had been married. The two had written, of course, but neither of them could wait to see each other. After the tears were shed, the ladies sat down in the drawing room for tea. Clayton was speaking with Jared in his study and would join the ladies later.

"You know, I wanted to send all those clothes back the minute I discovered your ploy," Briana said, smiling as she referred to the new gowns Emily had sent to Grimstoke Hall.

"Well, Bree, I can't say they didn't help my plan. You did marry my brother. Not that the gowns did it, but I am certain they caught many gentlemen's attention. And if I know Clay, he has more than one jealous bone in his body. He never liked to share, you know."

Briana laughed. "Yes, I can see that."

Emily paused, setting her teacup on her saucer. "But there is something different about you, and it has nothing to do with the beautiful gown you are wearing." She lifted an amused brow. "A gown my brother bought for you?"

Briana blushed. "Different. How different?"

"Like a woman who is about to have a baby different?"

Briana paled. "A baby?"

Emily laughed. "I was only jesting. You seem as nervous as I did before my child was born."

"Oh."

Emily's lids fell halfway over her eyes. "Is there something you wish to tell me?"

Briana circled her finger around her teacup. "I'm carrying your brother's child."

Emily squealed. "But it's only been—"

Briana took in a deep breath. "I know how long it's been. But Clayton didn't want a baby so soon. He was determined to spend time alone with me. He mentioned having children, but only in the future."

"That's silly, Bree. It will be the future. Sometimes Clayton is an idiot."

Briana fought back a smile. "You're talking about my husband." Then she started to cry. "But truly, I am thinking of telling him in a few months. You know, prepare him." She dabbed her eyes with a handkerchief. "I cry one minute and laugh the next. I don't know what's wrong with me."

Emily smiled. "You're having a baby. And nothing's wrong with you. Go on upstairs to see Gabrielle for her tea party. Clayton will be here in a few minutes to join you."

Briana swayed, trying to settle herself against the arm of the chair. Emily was at her side in a second. "And depend upon it, if you don't tell him about the babe, I will."

About ten minutes later Clayton walked into the drawing room, greeting his sister. "Jared will be here in a minute," he said. "And where are the little ladies who desire a tea party?"

Emily stood, looking out the window, barely glancing at her brother as he strode across the Aubusson rug. "Gabrielle is upstairs, readying the table," she said. "Briana is there, too."

Clayton knitted his brows and sank into the wing chair beside the hearth. "Is that cursed dog going to be up there? To tell you the truth, Em, I think Stonebridge should keep the beast in the country. Nigel doesn't fit into city life."

Emily whirled around, her eyes flashing. "We love Nigel! We love babies! And would you please stop complaining!"

Clayton folded his arms over his chest. "It isn't like you to keep silent." He waved his arm in the air. "For the love of the king, don't be civil for my sake. And might I say, I am overwhelmed at your loving welcome."

"Oh! If I were not a lady I would box your ears!"

His lips twitched. Had Jared forgotten her birthday? An anniversary perhaps? "Ah, the claws come out."

"You oaf." She strode across the floor and swatted his shoulder. He didn't flinch. "I never knew someone so pigheaded in my life."

"Hell's bells, Em. What are you so angry about?"

"You love her, then?"

"Briana?"

"Yes, you idiot."

" 'Course I love her."

"Well, you ninny. She's upstairs right now, wanting to tell you something."

He jumped from his seat. "Is she ill?"

"She's miserable."

"Then what is she doing in the nursery?"

"Having a tea party."

"I know that. But what the deuce is wrong with her? I knew something was up. She's been acting rather strange the past week. Crying at the drop of a pin."

Emily spoke between clenched teeth. "Sometimes I wonder where men come from."

Clayton didn't hear his sister, for he was already taking the stairs two at a time, practically running down the hall, and then slowing to a sedate pace as he came upon the nursery.

"Oh, hello, Uncle Clay," Gabrielle said, walking down the hall from the other direction.

"Hello there, Gabby." He swung her into his arms. "I'm looking for someone. Do you think you could help me?"

Gabrielle clapped her hands in excitement. "Oh, you're looking for the Fairy Lady? Mama told me you married her."

"Yes, the Fairy Lady. I need to tell her something."

"What do you want to tell her? I can do it for you."

"You can?"

The little girl nodded.

"Well, let's see. I want you to tell her I love her. Oh, and don't forget to tell her I miss her."

"I can do that." Her lips puckered in thought. "Do you miss

her this much?" she asked, opening her fingers about an inch. "Or do you miss her this much?" Her arms went wide.

He chuckled. "The second one because I haven't seen her for almost thirty minutes."

"That's a long time, Uncle Clay. I think it would be better if you just touch her feckles and make a wish."

Clayton let Gabrielle slip to the floor. "Could I?"

She nodded, her blue eyes dancing. "The Fairy Lady is over there." She pointed to the open door of the nursery. Her small hand slipped into his, and he let her direct him into the room.

He drew in a ragged breath when he saw Briana standing near the window, her back to him. She had been crying. Was she ill? Or could she be regretting their marriage now that she was back in London? He didn't want to think about either of his two choices.

"There she is," Gabrielle whispered.

"I see her," Clayton said calmly. "Why, she's even more beautiful than I remember."

"Yes," said Gabrielle gravely, running to Briana. The girl looked back at Clayton, her blue eyes tearing up. "But I think she's sad. She's crying, Uncle Clay."

Clayton strode across the room. "Well, did you know when a Fairy Lady cries, there's only one thing to do?"

The girl put a finger to her own cheek. "Mmmmm, what?"

"A prince must kiss the tears to make them go away."

Gabrielle jumped up and down. "Do it! Hurry, Uncle Clay! Do it! Do it!"

Clayton slipped a firm arm around his wife's waist, taking in the subtle scent of vanilla. "Will you let me kiss the tears, Fairy Lady?"

Briana threw her hands to her face. She had heard Clayton in the hall. How could she tell him she was going to have his child? She wanted this baby more than anything. But it made her think of Clarice. And she was frightened. What if Clayton didn't want the child? Of course he would. Oh, why couldn't she think straight?

Gabrielle's bottom lip formed a shovel as she tugged at Briana's skirt. "He wants to kiss them, Fairy Lady. Please, don't cry."

Briana smiled, wiping away the tears. "I won't cry."

Clayton turned Briana slowly in his arms and kissed her cheek. "That was one tear."

"Oh! Oh! There's another one!" Gabrielle cried.

Clayton touched the outside of Briana's eye. "Here?" he asked, smiling.

Gabrielle pointed to Briana's face. "Yes!"

Clayton's lips touched Briana's skin with such gentleness, she buried her face against his cravat and cried even more.

"It's not working!" Gabrielle said, her bottom lip starting to quiver. "You're doing it wrong!"

Clayton looked down at the girl. "Hell's bells! I'm trying, Gabby!"

"Oh!" the girl cried, pressing her hands to her flushed cheeks. "I'm telling Mama! You said bad words!"

Gabrielle squared her shoulders and turned swiftly around, dashing toward the door before Clayton could catch her.

He hurried after her. "Gabby!" He thumped his hand against the wall when the girl disappeared down the stairs.

Briana couldn't keep from laughing. "You want to try again, *Uncle Clay*?" she said sweetly.

Clayton glanced over his shoulder. "Why, bless my soul, it worked," he said with a wicked grin, walking toward her.

He kissed her again, making her world tilt. "I've missed you for all of thirty minutes. Now tell me why you're so miserable."

"There he is, Mama! Tell him to go to his room! He said bad words!" Gabrielle's little feet came thumping into the room, along with a laughing Emily and a barking Nigel.

Clayton threw his hands into the air and winked at Briana. "I confess. I will go directly to my bedchamber as soon as I return home."

Gabrielle wagged her finger at him. "I love you, Uncle Clay, but next time, no bad words!"

Briana eased an arm around her husband's elbow. "I shall accompany him, Princess, and make certain he talks nice."

The little girl nodded her head in satisfaction. "Good."

Emily's violet blue eyes gleamed. "And make sure you don't say those words around the baby fairy."

Clayton stiffened. "Baby fairy?" he said, turning to Briana.

Emily frowned. "Ooops. Sorry." She grabbed Gabrielle and hurried back down the hall.

"Baby fairy?" Clayton asked again, his brows knitting into a frown. "Is that why you're crying?"

Briana swallowed. "Now, Clayton—"

She tripped over a chair and he caught her.

"What the devil do you think you're doing?" he growled.

For a long moment she stared back at him.

"A baby?" he asked softly. Pride and joy danced in his eyes.

She nodded, her heart too happy to speak.

"Well, well!" He seemed very pleased with himself and started kissing the freckles on her nose.

"You don't mind?" she said. "I thought you wanted to wait."

He looked up. "Of course I don't mind. What do you think I am, an idiot? Besides, I'm making wishes on your *feckles*. Wishes for a magnificent life, and wishes for a very large family."

Overwhelmed, Briana pressed her face against his chest. A sense of peace filled her. She had even told Clayton all about Alistair and he had been wonderful. Briana wished Clarice had loved such a man. "I love you, Lord Clayton Clearbrook."

His eyes were blurry. "And I you, wife."

"He has fairy tears, Mama," Gabrielle whispered from the doorway. "Those are very special. Papa told me so."

Emily wiped the tears from her own eyes and smiled. "Yes, dear, they are very special."

The door closed and Clayton's smile grew as he wiped his wife's tears away. "I think it's time to return to our castle."

Briana's heart swelled. "And live happily ever after?"

"Hmmm, I'm not certain about that. I had better make another wish on one of those feckles first. For my safety, you see."

She grinned. "And why is that?"

"Had a talk with Stonebridge. There's danger in the air."

"Danger?" she asked, frowning.

"Your sweet godmother has bought another blasted parasol."

Briana burst out laughing. "My hero."

He opened the door. "You think that funny—"

"There you are!"

Clayton's head snapped up at the sound of the all-too-familiar voice. "Miss Appleby, how nice to see you again."

A shiny black parasol swung by her side as she marched toward him. "Is it, now? The last time I saw you—"

With a quick jerk of his arm, Clayton pulled Briana into the nursery and locked the door. "By Jove, she looks mean."

Briana giggled. "She is not mean."

"She looks as if she wants to hit me. What did I do?"

"You made her cover her ears."

He smiled. "That was a month ago. But I think I better make a few more wishes, er, for my safety. What say you, Fairy Lady?"

Smiling, Briana wiped her eyes. "I was wrong. She might be a little mean. You'd better make a lot more wishes."

"A lot more!" came the voice from beyond the door. "And Tinkles and Turneys has a multitude of parasols for me to choose from! Do you hear me, my lord?"

Briana bit her lip. "I think she's going to stand by that door until we come out."

"Dash it all, she can wait all day and all night, for all I care. I have more than a few feckles to kiss."

Briana suppressed a giggle as his lips covered hers.

"Open up this door, you young puppy! I have a few things I want to say to you! Now that you're home—"

With a quick turn, Clayton whipped the door open. Agatha stumbled into the room and he caught her. "And I have something I want to say to you, Miss Appleby. First, I think you should return to Tinkles and Turneys to buy yourself some more parasols." Her jaw dropped. "For the baby, my dear lady. We don't want your goddaughter's child to have too much sun, do we?"

"Child?" the lady said with a squeak in her voice, peering intently at Briana's stomach. Agatha surprised Clayton and headed toward the door. He started to follow her, and she whacked him in the shin with her parasol.

His eyes grew wide. "What the devil was that for?"

"Don't just stand there, my boy! Go kiss those feckles."

With those last words, Agatha slammed the door closed, leaving the couple to stare at each other in stunned amazement.

Clayton grinned. "Do you think she will ever like me?"

"Get her a new parasol, then see what she says."

He tugged playfully at his wife's hair. "Do you like me?"

"Hmmm, get me a new parasol and see what I say."

Without missing a beat, he lifted her off the ground. "Madam, I will never buy you a parasol. Do you understand me?"

"Yes, dear. Anything you say."

"I thought you would see it my way."

There was another knock and Clayton put his wife down once again, yanking open the door. "What the—"

To his surprise a parasol came flying into the room.

Agatha's head popped around the corner. "Hit him with that if he causes you any trouble, child. Always works."

Clayton's eyes flashed with mirth as he picked up the parasol and handed it to Briana.

Briana shook her head, laughing. "I don't need it. If you cause me any trouble, I'll just call Agatha." A bark sounded in the hall and Nigel appeared by her godmother's side. "Sorry, boy," Briana said with a chuckle. "And Nigel, too."

Clayton tugged his wife into his arms. "There won't be any trouble your feckles can't handle. And you're not a convenient bride at all, sweetheart. You are definitely, absolutely, positively essential to my heart and soul."

Tears flooded Briana's eyes. "Clayton, that's beautiful."

Agatha cleared her throat. "Thank goodness for *feckles*, you young puppy, or you would be in the suds!"

There was another bark as the door clicked home.

Briana tucked her head below her husband's shoulder and giggled. "I think she likes you now."

Clayton tipped his wife's chin and kissed her freckles with all the passion of a husband in love with his new bride.

"Well," he grinned, "all I can say is thank goodness for Fairy Lady feckles—and young puppies."

Briana looked into those twinkling violet blue eyes and smiled. It was the most perfect day of her life. She was definitely, absolutely, positively in love, and it felt wonderful.